BEYOND HONOR AND OTHER STORIES

GODDESS'S HONOR
BOOK ONE

JOYCE REYNOLDS-WARD

THE GODDESS'S CHOICE

THE GODDESS'S CHOICE

Setkin stared at Vered across the Captain's table. The amethyst die with two white spots—Vered's number—lay between them. Vered shivered with a mix of anticipation and fear as she studied Setkin's dark brows framed by his gray watch cap. It was less stomach-clenching to look at his brows than at what lurked in his dark brown eyes.

The ship plunged into a deep trough between the waves, crying out in response to the storm's growing strength. Vered wanted to stroke the ship's heartbeam to sing courage and steadiness into her.

Not my ship, she reminded herself.

She had to go through this ordeal to get her own ship. Much as she loved to talk to Setkin's *Heart Desire, Desire* was not her ship and would not respond to her voice.

"I'm ready," she croaked, her throat dry and tight.

Next to her, Hagni, her friend, her lover, and the other remaining Sorcerer-Captain candidate on this voyage, groaned.

She ignored him.

"Swear to it." Setkin lumbered to his feet, bracing wide as the ship climbed the next wave.

Desire creaked, calling to him once again for reassurance, but his focus remained on Vered instead of his ship.

Vered rose and fitted her right hand to Setkin's. His skull-shaped amethyst ring glowed as her hand met his, a final confirmation that this roll of the God's die spoke true.

"I swear to follow Terat's verdict in this my final test for Sorcerer-Captain," she repeated after Setkin. "My heirs and family renounce all claims against the Guild of Sorcerer-Captains should I fail this final assessment by the Goddess." *Not that my family will care about this failed daughter.* "So do I swear, this fourteenth day of the tenth month of the Twentieth Year of our Emperor Etikar, may the Seven Crowned Gods keep him safe."

Corrupt bastard that he is. His son Dunaran is only slightly better.

"There." Setkin reached for the waiting scroll and pen tucked in the cubbyhole that held only the agreements for her and for Hagni. "Sign."

Vered dipped the pen into the inkwell set into the table. Her hand trembled slightly and she took a deep breath to steady it before scrawling *Vered ea Kachtin* at the bottom of the agreement. *Vered-without-family.* Better not to reveal those who had rejected who and what she was. She had begun to worry during this trip that she would fail, that the Goddess would not choose her. Then she might have to return to those who would deny her.

Setkin signed, then sprinkled sand over the ink to set it. After that, he rolled the scroll, affixed his seal, and placed her scroll into the crowded cubbyhole, along with the three agreements from those candidates who had gone before her.

"Prepare yourself," he said. "The Goddess approaches." He dismissed them from his cabin with a wave of his hand, turning now to *Desire*, stroking her heartbeam and crooning to her as they left.

"REFUSE THE TESTING. PLEASE." Hagni helped Vered put on the flowing white candidate's gown. "I would not lose you, my dear."

"I want to be a captain as much as you do."

"More than you love me?"

He kissed Vered. She held the kiss for a few moments, then pulled back. She stroked his long red hair and beard, studying the heavy-framed face of the man she had grown to love.

The *only* man she had ever loved.

"I've worked for this all my life," she reminded him. "I have nothing else. Do *you* want to be a captain more than you love me?"

"I'm still thinking about it," he admitted. "The Goddess has been slow to call me, perhaps for a reason. Perhaps the same reason for both of us. Perhaps we're not called to be Captains. Vered, there is no dishonor in choosing not to test."

"No. I will not refuse."

I have no other choice. I am called.

They had talked about this throughout the voyage. Why was Hagni being so stubborn now, when she most needed his support?

"Hagni, if you choose not to test, then being a captain's consort who has been through captain's training would be of great value."

"Ah, Vered, Vered, you won't let go of a flawed dream. Besides, what if you fail?"

"I won't fail. I can't go back, and I would prefer not to lose you, too. Would being my consort be such a horrible thing?"

"I do not know for certain, dearest." He hesitated. "Are you certain that living the land life would be so horrible? We still have our skills and abilities. We could become healers, or Speakers for one of the Gods."

"Would you settle for that life?" she countered.

And my not-so-beloved cousin Etikar would find a means to kill me at the first opportunity.

But she couldn't share that with Hagni, because then he would know who she really was. That was something she would not reveal to any lover, not until they joined in a life bond. Her only safety was in the ranks of the Sorcerer-Captains. Etikar could not reach her there. She would be a Captain…or suffer whatever fate failed Captain candidates endured, before she would risk the not-so-tender justice of her cousin the Emperor.

Hagni shook his head.

A heavy fist pounded on the door. "Cap'n says it's time," the first mate Marna growled through the door, her tone carrying a hint of warning.

"On my way," Vered called to Marna.

She went into Hagni's arms for a last caress.

"May luck and the Goddess Terat be with you," he breathed into her ear. They separated and he offered her his arm.

VERED WAS grateful for Hagni's support as she walked onto the deck. This storm was stronger than the ones the other candidates had entered.

Good omen or bad?

Vered took the rope Hagni placed into her hand for support and made her way to the bulwark. She held the rope tight, using it to keep her balance as the ship bucked underneath her. It wouldn't do to meet the Goddess as a supplicant. She had to face the Goddess proudly, as an equal in his own element.

At last she reached the position she wanted and clung to the bulwark, measuring the mounting waves for strength and intensity, searching for the Goddess who awaited her.

"The Goddess! She comes!" Setkin bellowed from the forecastle.

Vered dared look at him, cherished one final glimpse of Hagni reeling around the deck, clutching at another rope. The shark's jaws mounted on the forecabin's wall behind Setkin caught her attention. Setkin treated the jaws as important but would never say why.

Remember the shark, was all he would say.

Then even that memory fled as Setkin pointed toward the ship's stern. Vered looked into the waves again, holding the bulwark with her left hand, gathering her gown with her right.

The Goddess's shape formed in the dark blue depths of the cresting wave. Vered crouched. She let go of the bulwark and leapt as far as she could, bracing herself for the shock of her impact in the cold water.

Impact never happened.

Instead, the pressure of warm, wet arms wrapped around her body. Then the Goddess's lips pushed against hers. Vered gasped, and water rushed into her lungs as Terat blew the liquid into Vered's mouth. Her first instinct was to choke on the water.

Sorcerer-Captain's First Rule. Water is as air in the Goddess's embrace.

She continued breathing, letting the water rush into her lungs and sustain her, trusting the Goddess bearing her.

Vered felt rather than heard Terat's approving whale-like rumble as they sank toward the bottom. With each fathom they dropped, her confidence grew. Vered ventured further from the

Goddess's grasp, until they barely maintained a fingertip contact.

Time for the second test.

Sorcerer-Captain's Second Rule. Once accepted by the Goddess, move forward boldly. Do not let fear rule you.

Vered glanced down toward the ocean bottom she could not yet see. She examined herself, ensuring that no doubt lay within her. Water pulsed in and out of her lungs as if it were air. Her limbs moved confidently through the water, controlling the element despite the currents that pulled at her.

I can do this.

Vered let her fingers slip free from the Goddess's. For one moment she wobbled, and almost reached for Terat's fingertips. The Goddess flowed out of reach to let Vered succeed or fail on her own.

Vered steeled herself against the icy fear that oh-so-quickly stabbed at her gut. She stabilized her breathing and corrected her wobble. Looking down again, she bent over double and kicked off straight down, pushing hard against the water, seeking the fastest way to the bottom.

The Goddess swam next to her. Again, she was aware of Terat's rumbling approval, sounding just like the whales Vered had swum with during her training.

And now, the third test.

Sorcerer-Captain's Third Rule. No one, not even the Goddess, can show you where your ring lies.

If she were to gain the ring that made her a Captain, it would be on the bottom.

Without that ring, she could not return to the surface.

But how was she to find her ring? That was one aspect of

Vered's training that no one had bothered to explain, save that she would find the ring on the ocean bottom. What skills could she use?

You want to be a Sorcerer-Captain. That means you need to apply sorcery.

Sorcerer-Captains sought the best routes for their ships through even the roughest waters. They did it by speaking to the Goddess, to their ship's heartbeam, to the elements, and to the creatures of the deep.

I need to find a whale. Dolphin might do. No. A whale.

Vered cupped her hands to her lips. She tightened her stomach, concentrated on projecting her wishes over a distance, then emitted a short passage of whale song.

Nothing.

She tried again. This time she thought she felt a distant vibration.

A third time. She could see something moving toward her through the deep. She eagerly swam toward it, then stopped.

Shark!

Vered steeled herself to repulse the likely attack. Instead, the shark circled her.

Why wait, Candidate? Don't you have a ring to find?

You came to my call?

Wordless humor flowed over Vered. The shark was laughing at her.

Vered resumed her passage down as the shark matched her movement.

I called a whale.

The sensation of wordless humor washed over her again.

Whales don't know what you need. Whales won't tell you anything useful.

So what are you going to tell me?

Think as a predator does.

Is that all?

Disappointment surged through her.
Then she recalled Setkin's words.

Remember the shark.

A shark had come to her call. Perhaps she should listen to it.

Sorcerer-Captains are predators. The ring is your prey.

With that, the shark twisted away from Vered.
So I must hunt my ring as if it's prey? Very well.
She finally reached the bottom, and dug her toes into the sand to steady herself.
Now where do I start?
The area where Vered had touched down was rock and sand, with a few small plants waving gently in the strong current. Cloudy shapes gathered around a rock formation a short distance away. She squinted. They appeared to be human, most likely lost souls killed in a shipwreck.
I'll hunt answers from them.
Vered strode boldly towards the rock formation. As she drew closer, she recognized one of the shadowy shapes as that of Keander, another candidate from her voyage.
What is this?
She stopped. Keander was a strong sorcerer. Had he failed, or had he just not found his ring yet? The stop saved her, as

Keander took the shape of a moray eel and snapped at where she would have been. He writhed and lunged at her again, barely missing Vered as she ducked away.

She grabbed moray-Keander behind the head, holding on tightly as he twisted in her grip.

The other shapes swarmed around her, taking the forms of octopi and other deep-sea predators. Vered grasped moray-Keander's body between her knees and thrust his head at them to fend off their attacks.

He wounded one of them. The others turned on their injured compatriot. Moray-Keander pulled toward it. Vered let him go. She turned away from them and swam toward the rock formation.

Maybe this is where my ring will be.

But no ring called to her around the rocks. Besides, if rings were that easy to find, wouldn't Keander and the others have found their rings by now?

She left the rock formation. Where was her ring? She could feel its song, tantalizing her, whispering her name.

Hunger came to her, along with *longing*.

Mine.

Vered bounded along the ocean bottom, rising a few feet with each stride. The faint shadows of a broken ship lay ahead. She paused, then continued on. That wasn't the source of the ring's song. She glimpsed faint shadows flitting in and around the ship, and circled wide around it, not wanting to waste time on another battle.

She finally spotted a gleaming rock in the distance. Vered slowed her steps. Was there anything else here? She approached the rock slowly.

No ring.

But the nameless hunger and longing calling her told her that the ring was near. Vered lightly tapped the rock, using several different sequences.

Looking for something?

The nurse shark who had followed Vered earlier swam around her in tight circles. *Hunger* and *longing* radiated from it, almost overwhelming her in its intensity.

The shark has my ring!

Why hadn't she felt that call from it before?

No time to question. Vered jumped at the shark. It dove at her, aiming for her midsection. She wrestled with the shark, tearing at it with her fingers and teeth, savagely seeking some clue to the source of her ring. The shark's teeth rent her flesh, but she didn't feel it. She ignored the raspy thickness of the shark's skin as she gnawed on the shark.

Remember the shark.

The shark jaw mounted on Setkin's ship.

The missing tooth.

The way Setkin caressed that socket where the tooth had been—tooth.

That tooth.

Instead of flinching away from the next swipe of the shark's teeth, she thrust her hands inside its mouth. Her right hand struggled to keep the shark from biting down while her left hand fumbled among the teeth.

One tooth worked loose. As it fell into her hand, something heavy slid onto her finger. The shark went limp, and she was able to extract her hands from its mouth. Vered lifted her left hand high, ignoring the blood streaming away from her arms in crimson ribbons.

It didn't matter now if the blood attracted predators. Her ring would protect her. Its song pulsed through her as it twinkled on her finger and she gave voice in the depths, singing as boldly as any whale, proclaiming to all that a new Sorcerer-Captain had emerged.

As she finished her song, Vered swayed, suddenly exhausted. The shark transformed into the Goddess Terat.

She took Vered into her arms.

> Vered, my dearest Vered. You have done me honor. Rest now, and let me return you to the breathing world. Your ship awaits you.

Water rushed by them. Vered strained to remain awake and see the glories of the underwater world through the Goddess's eyes. Terat laughed, a wild and jubilant note more akin to that of an air creature than a water creature.

> Not yet for you, my dearest. Time you rested.

Vered slept then, her dreams filled with wild and fantastic undersea images.

SHE WOKE ON THE SHORE. Vered blinked at the sky above her, surprised to be breathing air instead of water, vague memories of a great banquet with Sorcerer-Captains of the past in a gigantic coral castle fading.

Real memories, or simply a dream left by Terat to soothe her while the Goddess brought her here?

Not important. She needed to figure out where she was. Vered analyzed the clues she could discern before calling on the new sorcery stirring deep inside her. Early morning on an eastern shoreline, the sun rising over the ocean. Cool air, neither the stifling heat of a tropical location nor the bitter cold of the arctic. Echoing squawks of seagulls squabbling over food.

Something was beached not far from where she lay. Where was she? She closed her eyes, *feeling* the world's ley lines around her.

Principality of Fenras, her location sense told her. *Not far from the port of Fenras.*

Fenras was where they had started their voyage.

Sharp points poked her left hand. A bony structure. She picked it up. A shark's jawbone, with one tooth missing. She raised her hand to look at her ring.

An emerald skull glittered on her ring finger, almost hidden by her lace cuffs. Vered sat up slowly, staring at her ring and clothing.

Perhaps she hadn't dreamed that great banquet, because she now wore the formal attire of a Sorcerer-Captain in place of her candidate robe. Not the working garb Setkin had been wearing when she had gone out on her quest, but the formal dress of white blouse with lace jabot and cuffs, matching black coat and breeches, and knee-high boots.

She stood up carefully, brushing off her clothing. No sand adhered to it. She reached back and checked her hair, neatly braided and tied off with a ribbon of exquisite softness. A flash of green light attracted her attention back to her ring, and she stared into it, entranced.

I've made it. I'm a Sorcerer-Captain.

Whatever the gulls were squabbling over at the far end of the beach caught her attention. Not big enough to be a whale or a sea lion. Probably a seal. Whatever it was, the gulls were feeding. Not her concern.

What next? She needed her ship assignment. Vered started toward Fenras.

Remember the shark.

She turned back, picking up the shark jawbone. She paused, staring down the beach toward whatever the gulls were feeding on. She squinted at it.

Human, she decided.

She took two steps toward it, then shook herself.

Some poor soul washed overboard.

It was too far away from their ship's course to be anyone from her class of Sorcerer-Captain candidates, even Hagni. Best to tell the authorities at Fenras port about it. Otherwise, she would be pulled away from the more important task of meeting her ship.

Her ship.

That came first now. A joyous surge flowed throughout her whole body and quickened her steps. Vered swung the jawbone from her fingers, looking forward to nailing it on the forecastle of *her ship.* She sang a song of thanks to Terat as she marched toward Fenras.

Her ship.

She had done it. She was a Sorcerer-Captain. Her ship waited for her at Fenras. Perhaps Hagni would be there as well.

Her ship.

She danced along the sand, celebrating her escape.

Let Etikar do his worst now. He dared not touch her as a Sorcerer-Captain. Vered was free of the Miteal family and their eternal disapproval, this time for good. For better or worse, she was the Goddess's choice.

Today, that tasted sweet.

THE END

DELIAN'S GIFT

DELIAN'S GIFT

"Lady Inharise, a message for you and Leader-Designate Heinmyets."

The unfamiliar, soft-spoken voice came from one of the curtained window alcoves in the dark hallway that connected Inharise and Heinmyets's suite in the Leader's residence to the Great Hall.

Inharise spun, her right hand going to the handle of the poniard she wore at her belt. She did not immediately see the speaker amongst the wooden statues which lined the hallway.

"Who speaks?" she asked, keeping her voice lower than the speaker's. *Goddess Terat, aid me!* "Show yourself!"

"One moment." The heavy blue curtains billowed as the unseen speaker fumbled to find the opening. "By Dovré's golden tits," he growled. "Where does this cursed curtain open?"

Inharise eased her grip on the poniard's hilt at his mention of the Goddess Dovré. While neither she nor Heinmyets were dedicated to Dovré's service, the Goddess had made her favor known to them.

An ally, then.

Still, she continued to rest her hand on the hilt as the speaker kept muttering and poking at the curtain, which was partially secured at both ends to help keep the winter's cold out. Inharise and Heinmyets had also cast minor spells on the curtains, to slow down potential assassins. There was enough lingering magic from Medvara in these draperies that the spells were somewhat effective.

Soon enough the magic would fade, and then what?

She missed the simplicity of her Clendan people's long-houses and lodges after spending six months in Keldara's capital city of Dera during the last stages of her pregnancy and Cenarth's first months. True, the big lodges of Clenda had less privacy than the big houses common in Keldara, but these multi-story wooden buildings that Heinmyets's people favored felt full of traps.

Given Nateri's history, I've reason to worry.

The curtains parted as the speaker found the center opening, letting light through from the window on the other side of the curtain. The brightness briefly illuminated the dark hallway, bringing a fleeting flash of cheer to the gloom. A buckskin-clad courier with the darker skin of Heinmyets's kin slipped out from the window seat. Pinned to his fur hat was the blue and white moon and stars badge of the border patrol Heinmyets commanded, the Mer Galad.

"I am Patrol Rider Yamick, under Delian's subcommand." Yamick knelt, then rose, offering Inharise his badge. She took it, running her right index finger over it to query its credentials. The faint trace of magic within the painted metal badge confirmed that Yamick of Kinherit Village was sworn to Delian.

That's why I don't know him.

Delian's Mer Galad patrol rarely came to Dera, in part because his beloved, Heinmyets's sister Ciren, was second-in-command of his patrol. Ciren chose to stay as far away from her father and stepmother—primarily her stepmother—as she could arrange, and Delian respected her wishes.

"What message brings you here, Rider Yamick?" Inharise handed the badge back to him.

Yamick hooked the badge back onto his hat. He extracted a sealed packet tucked inside his heavy fur-lined jacket, offering it to Inharise. "This message from Captain Delian."

News from Delian.

Excitement rose within Inharise. Heinmyets had sent Delian, the out-of-favor Medvaran prince, back to his home to seek support from Delian's sister Alicira, next in line for the leadership of Medvara after their father Richenax.

If we could ally with our distant kin in Medvara, that would strengthen the Two Nations, Heinmyets had said in that quiet meeting between the three of them before Delian left.

Delian had taken three men from his regular patrol to ride with him, leaving Ciren to lead the others.

Yamick rested his hand on hers before she could break the seal. "Would be best to read this in your quarters, madam."

Inharise hesitated. She needed to join Heinmyets in the Great Hall, along with his father Thenil and stepmother Nateri, for the daily audience the Leader of Keldara held for petitioners who wanted their concerns to be brought to the Great Council. Stopping to feed baby Cenarth could only excuse her absence for so long.

"This news needs to be private," Yamick added.

Well, Tewasnin's delegation seeking greater concessions in the daranval trade had yet to arrive from Clenda, so she didn't need to be present right away to promote her kinfolk's cause. She couldn't think of any other pressing petitions that required her specific presence. Thenil and Heinmyets would not object, but Nateri—

Nateri can just fume. News from Delian comes first.

Inharise marched back down the hallway toward their suite, Yamick on her heels. She kept one hand on the hilt of her poniard. Yamick might be Mer Galad, but she didn't know him well, and he would be coming close to her infant son.

Most of Delian's subcommand were from the Keldaran border villages, while the majority of Heinmyets and Inharise's Mer Galad guards in Dera came from her Clendan kinfolk. Still, that isolation didn't guarantee that someone couldn't have encountered Yamick along the way, twisted him to their way of thinking. Little Cenarth was an heir to two nations, and if Nateri had a notion to eliminate him....

But Yamick gave Inharise no reason to worry as he followed politely behind her. They reached the door of Heinmyets and Inharise's suite. Netam and Kerait were on duty, Netam the son of one of Inharise's cousins, Kerait a second cousin's daughter. They saluted her, then Yamick. She inclined her head in return.

"How fares the border?" Kerait asked, smiling at Yamick.

"Your sister Kenseth sends her regards," Yamick said. "She's still envious of your assignment to Lady Inharise."

Good. Kerait knows him.

Inharise relaxed just a little more.

Kerait laughed, her voice high and clear. "Tell her that Dera is boring. Most battles here are fought with words, not action."

Yamick winced. "Words can be enough of a battle, Kerait."

Kerait sobered. "Certainly enough, Yamick, certainly enough." She opened the door for them.

Inharise swept through the door, glad to see that the door to Cenarth's nursery was firmly closed. The suite door had barely shut behind them before she broke the seal and slid the message out of the packet. There were only a few hastily scrawled lines on the paper, written in her own Clendan language rather than Heinmyets's Keldaran.

Burn this after reading. No help possible from Alicira; she is constrained. Yamick knows the old ways. D.

Old ways. That meant Yamick was one who spoke the High Tongue of Delian's Aireii kin. Another testament to his trust-worthiness, as Delian did not teach the High Speech to all of his riders.

"What further word?" she asked him in that speech.

"Captain Delian would have you meet him near Wickmasa," Yamick said, his voice hesitating as he thought through his words in the difficult phrasing of the High Speech. "I am to guide you there. The situation in the message is not entirely as represented due to the Captain's caution. Things are roiling in Medvara, and she who he speaks of has sent her own request. And more."

"How soon?"

"When I left Delian, he was planning to leave Wixtnal in two days. He has—encumbrances. A wagon." Yamick paused. "It will add several days to his travels, he says. I made the ride in three days."

Three days. Delian would have been on the road for one day by now. Wickmasa was a solid three-day ride from Dera, plus whatever time it took to ride to that meeting space. Even with Delian traveling with whatever encumbrances he might have, Heinmyets would need to leave right after this afternoon's Council in order to reach that meeting site without making Delian wait around and possibly attract attention from those who would whisper rumors to Nateri.

"I will have Heinmyets ready to ride as quickly as possible," she said, already thinking about who she should send with him, who she should keep with her for protection. "Rest and prepare yourself."

"Lady Inharise, Captain Delian requests both of you to come."

"My son is yet young and has not gone on a long trip," she demurred, trying to keep the excitement out of her voice.

Cenarth could ride in the cradleboard her father had sent as a birth present. She had been taking him out on short trips to accustom him to the cradleboard and her horse, but sedate rides around the Keldaran valley weren't the same as a *real* ride in the mountains.

Nateri would object to Inharise and Cenarth going with Heinmyets.

On the other hand, what power other than disapproval would Nateri have over her? Inharise had not rebelled before now, biding her time for the right occasion to exercise her independence. She was no delicate flower like Nateri.

It was time to assert herself.

"What he has to say concerns both of you," Yamick said.

"I understand."

Her heart pounded in her ears. Two years ago, the Gods had spoken to Inharise, telling her that a full marriage between herself and Heinmyets was auspicious, but not yet enough for them to avert the danger they both saw approaching. They needed a third member to help spin and weave the magic fabric which would ultimately protect the Two Nations of Keldara and Clenda.

But first, they needed access to the magic fleece from Medvara. Neither Thenil nor Nateri were able to spin or weave it, the magic in the wool evading both of them. Without the magic activated by spinning and weaving, protection against the wrath of the Seven Crowned Gods and of the designs of sorcerers empowered by a God was incomplete for any Leader.

Inharise could weave magic using the fibers from various plants. So could Heinmyets. But for full protection, they needed wool from the fleece of the specially bred sheep the Medvaran exiles had brought from Empire-over-Sea when they fled the crazed Darani Emperor Etikar, who had sought to murder his Aireii kinfolk.

"Provision yourself for the return trip," she said to Yamick. "Take Kerait with you." She followed him to the door. "Kerait. Settle Yamick with provisions and a place to rest. Then go to the stables to prepare horses and our riders for a trip. We ride this afternoon."

"How far?" Kerait asked, using their native Clendan language.

"Three days—and perhaps more."

Kerait's face lit up in anticipation. "All of us?"

"All of us," she confirmed. Inharise turned back inside, first to throw the message into the fire, then to tell Danetna, Cenarth's nurse, about the upcoming trip.

But before she spoke to Danetna, she picked up her son and hugged him.

"It is time you learned your Clendan heritage," she whispered to Cenarth in Clendan. "No more being choked up in the city!"

Until now, she hadn't realized how constrained the past few months had been.

THE MEETING PLACE Delian had told Yamick about was north of Wickmasa, near a hot spring. Reaching it added a half-day to their ride. Not that Inharise minded. Cenarth's cradleboard hung securely from the saddle horn of Inharise's blood bay daranval mare. Lailsa had been a bonding gift from Heinmyets, along with ten sheep and five cattle to set up her own independent wealth, as was the custom in Clenda.

Both Lailsa and Heinmyets's young black daranval stallion

Elantai eagerly trotted along the trails leading to the hot spring near the mountain pass, their swift smooth gait much faster than that of an ordinary horse. Fortunately, Heinmyets's guard all rode daranvelii as well-bred as Lailsa and Elantai, and they brought no pack animals with them, choosing to ride swiftly with stops at the villages along their route at nightfall, so no ordinary horses slowed them.

Still, Inharise was glad they approached the hot spring, climbing up the ridge to the great flat where they would meet Delian.

Only in the saddle until midday.

She had lost her endurance for long rides during the last months of her pregnancy, and the short rides since then were nothing like being in the saddle all day. Fortunately, Cenarth settled quickly into the traveling routine, fussing only when hungry or needing to be cleaned.

A true Clendan in that respect.

"Not much farther, dear one," Heinmyets said, as if he had read her mind. "We should be able to rest for a day or so at the hot spring."

She laughed. "I'm happy to be in the saddle again!"

And away from Dera for at least a short time.

Heinmyets nodded. "I am as well. Being away from Nateri for a while only makes this ride sweeter."

"I agree," she said. They had avoided talking much policy before spending last night at Wickmasa. By this point they were far enough away from Dera that even Nateri's small magics could not eavesdrop on their conversations. Plus there were the special spells that had protected Wickmasa over the years.

Metkyi, the young Wickmasan shaman who followed the God Staul, had helped Inharise and Heinmyets check to ensure that no traces of Nateri's listening spells lingered amongst their things.

Inharise continued. "Now that I can ride again, we need to be traveling to see our peoples. Not everyone can come to Dera. Enough snow has gone from the mountains that we could begin our rounds after talking to Delian."

"I've mentioned the need to Father."

"And Nateri?"

He grimaced. "What do you think? She still wants to keep us tied to Dera. But our treaty obligations to your people are greater than Nateri's desires, no matter what she whispers into my father's ears. He's not so entranced by her that he doesn't see the need. We discussed the necessity for you and me to go to Clenda and the border villages when I told him there was a call for us to come to Wickmasa." He paused. "I think we should go out with the herds this spring as well, stay away from Dera until fall."

"Yes. Get our herd away from the others."

Ever since her magic had returned with Cenarth's birth, they had used the cover of rebuilding Inharise's riding strength to examine the Keldaran herds for any sheep with the faintest hint of magic in their fleece and trade for them. Oh, there were sheep with magic in their fleeces, but it was weak. Only a handful had sufficient magic to potentially provide the wool for spinning and weaving a Tapestry. By separating their herd from the others, both she and Heinmyets hoped to rebuild its magical strength.

As they reached the top of the ridge, Inharise thought she heard the distant bleat of sheep.

"Yamick, I didn't think there were any herds out yet," Heinmyets called to him. "There's still snowbanks!"

Yamick reined his daranval in to wait for them, now allowing a faint smile to twitch his lips. "I should let Delian tell you—but that's the reason for his delay."

"Sheep?" Inharise asked. *Why would Delian have sheep—* Excitement rose within her. "From Medvara?"

Yamick nodded, his grin spreading.

Inharise and Heinmyets exchanged a glance. Then he urged Elantai into a gallop. Lailsa followed, Inharise urging her to greater speed, though she could only gain to Elantai's flank. Yamick and the other riders whooped, joining them.

At that speed it wasn't long before Inharise spotted the camp at the edge of the trees, with picketed and loose daranvelii, two wagons, five tents—and a milling group of six sheep by the wagons, stirring anxiously at the sound of hooves, barely kept from bolting by two black and white dogs and three people.

Heinmyets eased Elantai back into a walk. He uttered a deep, ululating call that was answered by a higher-pitched voice—Ciren. She waved at them, then whistled. Two of the loose daranvelii trotted toward camp. Ciren and Delian swung up on their mounts bareback, trotting toward Heinmyets and Inharise.

Ciren reached them first. Heinmyets dismounted and hugged her, then Delian. Inharise carefully got off of Lailsa and unhooked Cenarth's cradleboard from her saddle horn.

"This is the little one?" Ciren joined Inharise.

"This is your nephew Cenarth."

"May I?" Ciren asked. Inharise eased the cradleboard into Ciren's waiting arms, pausing until she was certain Ciren held his weight. Aunt and nephew gazed at each other. Delian joined Ciren as she stroked Cenarth's cheek, her fingers dark against Cenarth's red-brown. "He favors you, Inharise."

"Better her than me." Heinmyets slid his arm around Inharise and pulled her close. "He has travelled well. We will be able to take him out with the herds this spring."

"And I bring him a gift," Delian said softly. "Or, rather, Alicira and I bring little Cenarth a gift for the future of the Two Nations." He gestured toward the agitated sheep. "Two ram lambs and four ewe lambs, all that we could slip away from the Medvaran flocks. All strong in magic, the strongest that Alicira dared sort out. Go look."

Inharise hesitated.

"I have Cenarth," Ciren said.

"Bring him, please."

Maybe she would have the chance to do a proper introduction of Cenarth to the flock. They had been under too much observation by those who would run tattling to Nateri for Inharise to present him properly to the herd leaders. This would be a perfect opportunity to do that to this small flock, at least.

Inharise tucked her hand into Heinmyets's elbow as they walked toward the now quiet sheep. When they were ten paces away from the little flock, she slipped her hand free and moved more slowly, murmuring soft reassurances and copying the soft call of a mother ewe. She knelt three paces away from the sheep, continuing to make reassuring noises. One of the dogs guarding the sheep ran up to Inharise and inspected her before returning to her duties.

Heinmyets stooped next to Inharise. The sheep had the blond face of the standard Medvaran breed, with a faint golden sheen to their fleeces. But that didn't necessarily mean these sheep had magic in them. She and Heinmyets had blond-faced and gold-fleeced sheep amongst their herds. The only way to tell if these were truly bearers of magical fleece, especially at this age, was to touch them. As wild and skittery as these half-grown lambs appeared to be, that might take time.

Delian joined them, stiffly dropping to one knee. "Alicira chose them for me," he said quietly. "They come from Alexran's own flock. I wouldn't know magical fleece from non-magical, but Alicira knows the pedigrees and tried them each herself."

Inharise caught her breath at the mention of the Medvaran leader Alexran, the grandfather of Alicira and Delian. *Does this mean—*

"Are you certain you didn't put her at risk?" Heinmyets

asked. "This is a gift beyond belief, but at what cost? Or does Alexran look with favor upon our suit of Alicira?"

Inharise made herself breathe again.

Please, dear Goddess, let this be true.

Reports from Medvara hinted that Alicira was not viewed with favor by Alexran, even though she was his only descendant with magical ability. Rumors insinuated that the ruler of Medvara sought to wed his granddaughter to any faraway leader who would keep her occupied and away from Medvara.

So why not bring Alicira into the Two Nations as our spouse? Inharise had suggested when they first heard this news. *Terat has said we cannot fully bind ourselves to each other without a third who will bring us power greater than we imagine. That could be Alicira.*

We have to overcome Nateri's opposition, had been Heinmyets's answer. *Nateri may be Aireii, but her family was a rival to Alicira's in the Empire.*

Never mind that Nateri was exiled from Medvara due to her destruction of the Cooscol berry trade, another source of magical power in that nation. She brought a faint glimmer of legitimacy to those exiles from the Empire-over-Sea in Keldara who had left Medvara, seeking to be free from Alexran's constraints. Nateri might be from the Ralsem instead of the royal Miteal, but she still claimed kinship to the Emperor-over-Sea.

Thenil's marriage to Nateri added to his legitimacy as Leader when he dealt with nations such as Larij to the north and Keratil to the south. No longer was he considered a poor relation of the lower-class Aireii in Medvara who had come to bolster the native Keldaran population after the Great Plague.

"It's—complicated."

Delian started to say more, but one of the lambs ventured toward Inharise. The three of them stayed quiet as Inharise coaxed the ewe close enough to scratch her forehead and run her fingers through her wool. She inhaled sharply as the magic pulsed against her fingertips.

The other sheep followed the ewe's lead. Heinmyets ran his fingers through the coat of one of the rams.

"Amazing," he murmured. "Their magic is so strong."

"This is a marvelous gift, Delian. So Alexran looks with favor upon our petition to marry Alicira?" Inharise asked.

Delian scowled. "Alas, no, he does not. My grandfather listens to a recent arrival from Daran, Zauril, who aggressively pursues my sister. Alicira is doing her best to evade Zauril, even talking to Haran of Larij in hopes that Alexran might view that marriage with some sort of favor." He grimaced. "Unfortunately, Haran's preferences are too well-known. Alexran does not support that alliance."

Inharise nodded. Haran of Larij was the youngest son of the ruler of Larij, known as the Mershaunten. She had met Haran and Orlanden en Selail, Haran's companion of the heart, in Wixtnal, on the border between Larij and Keldara. Larij and Medvara were not as flexible about same-sex or multiple-partner relationships as Keldara or Clenda were.

Keldara had a history of taking in exiles for various reasons —such as Delian. Inharise had been privy to Heinmyets's discreet offer of refuge to Haran should it be needed.

Bringing in outsiders has made Keldara strong, Heinmyets had said on their ride back from the meeting in Wixtnal where he had made that offer. *Orlanden is an excellent negotiator, and Haran's almost his equal. If the Mershaunten and his eldest son are foolish enough to discard Haran because of his partnership preferences, well, then—*

A similar assessment, backed by Delian's concerns, had led to drafting their offer requesting Alicira's hand in marriage.

Perhaps Alexran didn't look with favor upon the alliances that Heinmyets was trying to create in Keldara and Clenda in preparation for his ascension to Leadership. But the sheer value of this gift suggested that Alicira was in favor of their proposal.

"Nonetheless, Haran remains close to Medvare-the-city as a potential protector for Alicira." A grim note deepened Delian's voice. "I would go back, to be a source of safety for my sister, except that she sent me away for my own protection."

"Oh?" Heinmyets raised his brows.

"We had to move quickly because Zauril got wind of what we were doing and tried to stop us." Delian tightened his lips. "I now bear the title of thief. I hope that Alicira has not come to any harm as a result. She had signed papers granting these sheep to you, but...." his voice trailed off. "I hope she's all right," he said finally. "Once things have calmed down a bit, I'll go back. With your leave, of course!"

"Of course." Heinmyets rose. "Well, we'll put these sheep in with our herds. A good thing that they're young. They'll adapt to our conditions much more quickly than adult sheep. You've transported them well—they're in very good shape."

"We've been carrying them in the wagon, especially over the rougher passages," Delian said.

"Good. They won't look like they've been traveling hard. No one will notice them amongst our herds," Heinmyets said. He and Delian walked away as Ciren joined Inharise.

Inharise reached for the cradleboard. She carefully extracted Cenarth, holding him in her arms as she crooned to the sheep.

"Come meet the one who will have need of your magic when older," she murmured to the little flock. She half-expected that the first ewe and ram to greet her and Heinmyets would be the leaders.

Instead, one of the ewes who had hung back moved forward, accompanied by the other ram. She nuzzled Cenarth, who startled, then clumsily brushed his little fingers across the ewe lamb's face. The lamb inhaled deeply of Cenarth, then stepped back. The ram nosed Cenarth more firmly than the ewe lamb had. Cenarth didn't startle but a random movement of his hand smacked the ram lamb's nose. A tiny golden spark flashed between baby and lamb.

Inharise caught her breath as the ram jerked back, then came forward again, nuzzling Cenarth more gently.

There's a link between Cenarth and the magic in these lambs. Oh Terat, this is better than I anticipated.

Even better, this suggested that magic would be strong in her son, for him to react to these sheep so powerfully at his age.

Delian's gift was marvelous—but to know this about her son was priceless.

Heinmyets joined her, reaching out to scratch the ram lamb's face as he talked. "I am sending Delian back with a gift for Alicira." His face tightened. "Given the circumstances and the value of this gift, I—I think we should give her a daranval."

"Perhaps the most powerful unbonded daranval we have?"

Heinmyets nodded. Then he looked at Cenarth, and a smile softened his expression. "Our boy has magic, doesn't he?"

"Yes—there was the slightest of sparks when he touched this lamb's face."

"Wonderful. And—yes. There's a palomino mare who has not bonded to anyone yet. I was surprised when she wouldn't bond with anyone during her training."

Inharise thought for a moment—oh yes, that one palomino mare who was cooperative but standoffish. No name yet—unbonded daranvelii were rarely named. "Perhaps she's been waiting for Alicira."

"Perhaps. She's young and fast, and in the worst case, would provide a safe mount for Alicira to flee on." His face clouded for a moment. "Although, if she chose to bond with Alicira…."

"Let's hope she does."

"In the meantime—let's settle for the night. You wanted rest and a hot spring soak." He winked at Ciren. "And since our son has his aunt here to watch over him, we can soak—*together.*"

Inharise smiled at Heinmyets. "Then let's hurry up. I hear that hot spring calling my name."

He laughed.

BEYOND HONOR

CHAPTER 1

"It's time to move on, my lady." Orlanden's voice was firm but apologetic as he shook Alicira awake. She jerked into sharp awareness of her surroundings, pulse pounding hard in her ears from her nightmare.

Did I really wrench my magic free from Zauril's control?

She lay on her back and stared at the wide gray sky above her, momentarily disoriented by the treeless surroundings so different from the damp forests of her former Medvaran home.

This definitely wasn't Medvara. Orlanden's fur-lined cloak cushioned her against the chilly dirt and bunchgrass. Sagebrush loomed over her, its faint acrid fragrance strangely soothing as it framed the thick white clouds skittering across the restless backdrop of higher gray clouds.

Storm coming.

Worry clenched her gut.

Natural or magical?

Without thinking, Alicira reached for her connection with the land, the enhanced natural senses that would answer her concern about the oncoming storm's origin. Then she flinched away from contact with the raw wound in her magical senses.

Even though she knew the land's magic was gone from her, reaching for it was still a reflex.

You cursed Zauril and banished Medvara's magic.

In doing so, she had cast away her magical link to the land that grounded her. Only the tiniest of connections to her homeland's magic remained now. Not enough magic was left to answer her question.

However, now that she was more awake, she doubted the likelihood of this being a magical storm. Zauril's magic couldn't build a storm. Was it strong enough to shape a naturally developing one?

In Medvara, she knew the answer would be no. Out here in the high desert ruled by the Saubral and their sinister Shadowwalkers, the possibility seemed all too likely.

Alicira shuddered and drew in a deep breath. Storm magic was a matter of legend. Not even the Saubral Shadowwalkers could control weather, in spite of the traditions they claimed.

But that knowledge didn't rid Alicira of the creeping worry about *just what can Zauril do.* Not after six months as his prisoner. She wrapped her hands in her scarf, the first magic weaving she had created from her own spinning, and called upon the power within it to scan the storm. Her magic responded slowly at first, sparking a deeper worry.

Was the dream true after all?

Had she lost all her sorcery to Zauril's machinations, even the oldest and most familiar?

Warmth pulsed through her hands and she could see deeper and farther into the world about her, able to scan the storm with her othersight. No telltale trace of magic rode those thick white clouds.

She pushed her magic vision a little harder, now seeking the whereabouts of the rest of their party. Orlanden still knelt next to her. Five of the six riders Haran had sent with him stood guard, scattered around the sagebrush near their grazing horses.

But her brother Delian and one of the riders were gone. Their absence sent a quick spasm of panic through her.

Alicira took another deep, calming breath, focusing on the sharp sage scent to steady herself. Delian and the rider Witmohan must have scouted ahead while she rested. They had talked about doing that at lunch, so they wouldn't be far away. Could she find them? Alicira quested further, seeking that faint blue-gray trace that marked her brother in the world that her othersight showed her, magicless though he was.

Then the child within her stirred, pushing back against her mother's magic. Alicira's stomach tightened as the sour, half-digested remains of the lunch she had eaten before her nap threatened to come back up. She swallowed hard to keep it down, but the spasms were stronger than her will, pushing acid liquid and foul chunks into her mouth. She rolled off of Orlanden's cloak to hands and knees, and vomited under a bush, thankful when Orlanden pulled her heavy braids out of the way to keep them clean, just like he had after breakfast.

I can't use magic to keep going for much longer.

Her remnant of Medvara's magic warred with the child's growing power. By next full moon, she would have to give up all use of it. Normally this would be good news. The child's lack of tolerance for her mother's magic was the mark of a powerful sorcerer-to-be.

But whose power did her daughter carry—Alicira's or Zauril's? By this point in her pregnancy, she should know—and she didn't. The Goddess Dovré, Alicira's patron, was silent. Was it a sign that Alicira still carried Zauril's taint in spite of fleeing him? Or did Dovré's silence mean that his magic dominated in their daughter?

It can't be his magic. Otherwise, wouldn't I be sensing Nitel?

The bloody goddess Nitel was Zauril's patron, and very different from Dovré. But no taint of Nitel lingered in her contact with the child. No red shadows hung around her.

It is all right. It will be all right.

Or it would be all right once she found shelter and a new home to bear and raise her daughter.

"Here, my lady." Orlanden offered a waterskin.

Alicira nodded thanks as she took it, easing back on her heels. Worry made his normal owl-like expression even more solemn as he studied her. She had not been able to keep down most of her meals during their flight from Medvare-the-city, where she had been imprisoned.

She swished water in her mouth, then spat it out before chancing a couple of swallows. The cold water settled in her unhappy gut, sitting hard like she'd swallowed a stone.

At least it didn't want to come back up.

"My brother?" she asked.

"Rode out with Witmohan to scout for tonight's camp," Orlanden said. "We should be close to meeting with Haran soon." His voice lightened at the mention of his lover, the youngest son of the Mershaunten of Larij. "Perhaps he brings news that the Mershaunten offers you asylum, after all."

Alicira stood, brushing off the knees of her leather breeches. "I hope you're right, Orlanden."

He was being optimistic. According to the Mershaunten's beliefs, she should stay in Medvara under Zauril's thumb. And yet—

He did not send representation to that travesty of a bonding ceremony.

The Mershaunten hadn't recognized Zauril's overthrow of her grandfather Alexran, either. There was that small hope.

But even though she had refused to complete the bonding ceremony that truly tied her to Zauril, there was the child.

Zauril's child.

And Zauril's magic, whatever one thought about the man himself, held much power and strength. Even if the Medvaran army lacked the magic Alicira had banished from the land, it still possessed the weaponry from Daran, the Empire-over-Sea, that Zauril had provided and that no other nations here in this land of Varen possessed. Only the Mershaunten possessed battle strength close to that claimed by Zauril.

Tingles from her location spell alerted her, distracting Alicira from her worries.

Delian is near.

She reached to touch her brother's mind and reassure herself that he was all right. But the child objected again, as another sorcerous presence made itself known.

Who?

She and Delian were the last of the Miteal. The inquiry she felt belonged to a wielder of Miteal magic.

Who else managed to survive?

Nausea washed through Alicira when she tried to probe further, and she struggled to keep the water in her stomach. Lack of food she could endure for a time, with magic's help.

Lack of water, she couldn't.

One of the guards alerted before she could speak. He scrambled up a rimrock, peering down the coulee below their lunch spot. Then he slid back down.

"Riders," he called in a soft voice pitched to carry only to their small group. "Four of them."

Orlanden drew his sword. Three of the guards rushed toward Alicira, drawing their swords to protect her. The lookout and another guard gathered the horses and slipped the bridles back on them.

"No need to worry," Alicira said. "Delian rides with them."

But who's the magician?

Orlanden nodded acknowledgement as he sheathed his sword and stooped to gather his cloak before he took his place in the protective formation around her. The two mounted guards ponied the horses over to them and each person took their mount's reins. Alicira swung up onto her new mare

Narasin, who had been sent by Delian's patron, Heinmyets of Keldara, as a pledge of support.

Narasin bounced a little under Alicira, head high, ears flicking back and forth, nostrils wide as she measured the magic flowing around them.

"Steady," Alicira breathed, taking up a light contact on the reins.

She stroked the golden mare's neck, thinking soothing thoughts. The mare's mind pushed back against Alicira's, but there was no warning about danger amongst her excitement at the arrival of new horses. Narasin was one of the magic-gifted breed called *daranval* by the Keldarans who bred and trained them. She and Alicira were not fully bonded as yet, but so far Narasin's skills complimented Alicira's magic.

Other daranvelii were with the oncoming group. Delian's mare, of course, and Haran would also be daranval-mounted. But there was also at least one more daranval of high rank with that group, one whose presence reeked of a strong bond with a human magician, like Alicira hoped to develop with Narasin.

So who is it?

Alicira reached into the magic currents around her, drawing on her partial linkage with Narasin to scry who this rider was.

The magician with Delian unshielded as if he had heard her thought. His touch brushed against her mind, dark midnight blue in hue with silver highlights, familiar and beloved even though it had been ten years since they had last seen each other. Then, he had been raging and crazed as a result of his exile from Medvara, the midnight blue shot through with dark blood red. No sign remained of that dark red.

Then he mindspoke to her.

Niece, are you all right?

Oh Uncle. Oh Uncle.

Relief flooded over her, wordless joy mixed with sorrow that kept her from mindspeeching more than those two words.

Her uncle Alame. Her father's brother. The family hadn't heard even a whisper from him since his exile. When Medvara's magic had come to her upon her grandfather's murder last summer, Alicira had been certain that Alame was dead.

Not so, apparently. She and Delian were not the last survivors of the House of Miteal, despite Zauril's boasts. Unexpectedly tears blurred her vision and she gulped back a sob.

"What's wrong?" Orlanden asked.

"My uncle lives," she murmured. "Alame rides with Delian."

She urged Narasin forward, not bothering to wipe away the tears spilling down her cheeks.

Alame lived. She was not the last magician of the Miteal.

Not the last, despite Zauril's taunts.

Narasin bounded down the narrow trail winding along the coulee's steep slope, breaking into the daranval long gallop at the bottom, the smooth floating gait so much faster than that of an ordinary horse.

An unfamiliar blood bay daranval led the others coming toward them. Prickles of daranval magic swept through Alicira as Narasin challenged the oncoming riders through mindspeech, projecting an image of herself as larger than life, sparks and flame flashing from each of her footfalls.

Findel, partner to Alame!

The blood bay stallion swaggered as he boasted, neck arching as he added a deep whicker to emphasize his mindspeech, flagging his black tail high as he pranced in a big, showy, floating trot.

Narasin, partner to Alicira!

Narasin countered with a toss of her silvery mane at the stud's posturing.

Tears blurred Alicira's eyes. Her uncle opened his arms wide as Narasin marched up to Findel. Heedless of her balance in the saddle, Alicira leaned over and grabbed her uncle, burying her head in his chest. The sobs she had kept under restraint during the hideous events of the past summer and fall finally broke free.

Alame's arms tightened hard around her. He stroked her back as Narasin shifted under her weight.

"Niece, niece," he murmured. "I feared the worst until I encountered Haran on the road. Your light went out but the magic didn't come to me. I feared all was lost, that Zauril had destroyed you too. I was on my way to challenge him as the last of the Miteal, all hope gone, and then—" He choked and his arms wrapped themselves even tighter around her. "The sight of Delian this morning and his news of your escape were so very welcome."

Sooner than she expected, the tears ebbed away. Alicira was able to release Alame and slide back into a more secure position in Narasin's saddle.

"Your light went out too and the soul of Medvara came to me," she gulped. "I thought I was alone. I thought it should have gone to you next, not to me."

Alame's jaw tightened. "My father's curse stayed true. I am cast out from the line of inheritance. I only hold my personal sorcery, not the royal power." He studied her, frowning. "But your magic is shadowed and restrained. What has happened?"

"Zauril." Her tone went bitter and hard. "He attempted to force me to bond with him—and I carry his child."

Anger brought Alame's brows down into a tight line, lips thinning until she almost couldn't see them. "He dared."

"The bond was not completed. I refused the words and the final swearing. Nonetheless he acted as if it were done."

"Medvara did not aid your resistance?"

She shook her head. "The reddest of blood magic, uncle. Zauril used Nitel to block my awareness while he killed Grandfather Alexran. Then, while I was fighting my way free of that accursed goddess's power, he fed Mother to Karnoi and Cirdel. Only then did I get the land's magic—and it was too late for me to act. Between those three gods, he spun a restraining web that took me ages to break. But I still could not fully wield Medvara's magic."

Alame winced. "Not a good sign at all. So *he* wields the Twin Gods as well as Nitel?"

"No. The Twins chose to support him at first. But he did not honor them after mother—they withdrew their favor." She swallowed hard. "I owe the Twins a price. He considers himself beyond the need to honor the Gods. Any Gods, except perhaps for Nitel. He aspires to Godhood himself. He betrayed the Twins while he tried to use me to reach that power. Karnoi and Cirdel's wrath after Zauril twisted their power was enough to aid Delian when he came to free me."

"So none other stood with you?"

"No. Grandfather had been thoroughly enchanted by Zauril's sweet words and bright toys from Daran, enough to speak of pursuing those who have fled Medvara's grasp in Keldara. By the time Zauril acted, he had secured the support of the army and the Guards by speaking of invasion, conquest, and gold. None dared openly help me." She smiled bitterly at Alame. "Let us see how well Zauril can run Medvara without the land's magic. Once I crossed the borders, even with his babe quickened in my womb, I cursed him and his hold on the land. *My* curse held. He bound me from wielding Medvara's magic—but he can't use it either."

"So he is another rebel against Daran?" Alame's long fingers flickered in a quick ward at the mention of the great Empire east of the Great Ocean, that had once been ruled by the house of Miteal.

"It is—complicated. Originally, he came as an emissary from the Empire-over-Sea." Alicira used the more common phrasing for Daran, not wanting to exert her magic to protect herself against its mention. "He swore fealty to the Empire as he killed Grandfather. He claims he bears the sanction of the current Emperor. Except—when he got this child on me while trying to raise himself as God, I was briefly able to see into his thoughts. He wants more than human rule. He wants divinity—and, since he failed with me, he thinks my daughter would be his tool to achieve it."

She shuddered, the memory of that glance into Zauril's mind even more frightening than his physical abuse. Remembering the bloody sacrifices and vile ceremonies that Zauril had been contemplating in order to make himself a God. What he would do once he gained Godhood haunted her more than the abuses that he had inflicted upon her.

What if he succeeded in bending my daughter into those pathways from her earliest moments? What if her conception is cursed from the beginning?

Alame's face tightened even more. "I see just enough of it from your thoughts. Oh, niece. If only I had been there to help."

"You might have fallen along with Grandfather," she said bitterly. "Reddest betrayals. Better you were away from it. Better you are alive now."

"I should have been there." Alame heaved a heavy sigh. "But my father—the fool—oh niece."

She exhaled a long deep breath, centering and calming herself. "It is a long story, uncle, and Zauril may not have the support he claims. There are—things I learned about his connections to the Empire while his prisoner, things he may not be aware that I now know." She coughed, then changed the subject. "It does my heart good to see you alive after all these years. Zauril claimed you were dead."

Alame's lips loosened enough to give her a faint smile. "He tried to ensure my death just this spring. But I have studied well over these years of exile, and not all my power comes from the Miteal. There are other paths." He straightened up. "But we need to ride fast and hard. The news Haran brings—well, best you speak to him."

Alicira nodded, though she thought she knew what Haran would say, given her uncle's expression. No asylum from Larij. The Mershaunten had chosen to exercise his famous caution. Otherwise Alame would not have been so careful not to speak for Haran.

Nonetheless I will find a way to endure and earn my vengeance on Zauril. With or without the Mershaunten. I will remember the choice he has made.

She rubbed Narasin's neck. Larij was not an option for refuge. That left Heinmyets and Keldara. A gift of Narasin's value had to be some measure of his willingness to grant her asylum—wouldn't it?

CHAPTER 2

THE OPPORTUNITY TO SPEAK OF POLICIES AND ASYLUM WITH
Haran did not arise until after dinner that night. Haran's men
set up a rough camp in a cottonwood grove and meadow at the
bottom of a narrow little draw that opened into the coulee. The
tiny creek trickling through the meadow poured into a small
pool just big enough to provide horse and human water for a
night's camp.

Alame concocted a broth for Alicira from grouse captured
during the afternoon's hunt, plus herbs and seeds gathered from
around their camp. He blended them with a spell to quiet the
child so that Alicira could rest further.

To that end, he insisted she sit. Her fatigue and the relief at
holding down solid food seconded that urging, even though she
itched to help with camp chores and prepare for the next day's
ride. Alame and Orlanden arranged her bedroll with brush and
downed cottonwood limbs so that she could sit next to the fire
with a back support, and stay warm.

Alicira took over fire tending duties while the others
worked. At least that was something useful she could do. The
food and warmth made her sleepy, but anticipation of the

conversations she needed to have about what would happen tomorrow and afterwards kept her awake.

At last Haran dropped onto his bedroll next to hers, offering the shy smile he hid from others. She smiled back at him, noting how Delian and Alame and the others busied themselves away from the two of them.

As if we were courting.

She bit back the bitter chuckle she wanted to make. Haran's somber expression told her what she needed to know. She knew him too well after her three years of fostering in the Mershaunten's court.

His lips tightened and he shook his head, looking down and away from her, jabbing at the dirt in front of him with a stick, obviously struggling with what he had to say.

Oh Haran.

She wanted to reach out and hug him, wanted to tell him this wasn't his fault. They had discussed a threefold marriage last spring, to cover his relationship with Orlanden and to keep Zauril away from her. If there had been more time to arrange it—

But there hadn't been, and past was past. If she had known what Zauril was capable of doing, she would have fled Medvara a season earlier with Delian, in spite of parental disapproval.

Two seasons, even—but she hadn't, and *past was past*, she repeated to herself.

"A long ride, my friend?" she said finally.

"All the longer for what I have to say." Haran took her hand and raised it to his lips. "I wish I brought you better news," he sighed, still holding her hand as he lowered it. "The best I could do was to keep my father from acknowledging Zauril's acts as legitimate. At least he fears Zauril's ambition."

"That was no little thing," she said, giving him a small smile. "Then no asylum, not even if we were to marry?"

His mouth twisted. "I suggested marriage as a means of

rescue even before Delian came seeking assistance, and earned a rant from my father which went on for the entire evening. My father has no love for Zauril, no desire for an alliance with him —but neither does he believe it's safe to harbor you in any way, even if we were to marry." He dropped her hand and stared into the fire. "Worse yet, he's aware of the ties between me and Orlanden."

"Oh no. How?"

He shrugged. "Gossip rules supreme at the Mershaunten's court. Orlanden is under edict." He sighed heavier than before, and met her eyes. "I have to withdraw my riders from Orlanden's command and sever all ties with him. Delian managed to negotiate a small concession on how soon I have to return and submit to my father's will, or join Orlanden in the ranks of the outcast. I have a couple of days to say farewell to him, no more."

"So he's completely cast out?"

"I may be able to secure a position for him in Wixtnal, administering the springs. It may take a year before Father will allow me to do so, though."

She nodded. Wixtnal was a small hot springs resort near the border of Larij and Keldara. It had been many years since she had visited it, but she remembered Wixtnal as being small and isolated.

"It may be the best place for him."

"Trust me, my father's gossips will ensure we have no connection once he is there," Haran said bitterly. "The Court is already developing a fascination with the place. But, until then —he is under edict."

Under edict. The words echoed heavily in her heart. Under the Mershaunten's rule, Orlanden could not return to Larij under pain of death until the edict against him was lifted. True, he might find his way back to favor after a few years, but until then? Winter was coming. No options except—

"He's been a great help to me," she said in a low voice. "I can't promise where I will take him or what his fate will be, but if he would want to ride with me, he's welcome."

The Goddess knows I can use every person available.

Haran heaved a relieved sigh. "That helps to relieve my worries over both of you. I have worried about my friend Alicira ever since the horrors of this Midsummer, and with Orlanden in your service, I know you will both do well."

"And you have been right to worry." She sat up taller. "Medvara is lost." Her voice broke. "Medvara is lost and I have not the faintest notion where I will next find a home. I can't promise much to Orlanden. Maybe a place in Keldara."

"Keldara?"

"Heinmyets sent me a daranval and hints of more help. He had approached my grandfather for a marriage between us before Zauril—acted— and had been rejected." She closed her eyes for a moment as bleak memories stirred of Zauril and his ambitions. Would Heinmyets be able to protect her? There were other problems as well. Keldara had taken in rebels against her grandfather's rule. How many of those refugees might hold a grudge against her, enough to undermine any sanctuary she might find there?

"I wish I bore better news. If Heinmyets can keep you safe—" His voice trailed away and from his expression, she suspected he felt many of the same doubts about Keldara's potential as a refuge as she did.

Alicira dropped her head into her hands. "Where do I go now?" she breathed, trying to keep her voice from sliding into a whine. "I carry Zauril's child. It will be a strong magician. I just don't know whether it carries my magic or his. Can I at least cross the River with you, and travel as far as possible on that side on my way to Keldara, away from the Saubral?"

"No. Guards are stationed at all the ferries to take you into custody and return you to Medvara should you try to enter

Larij. My father will not aid in any pursuit as long as you stay out of Larij—but you are under edict as well."

Haran's hands closed convulsively on hers. Alicira raised her head, taking in Haran's stricken look. Since her escape she had been focused on riding to meet Haran, with no thought beyond evading Zauril and a vague hope that just as Haran had sent Orlanden with Delian to free her, he would sweet-talk his father into providing a place for her to hide and bear her child.

The Mershaunten's court would have been a good place to raise her daughter in opposition to Zauril, even though her conception went beyond all honor. Alicira had hoped that the Mershaunten would have understood that reality, honor be damned. Keldara was an option, but Keldara, despite Heinmyets's apparent friendliness, was unknown.

Now Keldara was her best choice. If she even had an option other than Keldara. Nothing else seemed promising.

Ride north? Larij blocked that possibility. West lay Medvara and the ocean. No help lay over Sea. The lands to Medvara's south would be of no assistance, weak as they were in the face of Zauril's wrath. Treaties of alliance had been signed in her presence, in part to break her, she was certain. The Saubral controlled this inland sagebrush desert for days of riding to the south, and she knew nothing of the lands beyond the Saubral influence.

Two nations south and east of Keldara were her only other alternatives. Keratil, to the southeast of the Saubral. Or directly east of Keldara and its partner nation, Clenda, to Waykemin, the land of the witches.

Keratil and its capitol, Nere—well, she had little reason to expect safety there. Nere's openness as a trade city would mean easy refuge with little analysis or resistance. But she would need to be on constant guard. Alicira and her child would be targets for ambitious magicians and travelers seeking Zauril's favor, not to speak of conspirators seeking to exploit their magic to bolster their own goals.

And Waykemin? Alicira shivered. Zauril's bloody goddess Nitel ruled there. The price that Alicira expected the witches of Waykemin would demand for the safety of herself and her daughter made her hesitate to consider that option. Waykemin would absorb both of them. Worse, she still might fall prey to Zauril's ambitions through Nitel's intervention.

Perhaps Heinmyets was the best choice.

But Keldara was not what she had hoped for.

Larij was familiar. Haran and Orlanden would not pressure her. For all the Mershaunten's barbaric notions about there being a solitary God, Larij was an understandable entity, with risks and benefits she understood from three years of fostering with the Mershaunten's household. Keldara and Clenda carried their own perils beyond the Medvaran exiles. From all reports both nations still were rough and undeveloped, a place of wandering herders and small villages, except for the main city of the Two Nations, Dera. A wild land.

"I wish I could help," Haran said, slipping his hands from hers. "But I dare not bring you to my father. Not now. He'd hand you back over to Zauril without hesitation."

"Sending Orlanden was more help than you could have imagined. Without him I could not have escaped Zauril." Alicira bit her lip. "Helping me may have given Zauril's sympathizers in your father's court a reason to cause you problems."

"Possible," Haran acknowledged, staring down at his hands.

She leaned over and rested her hand on his shoulder. "Why are you spending time with me now that you've delivered your message? Off with you. Go be with your love. Better that you not know what I'm doing next. Then you can honestly report to your father's lackeys that you have no more involvement with either one of us."

"I hate this," he growled. "I hate what this is doing to all of us. I hate worrying about you and Orlanden."

"Haran. Don't worry. You have done what you can, which is more than most would. You have to protect yourself, too. We will worry about you—don't be reckless. Please take care of yourself. Should any harm come to you for my sake—" Her throat tightened and it took a few moments before she could speak again. "You've done what you can for me, and I am grateful for it. But for now—go. Be with your love."

He gave her a sideways smile, then rose, slowly, brushing off his seat. "I will find a way to help you further," he said. "By one means or another."

"Orlanden to ride with me will be more than enough." Her voice softened. "Protect yourself. I don't want to lose my friend Haran."

He raised her hand as if to kiss it, then pulled her close, hugging her hard and kissing the top of her head.

"I wish I was brave enough to do what is right for you," he whispered. "Even with my father's opposition."

She leaned back and stroked his cheek. "It takes courage to love where you do. You've already done enough to help me. Stay strong for your love. Go be with him now. I'll make sure he stays safe after you part."

"But who will watch over you?"

"I have Delian and now Alame and your Orlanden. Don't worry. Go! Your time is short!"

He smiled sadly and left. Alicira awkwardly tucked her legs to her chest, wrapping her arms around her knees as she stared into the fire.

Keldara and Clenda. Her best choice now. Delian's choice to ride with Heinmyets's guard had earned him exile. Her family had scoffed at his decision to work for the descendants of Aireii servants. But Delian had preferred to join the handful of Aireii who had merged with the native Tauri families in Keldara, rather than continue to be scorned in Medvara for his lack of magic.

She scowled at the flames. Magic. She needed magic and the favor of the Gods to protect both herself and her unborn child from Zauril's wrath. She was beyond all honor thanks to what he had done to her, unless she could find a sponsor and protection somewhere.

Did Heinmyets have magic? Her grandfather had mocked the possibilities of her marriage to him for just that reason. Delian had formally conveyed Heinmyets's interest in marrying Alicira last spring when options other than Zauril had seemed possible. But he had not mentioned any sort of magical ability on Heinmyets's part. Heinmyets's magical abilities—or lack thereof—were even more important now.

As if summoned by her thoughts, both Alame and Delian came up to the fire to warm their hands.

"Haran told you that the Mershaunten refuses you asylum," Delian said, no question in his voice.

Alicira nodded. "I can't see any option other than going east. To Heinmyets—or beyond."

Alame frowned. "Isn't Heinmyets already pledged to Inharise of Clenda?"

"Heinmyets and Inharise are married, though she is not designated as his First Wife. The Clendans as well as the Keldarans openly acknowledge threefold marriages," Delian said. "Especially when it is a matter of policy and alliances. As my sister, Alicira would be honored even without her magic." He hesitated. "And—"

"Do you really want that?" Alame broke in, interrupting Delian. "If he is already contracted, you would be a second wife."

A bitter chuckle tore free from her throat. "Have I any choice, uncle? I'm carrying Zauril's child, remember? That makes me spoiled goods in the eyes of those who might otherwise see a use in marrying a renegade Miteal heir."

"You deserve better than a lesser wife's rank," grumbled Alame.

"That may not matter." She pulled one of her braids forward, twisting it around her finger. "Not given Zauril's attempt at bonding with me. Magic holds truer than marriage in some circles."

"Heinmyets is better than that," Delian said softly. "Remember, I am sworn to his service, and—"

"And how close of a tie is *that*?" Alame asked skeptically.

"Close enough. I—" Delian closed his mouth sharply, frowning. Then he continued, giving Alicira the impression that he had changed his mind about what he was going to say next. "We did not consult the Council before I left, but I can assure you, sister, there will be a place for you in the Two Nations. I do have that much status."

"As what?" Alame cocked a brow at Delian. "Niece, there are other options. The witches of Waykemin would take you on without judgment or concern for your honor. It is a long ride, but the reception would be certain."

Alicira shuddered. "They are dedicated to Nitel, and I do not want my child anywhere near *that* goddess or her followers." Why would her uncle suggest the witches? "How do you know what reception I would receive there?"

He *had* said *there are other paths.*

What had Alame been doing in the past ten years of exile? Could he have been so desperate as to study with the witches?

"Not all of them follow Nitel." Alame tightened his lips. "Terani their leader follows Karnoi and Cirdel."

"As if the Twin Gods would be any better!" Her fingers tightened on her braid, a chill spreading through her at her uncle's words.

He *had* studied with the witches, then, knew them well

enough to speak openly of their leader. A leader dedicated to the very gods who had devoured her mother.

Can I tolerate their presence after that experience?

Alicira wasn't certain she could do it, even for her daughter's sake.

"You may not have a choice." Alame squatted by the fire and picked up a stick to poke at the burning branches.

"I would have to be desperate indeed to choose the witches of Waykemin," she said. "How would you know what reception I would receive there?"

Alame grimaced, staring into the fire. "First-hand experience, niece. They took me in when I was first exiled, magic flying free and unbound, at risk of being consumed by it." He glanced up, glowering at her. "As powerful a child as you carry, you're even more at risk without the land's protection."

Alicira shivered. Her great-grandmother had gone insane when Daran had been wrested from her rule, losing both magic and sanity. The one moment she had seen Alame after his exile he had been ranting and crazed, in withdrawal from his ties to Medvara.

"I am not Elithtra," she whispered, trying to convince herself, reaching for that one tiny shard of Medvara's magic she carried in addition to her own powers. Even here in the Saubral it comforted her.

"You carry a foe's child, sired by one who usurped your homeland's magic. You need protection as much as I did. Terani has the strength to aid you."

"I would explore the options in Keldara first," she said.

"Heinmyets is young and strong, but even should he show you his favor, can he protect you from Zauril?"

"Do you think just anyone could breed a daranval like Findel?" Delian countered. "Or, gods be praised, Heinmyets's own Elantai? Daranvelii with that level of magical power don't happen by chance. It takes strong magic to control a stallion of Elantai's strength."

"Horsebreeder magic isn't the same as reigning magic!" Alame countered.

"Nor is magic derived from spinning and weaving alone!" Alicira snapped. "But there it is. We were gifted the magic wool in the sheep we brought from the Empire-over-Sea, part of the magic that I cursed and drove from the land. Our forebears made that magic. *Without spinning you cannot rule.* Isn't that what Alexran decreed for the rulers of Medvara?"

"But you are with child. Your magic will weaken."

"Heinmyets does not always stay in the capital," Delian said. "They breed magic sheep, and Heinmyets supervises those herds while his father rules in Dera. A partnership with Inharise allows Heinmyets and his associates to spend even more time in the middle of Clenda as the safest place for the magical herds. *That* would not be so horrible a place for you and your child to be, sister. Clenda holds its own magic."

"But will Clenda allow me my magic?" Alicira sighed.

"That would not be an issue in Waykemin," Alame argued. He would have said more but Alicira held a hand up to stop him.

"Let me think," she said to them.

"Your choice will affect our path once we separate from Haran's riders," Delian cautioned. "We'll need to follow the river even further to go to Waykemin."

"I understand. I just—" She looked up, noting the sliver of moon showing just above the ridge to their east. "When the moon rises halfway between full overhead and the horizon, I will speak. Until then, let me think!"

Her uncle bowed and drifted away from the fire. Delian frowned, as if to continue his argument, then followed Alame.

Alicira heaved another big sigh once she was alone. She rested her chin on her knees, staring into the fire. Keldara or Waykemin? Heinmyets or Terani?

Goddess Dovré, what to do, what to do?

No response. No different from what it had been during the nights under Zauril's control when she had cried to the Goddess for help. Alicira buried her head in her hands.

A horse snorted and stomped across the fire from her. Alicira lifted her head to look into Narasin's eyes. The golden mare flicked her ears and tossed her head impatiently.

"How did you get here? Escaped the corral? Silly thing." Surprising that no one had followed Narasin to take her back to the other horses.

The daranval mare tossed her head and stamped again. The image of Narasin with ears pinned drifted into Alicira's thoughts, followed by a blurry shape of a tall, elegant woman with russet-brown skin, waist-length straight black hair edged in silver that seemed to move with a life of its own, and deep golden eyes that held reproof. Her silver and copper skirts rippled as if a soft wind blew through them, as did the trailing edges of the sleeves of the fitted gold and copper tunic she wore over her skirts.

"My lady Dovré," Alicira breathed, joy flowing through her as she straightened. "You have not left me."

Follow my gift. Follow her lead to your honor.

Her gift? Alicira stared at Narasin, puzzled. True, Delian had spoken of daranvelii as Dovré's Gift, but for the Goddess to speak through one? That was something new to her.

Follow my gift. She speaks true.

Then the Goddess's presence faded away.

What did that mean? Ask Narasin for guidance? Ask a *horse*?

Then again, the Goddess had been silent until now. By choice, or by restraint because of the child Alicira carried?

Perhaps Narasin was the only means that the Goddess could use to communicate right now.

"So what do you think?" she asked the daranval, feeling silly to be asking a *horse* about her future, daranval or not. "Heinmyets and Keldara or Terani and Waykemin?"

The images that followed contained a tall, broad-shouldered man with compelling brown eyes, curly black hair twisted into braids, and reddish-brown skin. He sat on a black daranval with silver mane and tail, a young stallion from the look of his neck and body, still lanky and without the thickness of a mature stud's neck and shoulders.

Definitely *not* Terani. Alicira heaved a big sigh.

"You're certain of that?"

Narasin tossed her silver mane and snorted, baring her teeth.

Follow my gift.

At last, the Goddess had spoken. Alicira leaned back against her support. Keldara and Heinmyets it was, then.

And hope that it's the right choice.

CHAPTER 3

THE THREATENED STORM BLEW IN DURING THE NIGHT, ROUSING Alicira enough to burrow deeper into her bedroll, pulling the cover over her head to help keep her dry. She drowsed uneasily as the winds roiled around her, listening for the moan of spirits in the winds that drove the ice pellets on and around her. Worry coursed through her.

A select troop from Zauril's Own Guard could use the storm as a cover to sneak up on them.

If they do, they risk the Mershaunten's wrath.

If she told herself that often enough, maybe she would believe it. She still rode under Haran's protection, and his guard was large enough to hold off all but a war brigade.

Still, she lay there half-asleep, alert to any possible new sound that might mean an immanent attack.

Nothing untoward stirred, and the winds remained ordinary winds carrying ordinary ice pellets. After what seemed to be an eternity, the gusts eased back and the patter of pellets on her bedroll's cover faded.

But cold remained, along with a dampness in her nostrils. The faint sounds of the guards on watch seemed muffled. Then

Narasin's mind touched hers; bright, golden and softly soothing. An image of the golden mare standing guard came into her thoughts.

Warmth eased through her and Alicira slipped back into sleep, comforted by her daranval's reassurance even as Narasin's touch faded away.

At first light she roused fully, reaching to the bottom of her bedroll for her boots. Ice cracked and weight shifted off of her as she pulled them on while still remaining under cover. Snow had followed the ice.

Haran and Orlanden crawled out of their bedrolls next to her. Together, silently, the three of them worked together to shake their bedrolls free from ice and snow, then secured them on the pack mules Haran's troop had brought. For a moment Alicira wished she were marrying Haran and Orlanden, even if the Mershaunten would damn all of them for it. But she sighed, and Haran patted her shoulder, almost as if he understood her thoughts, as they walked back toward the firepit. Delian served them a mush that had cooked overnight in an iron pot placed in the fire's coals.

"You are still determined to go to Keldara?" her uncle asked as they ate while standing around the fire.

Alicira nodded. "But I will consider Waykemin if Keldara is not welcoming."

"That will be a rough road at that point," he warned. "We will have to divert around the deep canyons of the Kitskan River. It might be best to approach Waykemin more directly by following the Chellana around Keldara to the north."

She shook her head. "The Goddess has spoken through Narasin, Uncle. My route lies with Heinmyets and Keldara."

Alame nodded his head in acknowledgement. "Then may her way be true."

She chose not to answer the doubt in his voice. Her uncle

followed Artel the Judge, the Bright Warrior whose role was to question the Gods' choices.

It is what he is led to do, she reassured herself. *Not because it is an omen.*

"Our destination today?" she asked Haran instead.

He slurped down a spoonful of mush and swallowed hard. "From here we need to ride to the ferry at Nixyin. You will not be able to cross with my men, but at least I can protect you that far on your route to Keldara."

"Thank you," she said, swallowing her last spoonful of mush.

By the Gods she hoped she could keep her food down today. Her ride would go much better if she didn't have to use magic to sustain herself.

NIGHTFALL BROUGHT them to the small town of Nixyin, held jointly by Saubral and Larij. Haran led them directly to the barracks for those serving the Mershaunten, Alicira riding in the middle of his troop, her jacket's hood supplemented by a cloak lent by one of Haran's riders. Alame placed a glamor on Narasin to turn her coat into a barely remarkable dark brown instead of the easily remembered bright gold. The silver mane and tail that marked her as a high-ranking daranval strong in magic could not be concealed, but given the mixture of daran-velii and regular horses amongst Haran's troop, even that might serve as sufficient concealment.

Alicira was staggering tired by the time Narasin was safely bedded amongst the horses of Haran's troop, and it was only through the quiet support of Orlanden and Delian walking shoulder to shoulder with her that she kept concealed during the passage to Haran's private barracks. Even then she remained cloaked until the five of them, Haran, Orlanden, Delian, Alame and herself, were safely in Haran's own quarters.

Once the servants had kindled a strong fire and brought platters of roast meats, root vegetables, fresh-baked bread, and sweet cake, then retreated, she felt safe enough to uncloak. Alame helped Alicira pull her soggy coat off.

The snow had changed to an icy rain during the day's ride and she was soaked through. Riding that last distance with the additional warmth of the cloak had been a welcome relief. Her braids were soaked and tangled, and she longed for a bath to warm herself and become clean for the first time in days.

But was it safe? Alicira hesitated to request that service, fearing the risk of even more disclosure. Haran's troop was confined to quarters tonight. Tomorrow Haran and his riders would be safe in Larij, on their way back to the Mershaunten's court, away from the risk that one poorly spoken word would alert the Saubral to Alicira's presence.

However, tonight, one difference in how things were done might be enough to attract unwanted attention or betray her. There were still three hard days of riding ahead of them before they would be in Keldara. And until they met with Heinmyets, the Saubral might find it worth their while to pursue them.

Ah well, at least she could eat and perhaps keep it down.

Light food.

Light on the meat, more of that marvelous-smelling fresh-baked bread. Not warmed biscuits of uncertain age, or mush made from grains gathered around the campsite. *That* at least she could savor. She joined the men around the table and ate slowly, still shivering as her damp clothing steamed from the warmth of the room, taking its time to dry.

Haran frowned at her. "You need clothing."

She gestured at what she wore. "This is all I have left to me right now."

A pained look crossed his face. "I would do better by my friend—"

Someone pounded on the door. "Haran! My Lord! Nixyin's Shadowwalker Gegarth would have words with you!"

A knifing chill different from the cold oozed through her, one that couldn't be banished by heat or more clothing. A Shadowwalker. How strong was it? If it knew who she was, it would try to take her back to Zauril. And there was no other way out of this room. She started to rise but Alame shook his head.

"Sit." He gestured to Haran. "Change places with me. Delian, on my other side. I will hide us."

"Will that be enough?" she asked, keeping her voice low. "If that Shadowwalker is sufficiently powerful—"

"Let me worry about it." Alame slid in next to her and put one arm around her shoulder. "I won't be using Aireii magic."

Then what magic will you be using?

As Orlanden got up to open the door, face sick yellow with worry under his normal light brown, a foul sensation roiled through Alicira. She gagged at the sick stench rising from her, as if she had been drinking hard and heavily all day. Her clothing felt heavy and slimy, like it had moldered and hadn't been washed in ages.

The magic clung heavily to her, making her head spin. She slouched against her uncle as he burped, belching up alcoholic fumes. Her child kicked hard in rebellion and Alicira dared to rest a hand on her belly, hoping to soothe it. She almost jerked her hand away from the mildew and slime on her tunic.

What is this? What God is my uncle truly serving?

This was no magic of Artel or Dovré, not even of Staul the Destroyer.

"My lord Shadowwalker." Orlanden's voice was half a note higher than usual as he bowed low to the helmeted being who pushed him aside as he strode into the room.

A male Shadowwalker, in full maturity and strength. He wore a gray mail shirt over brown tunic and trousers, but no boots on his cloven feet. The red bull's head sigil of the Saubral glowed on his chest and the forehead of his horned helmet, the sigil two shades lighter than his dark, blood-red eyes.

Haran scowled as Orlanden stumbled and almost fell from the Shadowwalker's push, but the frown faded quickly as he leaned back in his chair, a languid smile playing on his lips, eyes half-shuttered. He picked up his goblet and toasted the Shadowwalker glowering at him from the other side of the table.

"So what brings you here, Shadowwalker Gegarth?" Haran slowly and deliberately sipped from the goblet, his every gesture implying that the Shadowwalker's presence was nothing more than an annoying imposition.

Gegarth growled and smashed one scaly, gray-skinned fist on the table between them. "I come seeking fugitives!"

"Fugitives?" Haran raised one brow as Orlanden warily skirted Gegarth and rejoined Haran. "There are no fugitives here." Haran pulled Orlanden close and kissed him full on the lips. The Shadowwalker growled again, scowling. Haran sat back up, gently stroking Orlanden's cheek. "We're having a farewell party. No fugitives."

"Then who are they?" The Shadowwalker pointed at Alicira, Alame, and Delian. "Not any of your captains or leaders. Who are they?"

Haran shrugged. "Do you honestly think any of my troop leaders would wish to be present in such decadent company?"

The Shadowwalker's lips curled contemptuously.

Alame hiccuped. "M'Lord, is this the new plaything you spoke of? He seems overdressed to me for our purposes." Delian yelped and Alicira flinched as their uncle pinched each of them. "He does allow us a balance instead of two for me and one for you. Though it does seem unfair as your other one is much bigger than mine." He shook Alicira. "Perhaps we should trade. I've a taste for something larger than young boy."

"You degenerate whelp—" Gegarth grimaced, leaving his sentence unfinished.

"I told you this was a farewell party." Haran's voice hardened. "I cross the River tomorrow and leave my beloved behind. Feel free to search my troops *then* for whatever poor soul it is you seek. Until tomorrow, don't waste my time with your quest!"

Gegarth rumbled, his fists clenching tightly. "You overstep your position here."

"Do I?" Haran's voice lowered. "I may only be the Mershaunten's youngest son, despised for my nature, but I am still his son." Menace crept into his tone. "As such, you've trespassed on Larijian royal territory in this room. To bash your way into here, demanding to know the identity of my companions—you have not the authority to do so without prior notice."

"Oh, did I forget my authority?" the Shadowwalker jeered. "Then perhaps you will acknowledge the express will of Zauril of Medvara as equal to yours." He threw a scroll tied in black ribbon in front of Haran. "Therein lies my warrant, Haran of Larij, Mershaunten's son. By treaty you must acknowledge his wish."

Alicira tightened under Alame's hand. A warrant from Zauril. She could feel the magic streaming from it, seeking, seeking—as the child stirred in response to her father's magic. Yellow streamers spread across the table, oozing toward all five of them.

Would you betray me to your father, little one?

She tried to shield but whatever magic Alame was using blocked her own. Alicira stared at the yellow trickle. It stopped an arm's length short of her, then wriggled back to the scroll. To her relief, the tendrils that had extended toward Haran and Orlanden did the same.

"Are you quite done?" Haran drawled. If Alicira hadn't known him like she did, she would not have noticed how tense his jaw was.

Oh friend of mine, does your father appreciate your skill in managing difficult situations?

She had seen Haran play the fop when under challenge during her fostering, and then again this spring at the court in Medvara, before everything fell.... Just not when the stakes were this high. Never had Haran played this role so well.

"Open the scroll." Gegarth's tone carried a compulsion.

Haran flexed his hands, staring at it. "I will not be forced."

The Shadowwalker laughed. "Do you then admit to harboring fugitives?"

"I admit nothing." Haran glanced at Orlanden.

Orlanden snuggled in closer to him. "Oh, open the damned thing so we can be rid of this beast, Haran dear. He's tiresome and he's wasting our time."

"Since you request it, my love—"

Alicira tensed as Haran picked up the scroll. Haran had no defenses against any spell Zauril might have put on it. He might be forced to betray her. She felt for the knife at her belt.

I will die rather than go back to him. Lady Dovré, please—

Then she noticed that Orlanden kept one hand on Haran's arm as he broke the seal. A faint flash of yellow light flared as Haran unrolled it, turning white before fading. She glanced at the Shadowwalker.

Did he notice?

And just how had Orlanden acquired the magic to counter the compulsion on the scroll? He possessed no magical ability. Her uncle must have passed him a charm at some point.

"I see that Zauril believes I still have a romantic or strategic interest in his lady," Haran said evenly. He snorted and tossed the scroll back to Gegarth. "Do you see either Alicira or her brother with me? Surely Zauril's charms still keep the lady entranced in Medvare-the-city."

"She fled Medvare-the-city seven days ago and was sighted crossing Medvara's borders two days ago, when Medvara's magic failed," Gegarth growled. "It is said that her brother rides with her, and you have been observed to meet with him ten days before that."

Haran laughed. "And did your spies tell you what resulted from Delian's plea to my father for the rescue of Lady Alicira? Yes," he sneered. "I met with Delian at my father's court seventeen days ago, to hear him plead his case for Larij to extend official aid to his sister. Which was denied, as you well know."

"You once sought to marry her."

"My father seeks many alliances beside the one I would prefer," Haran countered. "If I were to follow what all of my alleged spouses-to-be do, I'd never have time for my duties. Which, come to think of it, include my review of the ferry tolls the Saubral have collected in the past season. Orlanden, dearest, my scroll with the records from the Larij side is in my pack. Would you be a darling and pull it out?" As Orlanden got up, Haran cocked a brow at the Shadowwalker. "So do you bring me Hhranger's report, or will he provide it to me before I catch the ferry across the Chellana tomorrow? My father will be *most* offended to hear that Hhranger is behind on tracking the Nixyin tolls. The Mershaunten has been known to call for battle over even smaller offenses than this."

Gegarth took the thick roll of paper from Orlanden, glaring at Haran. "So you leave this one behind to administer the port? Has Nixyin grown to a greater priority in the Mershaunten's sight?"

"That I will share with Hhranger, not yourself." Haran waved at Gegarth contemptuously. "Produce the report now or begone until morning. I would prefer privacy for my farewells. Unless you would care to join the party?"

The Shadowwalker growled, then produced a roll almost as thick as the one Orlanden had given him. "There it is." He stepped back from the table, his eyes now lingering on Alicira, Alame and Delian. "See to it that your decadent companions are clear of Nixyin by sunrise. Such of that ilk are not welcome here. And if we find that the Mershaunten has been harboring Alicira and her brother, we will guarantee that both he and Larij will have cause to regret this action."

"Big words," Haran sneered in return. "It seems I'll need to review the paperwork tonight to ensure Hhranger isn't covering up a little toll skimming on the side by sending you to bluster and fuss over Zauril as a distraction, Gegarth."

"You *dare*, my lord!"

"I *dare*," Haran said coldly. "I *dare* because this is not the first time someone has tried to take advantage of me and my preferences while I perform my duties. I might also remind you and Hhranger of your predecessors' fate, and why it is that my father trusts *me* to monitor tolls for the Great River ferries, even given his dislike of what I am. Now. Go. You've used up enough of my attention for tonight, especially since I must be distracted by paperwork." He rose, dropping the foppish pose, one hand on his belt knife. "Leave."

Gegarth backed away from the table and turned for the door. At the door he turned. "I will conduct my examination of your troops before sunrise tomorrow, *Mershaunten's son*."

"As you will." Haran's voice did not waver as he met the Shadowwalker's eyes.

The Shadowwalker glanced over at Alicira, Alame, and Delian. "Meanwhile, that scum will be gone from Nixyin by then, or suffer the consequences."

"My friends will do what is needed." Haran tightened his grip on his belt knife until his knuckles showed white under brown. "Now do I need to call for weapons and my Second?"

"Not today." Gegarth opened the door and left.

Haran stood glaring at the door for a few moments. Then he sighed. "Orlanden. Please bar the door." He gestured at the open scroll on the table. "This changes things."

"Reroll it, please," Alame said. He said no more as Orlanden delicately rolled the scroll with his fingertips.

Orlanden tied the black ribbon around the scroll again, then tapped it. White flashed and the scroll burst into flame. No one moved or spoke as it burned, fading into ash. Orlanden carefully swept the ash into his hand and poured it into a small cedar bentwood box.

"That should contain any magic it holds," he said. "But that was my last protection charm."

"It proved to be very useful," Haran said, swallowing hard.

The foul stench roiled once more around Alicira and then was gone as Alame dropped his arms from both her shoulders and Delian's.

"Orlanden, I didn't know you had magic!" She studied him, looking for further signs.

Orlanden shook his head. "Merely a charm given me by the Lady Inharise in return for a favor. I have used it carefully, but this nearly exhausts it."

Inharise. Wasn't that the woman mentioned as already married to Heinmyets?

"I did not know Inharise of Clenda carried magic," she said carefully.

"It is not Aireii magic, but the power gifted to the Tauri peoples of Clenda," Alame said.

"Heinmyets shares a similar power," Delian said, stretching. "It is needed when we ride patrol on Keldara's borders—a means for holding the Saubral at bay. It is not as strong as your magic, sister, but it does work."

So Keldara and Clenda do not lack for magic.

This information gave her hope for further protection against Zauril.

"Meanwhile, we need to outfit you. I am afraid we need to send you out sooner than I had hoped," Haran sighed. "I mistrust what little control Hhranger may have over that Shad-owwalker."

"I will take whatever help you can provide," Alicira said steadily, even though she wanted to sink to the floor in exhaustion.

Until now she had not realized how much she had been looking forward to a night's sleep in a real bed instead of a bedroll without even a tent's shelter.

Sadly, it seemed even that respite would be denied to her for this night.

CHAPTER 4

THE BELLS OF NIXYIN'S NIGHT WATCH RANG MIDNIGHT AS Alicira, Orlanden, Delian and Alame rode out of town. Haran had wanted to send more riders with them but Alicira didn't want to take anyone whose absence would be noticed the next morning. At some point Gegarth's already heightened suspicions would be aroused further, and a group larger than the four of them might trigger a reaction. Besides, a small party could slip through the Saubral lands unnoticed better than a larger group. Haran had promised to send word to Heinmyets that they were coming, once he was safely in Larij and had reliable courier bird service to Keldara.

Alicira wore a set of Haran's clothing, including his heavy fur-lined riding jacket, stripped of his insignia, with spares on the pack mule Orlanden led. Somehow Haran had found a mule bred from a daranval mare, so it could keep up with the daranvelii without slowing them down. The mule also carried bedrolls and food stocks to keep them supplied for the ride to Keldara's borders. Each daranval also had saddlebags stuffed full of extra scarves, gloves, daybread, and enough of the dried pounded meat and berry cakes popular along the Great River for travel food mix to back up what the mule carried.

Haran had been overly generous, in Alicira's opinion, but she was not about to object to his open-handedness, not after the deprivations of their flight from Medvare-the-city. At least now they had adequate supplies for this journey. She wondered about the small soft pouches tucked in her right saddlebag. Magic radiated from those bags and tempted her with the possibilities—but until she had time to focus on what the three pouches contained, best not to even begin to look at them, lest she be lured down the tempting pathways of new sorcery. Perhaps when they stopped in the morning she would have the time to get a better idea of what she carried.

With the cloak over Haran's jacket, she was almost too warm as they rode out of Nixyin, especially with the hood drawn far over her face. But she dared not ride openly here, not with a Shadowwalker suspicious of their presence.

They reached the main road following the great river Chellana and struck up a long, floating trot comfortable to ride but covered ground without being particularly attention-gathering. Snow on the ground and the sliver of moon above just provided enough light to travel by, while creating shadows around them that made Alicira's heart jump. Zauril had used the shadows to spy on her far too often for her to trust what they hid.

Best to be used to it.

Until they reached the Keldaran border they would be traveling by night. Night travel was safer in Saubral lands. That way they might avoid Saubral travelers on this main road.

As long as they don't send houndriders after us.

If Gegarth was suspicious enough about Haran's companions, he might summon houndriders to hunt them down. But she could do nothing about that except focus on the road ahead and ride hard, helping to put distance between themselves and Nixyin.

Alicira kept her attention on the road, even as worry niggled at her. What if something about the scroll had triggered Gegarth's attention? What if Alame's protection had been incomplete? Gegarth had kept studying them, and she didn't think it was completely about his finding their guises offensive. Hopefully he would not attack Haran during this morning's review. Sometimes she had to wonder just how much protection from Zauril's ambitions that the Mershaunten's treaties with the Saubral could have for Haran—or for Larij itself.

You can do nothing but ride.

She had to ride. She had to stay free from Zauril, not just for her or her unborn child but for—Varen. Without her power to supplement his, without the power of the land that she had stripped from Medvara, it would take Zauril longer to achieve his goals. The best thing she could do was to stay out of his clutches.

Alicira made herself contemplate the hoofbeats as Narasin trotted along, counting each footfall. Forced herself to think of nothing but the smooth float as Narasin's stride covered the ground. Concentrated on the working of Narasin's muscles under the saddle, the evenness of her breath, her ears pointed ahead, a soft reassurance that *all is well* radiating from her entire carriage. Alicira slipped into a trance-like state, riding, riding, just riding, reassured by the confidence Narasin seemed to pass on to her.

Never had she ridden a horse like Narasin. Now she began to understand why the daranvelii of Keldara and Clenda were so prized.

The moon slowly moved across the sky until it was behind them. The horizon in front of them grew lighter. As the light of dawn brightened, worry once again stirred in Alicira, not triggered by shadows or anything explainable around her.

Concern about Haran, since he would be confronting Gegarth right now? Possibly.

Narasin tensed under her. The sense of well-being that had enveloped Alicira through most of the night's ride began to fade as Narasin raised her head higher, flicking one ear behind her. Alicira roused herself to look around. The other daranvelii appeared to be as concerned as Narasin.

Alame reined Findel in. He and Orlanden turned their mounts to face Alicira and Delian.

"You feel it too?" he asked, his eyes focusing on Alicira.

"Something's wrong," she answered. "One moment everything was well. Then Narasin became worried." She hesitated. "Or am I imagining that?"

Alame shook his head. "No. Narasin projects her moods quite strongly. What you've been feeling is truth, not imagination."

"I'm still not certain what to trust when it comes to—things I feel. Plus our bond is still new, and—" She looked down at her hands. "Zauril projects very strongly," she whispered.

"Oh niece." Alame's face softened. "Narasin is very sensitive to houndrider presence, more so than Findel or our other daranvelii. She told Findel she senses houndriders, but she is not certain if they are pursuing us or if we've just come close to them by accident."

"I wish I could hear more than just her projections. But I'm afraid to try that much magic right now, in case it attracts Saubral." She shook herself. "No matter. How close?"

Alame sighed. "Nearby, but not an immediate danger. No idea whether they are in front of us or behind us. I wish you and Narasin knew each other better. I'm only receiving what Findel understands of her warnings, and the details are unclear."

"Is there something I can do?"

Alame shook his head. "Not right now, not with houndriders close enough for Narasin to alert. You need guidance to bond with your first daranval, and a safe place to do that. Not out here on the road."

"There has to be *something* I can do to speak more clearly with her, uncle," Alicira persisted. "Some magic, some skill." She glanced at both Orlanden and Delian. "You two ride daranvelii and don't have magic. How do you speak with your horse?"

"Only like I would with spells or charms that others have given me," Orlanden answered. "But my Odilel is not as high-ranking or as skilled as Findel or Narasin."

"Emotions with Larasna," Delian answered. "Feelings."

"Work on communicating with her while we ride, Alicira," Alame said. "Try to understand her warnings. Meanwhile, we need to find a defensible hiding place." He looked around the forbidding cliffs and sagebrush canyon walls around them. "Orlanden, Delian, any suggestions?"

"Places to hide are not plentiful in this stretch of the Great River." Orlanden frowned, scratching his chin thoughtfully. "No caves along here that I know of." He squinted across the river, pointing to a faint rocky shape coming clear in the early dawn. "If that island over there is the one I think it is, then there's a small hidden canyon amongst those rocks. It would be considered safe from the Mershaunten's edict."

"That means swimming to get there, and swimming back later," Alame frowned. "Is it concealed enough that we could kindle a small fire to dry ourselves?"

"If there's wood," Delian said.

"And then there's the question of dealing with being wet after we return."

"We would also need to backtrack to avoid the rapids," Orlanden added.

"I don't like that idea at all," Alicira said. Her uneasiness increased.

Was it her own fear about swimming in this cold, or a warning from Narasin? She placed one hand on the golden mare's neck and focused on the uneasiness.

Response. The sensation of uneasiness rippled along Alicira's awareness as Narasin's neck muscles tightened. Alicira looked at the island. No change. She looked ahead. Nothing. Back down the road—and the sense of foreboding grew.

"I think Narasin is saying that the houndriders are behind us," she said. She dared not try to confirm Narasin's alert with her own magical senses. Houndriders often followed the use of magic to trace its users.

Alame glanced over at the island. "I'd prefer not to swim. Let's keep riding and look for something—even a small draw with brush at its mouth is better than nothing."

Delian drew his sword. "And ride armed."

"Agreed." Alame drew his sword. As Orlanden braced his short horseback bow, Alicira dropped her reins on Narasin's neck and brought out the new bow Delian had given her. She hadn't shot any bow since five days after Midsummer, when she had tried and failed to use her old bow—now broken—to protect her mother from Zauril.

Her thoughts blanked for a moment before the memory continued.

Then Zauril's spell had destroyed the protections built into the string and shattered her bow. She hadn't wanted to touch this new bow until now, just do nothing more than hang the handsome painted skin case for bow and arrows across her chest before riding.

This bow was different from her old one. She flexed it carefully, trying to get an impression of its strength. Shorter than her old horseback bow. Horn with sinew backing, not wood with sinew as her old bow had been. She felt the string. Sinew as well. She braced the bow and brought it up to shooting position, not pulling back as far as she had with her old bow, remembering Delian's caution about what these horn bows could tolerate.

More power with a shorter draw. That explained the shorter arrows in her quiver. She sighted at a bush off to her side and

Narasin responded to her weight shift, positioning herself so that Alicira's aim was better. Alicira eased the bow back down, and Narasin turned back forward.

"Can you take my bow for a moment?" Orlanden asked. Alicira nodded, and reached for his heavier wood bow. Once she had it, he untied the mule's lead rope from his saddle horn and looped it around the mule's neck, fastening it securely with a quick-release knot. Then Orlanden took his bow back. "You'll need to watch for old Sarail," he advised Alicira. "She'll stick with us—one of Haran's best pack mules, trained to follow riders. But without a lead she'll crowd you."

"Understand," Alicira said. The mule pushed close to Narasin. The golden mare pinned her ears back and tossed her head, forcing the mule to fall back. "Looks like Narasin won't let her do it."

"Good," Orlanden said.

Alicira didn't answer, straining her senses to track Narasin's awareness without raising her magic enough to either rouse the child or alert the houndriders. They continued in silence, the faint roar of the river and the footfalls of their horses the only sound present.

Narasin tightened under Alicira and threw her head high, flicking her ears back. Before Alicira could touch her free hand to Narasin's neck a distant howl echoed off of the cliff walls behind them. The houndriders had discovered their scent.

Without speaking they urged the horses into a gallop. Alicira thought about heading for the river to take their chances with the cold water.

"River?" she shouted at Delian.

"Not here!" he yelled back. "We have to ride back toward the hounds for safest crossing, and I don't want to get caught swimming!"

"There!" Orlanden pointed at a clump of trees to their right, turning his daranval off of the road.

They followed his lead, even though it meant slowing as they dropped into a trickle of a creek and followed its bed upstream. They stuck to the water as the tiny canyon closed in around them, the brush along the bank too thick for a rider to ride through.

Were they heading into a trap? Or would riding through that small creek be enough to hide their scent? They emerged into a small opening just wide enough for them to get out of the water before another thicket of willows and brambles closed around the creek. Orlanden chivvied the mule toward the back of the clearing, then took up a position on the other side of the creek from Alicira, on the lower bank. They nocked arrows as Delian and Alame waited with swords drawn. Orlanden whistled and caught her eye.

"Hound," he mouthed, calling his target. It made sense since he was on the lower side of the creek.

"Rider," she replied.

Danger. Danger.

Narasin's distress grew, her worry threatening to swamp Alicira's focus and feelings. The child stirred uneasily, fear echoing Narasin's unease. Alicira took a deep breath, projecting *calm, wait, steady* emotions to both horse and child. The houndriders were near. Did a Shadowwalker ride with these houndriders? Gods, she wished that at the very least Haran's father would have allowed her to cross the river and travel as far as she could in Larij.

Calm. Wait. Steady.

Narasin jigged her head up and down nervously but stood still. The intensity of her worry did not change, and Alicira hoped that this meant the houndriders were riding past them, that they had gone to water soon enough to put the riders off their scent.

Another long, wavering howl came from down the creek, followed by the telltale screech of a Shadowwalker on the trail.

No such luck.

Narasin quivered under Alicira and the child started kicking. *Steady*, she thought at both of them. *Steady.* If only there was something to quiet the child!

As soon as she thought more clearly of the child, Narasin mirrored the thought back with a question. Alicira pictured a baby within her. Narasin sent a fuzzy image of a little red foal, then of a child. Soothing and quieting thoughts flowed through Alicira. The child calmed.

Good.

Splashing and rustling noises echoed up the canyon walls, combined with the fell hounds panting and the muttered curses of the houndriders.

Alicira drew her bowstring and held the arrow steady, waiting. At most the houndriders could come through the opening in the brambles two at a time. Perhaps if she and Orlanden could pick off enough of them, then they could delay or discourage the pack.

Narasin tightened even more as splashing and panting sounds came closer. The first gray and brown hound burst through the opening. It was almost the size of a pony. A wizened gray and green-skinned rider wearing only a gray breechclout clung to the hound's back.

Alicira and Orlanden released together, both arrows striking their targets. Hound and rider keened as they fell into the creek, bleeding pale green blood that sizzled as it struck water. The hounds behind the first bayed. Three more tried to push through the opening. Alicira pulled another arrow and fired, then reached for another and then another, calling upon all the speed and accuracy she had developed over the years of target shooting, ever since she and Haran had first gone through weapons training and her aptitude for archery had become noticed.

Alame and Delian roared, charging forward to strike at the

hounds and riders who managed to escape Alicira and Orlanden's fusillade. As her arrows grew low, Alicira hesitated to shoot more. They needed to save arrows for the Shadowwalker.

Goddess, dear Goddess, give me strength!

She mouthed the prayer, unconvinced that despite the other day's vision Dovré would answer. The Goddess had been silent throughout her captivity so why would things change now?

Warmth flowed through her.

I do not forget, I am merely constrained. I have not forgotten my Alicira.

Then the Goddess fell silent. The warmth remained with Alicira. She sought the Shadowwalker, pulling together her othersight. Mercifully, the child remained quiet. Alicira extended her vision further, seeking, seeking—

It *was* Gegarth. He sat on a blood-red stallion just outside of the brush where they had first entered the creek, growling orders to the houndriders now hanging back as the foul green blood of their packmates oozed down the creek, sizzling and steaming.

Could she use her magic to drive him away? What else did she have to try? Perhaps with Narasin's help and the Goddess's continued presence—

Alicira brushed against the mare's mind.

Help me, give me strength.

To the Goddess, she thought:

If you can, please let me work magic without rousing the child.

For the child.

The warmth in Alicira concentrated around the child.

Alicira pulled out an arrow, her next-to-last one. She bound two spells to the arrowhead. The first was meant to scatter and confuse the hounds and Gegarth's mount. The second was a seeking spell to find the Shadowwalker. She lacked the magical strength to shape more than that, especially away from her land—now that she had no land. Otherwise, she'd have witched the land to strike at Gegarth.

Fly well.

She loosed the arrow. It screeched as it arced over the brush, making the daranvelii throw their heads up and snort.

"Whoa," Alicira breathed to Narasin as she tensed to bolt. "It is my magic, nothing more."

Steady. Magic of me.

She projected assurance as the mare fretted at the arrow's howl, straining to listen so she could follow how far it went, tracking its path with her magic.

The arrow stopped screeching. Howls and yelps replaced the scream of the arrow as Gegarth's stallion bellowed.

She'd struck his horse.

Alicira pushed her vision as far as she dared to see houndriders scattering and the red stallion galloping back toward Nixyin. Gegarth struggled to regain control of the runaway.

"Thank you," she breathed to the Goddess, dropping her vision.

Your daughter is most interesting.

The Goddess faded. Alicira dared send one last plea.

Is she of me or of Zauril?

No response came.

"You did it," Alame said, carefully sheathing his sword. "Niece, that was excellent work."

Fatigue pulled at Alicira as she swayed in the saddle. "But at a cost," she moaned. "I need sleep. That last spell drew too much energy from me."

It shouldn't have. Perhaps the child affects me as well.

Alame sidepassed Findel next to her. "You can't rest yet. We have to find a safe place."

"I don't know if I can stay on her," she whispered to him.

"You have to. We don't dare go back down the creek."

"Won't they circle around and come down the draw?"

"Possibly. But they'll either have to come after us or climb down those cliffs. That will take them longer, and Gegarth can't take his horse up those walls, just like we can't. We have to ride hard to get ahead of them before they can find a way to reach this draw. I'm sorry."

"I don't have much strength to call on my magic." Alicira grasped Narasin's mane as another wave of exhaustion washed over her.

Her uncle hesitated. Then he leapt off of Findel. "Orlanden. Delian. Help me secure Narasin's saddlebags on Findel. I need to ride behind Alicira. She's played out."

Alicira heard them talking but couldn't make out the words as the world swung around her. She grabbed Narasin's neck to steady herself as the swaying grew worse. Affection seeped into her, along with wordless encouragement from Narasin. Alicira clutched at those sensations, trying to focus on them instead of on the tiredness sucking her down.

Then her uncle's arms wrapped around Alicira as he slid onto Narasin's back behind the saddle. "I'll keep hold of you, niece. Sleep if you need to."

Alicira fought the fatigue as Narasin began to walk again. But the scent of Alame's leathers, spicy and potent with the rich odors of the spell makings he used, evoked memories of when she would fall asleep before him in the saddle when she was a little girl.

The Court had regularly examined the special sheep herds that provided the magical fleeces for Medvara's magic workings every spring. When Alicira was young, it had been a family outing. Later in the summer they would do the same after gathering wild herbs in the mountains above Medvare-the-city for potions. Her little sister Melaraen, named after their mother Melara, rode in front of their father, while Alicira often rode in front of Alame.

It had been many years since she had fallen asleep in the saddle in front of her uncle.

To do it again was oddly reassuring. She hung onto the saddle horn and helped her uncle keep Narasin balanced as they scrambled up the canyon wall at an angle away from the creek. Once they attained the top, and Narasin began her long, floating trot, Alicira let herself be lulled into sleep. She woke only when they stopped at an abandoned shack. Alame eased her off of Narasin, then helped her spread her bedroll on an old cot. Once her bed was laid out, Alicira collapsed onto the cot and immediately fell asleep, not even waiting for food.

CHAPTER 5

ALICIRA AWOKE AT DUSK TO REALIZE THAT ALL OF THEM; PEOPLE, daranvelii, and mule, were crowded into the small shack, the heat from their combined bodies making the space almost as warm as a summer evening in Medvare-the-city. Orlanden sat in the doorway facing the sunset, bow strung, his daranval and the mule standing next to him with their heads just outside the shack. Besides the doorway, the only light came from gaps between the hand-planed planks that made up the rickety walls. Narasin stood next to Alicira's cot, head low and hanging protectively over Alicira's body, left hind foot resting. Delian and Alame lay on the dirt floor by their daranvelii's forelegs, curled up in their cloaks.

Alicira sat up. Her body ached; her back and legs were stiff. Narasin raised her head and nuzzled Alicira. She stroked the golden mare's head and leaned on her neck for a moment. That much contact with the daranval seemed to ease the aches. Then she slid off of the cot and carefully made her way to the door, avoiding her uncle and brother and their daranvelii. Narasin cautiously followed Alicira.

Orlanden silently slid over to make room for her. She knelt

next to him, scanning the horizon. This shack sat on a plateau between two steep draws, sagebrush and long-stemmed grasses making up the ground cover, speckled with the occasional juniper. Ice crystals lingering on the grasses that poked through the knuckle-deep snow, as well as the sagebrush and trees, spoke of an earlier fog.

Probably why the daranvelii are inside with us.

A faint break in the gray-white clouds to the west stained the sky with the rose and orange tones of sunset. The draws around the plateau were filled to the brim with fog, marking their passageway toward the Chellana, the Great River also socked in from what she could see.

That'll slow pursuit.

But it would also delay them as they had to drop into those draws for passage.

Two more days, if we're holding to Delian's calculations.

"How are things?" she asked.

"We've been taking turns at watch." Orlanden kept his voice low. "So far we've seen no followers. Though it's been foggy until late this afternoon. Then the sun burned off the cloud cover here."

"How far off course are we now?" she asked.

"Not at all," he said. "Or at least not as much as I might fear." He turned east and pointed to a distant solitary peak with a dark crown of fir, past two fogged-in draws. "The Lone Peak. We're deep in Saubral country now, but that is where we would have needed to leave the river to cut across the plateaus for the quickest route to Keldara. We should reach it by tomorrow morning, and then it's a half day to the Keldaran border."

"So is this a shorter way than following the river?"

"Yes, and more dangerous. The River trails are acknowledged trade routes by treaty. If we hadn't had houndriders and a Shadowwalker after us, we could have travelled there safely without a challenge, with travel rights. Up here—it's a risk. No travel rights. If we come across Saubral herders they can kill us on sight."

"If they see us. Is there a trail we follow to the Lone Peak or are we just bushwhacking our path?"

"A little of both. Things weren't always so." He gestured to the shack around them. "Before the Miteal came, this was the barn for a wayhouse on the trade routes between the nations. We've been following the old roads to the Lone Peak."

She shivered.

Before the Miteal came.

That meant either war or plague had caused the change.

"How do you know so much about the history of this area?" She hadn't expected this from Orlanden.

"I am a scholar of trade routes and their history." Orlanden blinked at her, then sighed. "This was once Larijian territory. Larij when we had people and power. We ran herds of cattle and horses on these plateaus. Prosperous farmers lived along the river bottoms. And then the Plague came. Our people died. The Saubral moved in because we didn't have enough of our folk left alive to defend our land. Finally, the Miteal came to Medvara. Alexran's treaties with the Saubral ended our rule here."

Alicira leaned her head against the doorframe, biting her lip. The things she didn't know. Since Orlanden was a scholar, did he know of the Miteal role in the plague? Would that be something that might affect how he dealt with her?

For that was yet another change her grandfather had brought to this land over sea from Daran, after the plague caused by her great-grandmother's overthrow had spilled across the world. Alexran had been looking for a home for his family, perhaps a chance to nurture a potential challenger for the Miteal to retake Daran. He had claimed Medvara, striking deals and treaties with the native peoples diminished by the great plagues for the rights to it, using gold and magic freely to trade for ownership.

But it was still change the Aireii had imposed on this land. Was she now paying the price for that taking? Was Zauril simply a logical progression along the pathway of Aireii oppression of this land?

She grimaced at that thought. But she had time to consider that prospect and many others while in Zauril's possession. She had known that her grandfather—even her beloved father— held to models of government that would eventually lead to problems in this land.

The lands of Varen didn't view leadership in the same way that Daran and its neighbors did. Here, lifetime leadership came by the choice of the governed, though those roles often became inherited. She had argued over the years with Haran and Delian about the problems with the Aireii Empire.

Now that she thought about it, she had heard many of the same opinions from her uncle, when she was yet too small to completely understand his positions. She had distant memories of evenings when she curled up in a wrap and listened to her father and her uncle debate about whether the Aireii had been right to free their long-term servants to follow their own path when they first arrived in Medvara.

Alame had argued that letting them choose their way was the correct thing to do. Her father Richenax had countered with the reports of Saubral incursions against those who had left Medvara to join the Tauri, and how perhaps they might have done better if they had remained part of the Aireii domain.

Before the plague this was a prosperous and productive land. Now —well, the condition of the shack spoke to what the current circumstances were. But was that only because of reduced numbers in Larij, weakened by that virulent pestilence? Or was it the doing of the Saubral?

"How many more of these wayhouses are left?"

Dare she hope that if they could defeat Zauril, perhaps a reestablished order could rebuild these old routes? Zauril's occupation voided Alexran's old treaties, but new ones could be created. Perhaps the desert could once again be home to herders and farmers?

Orlanden shrugged. "Since the Saubral lay waste to these lands, destroying crops, buildings, and any survivors—I have no idea. For a time, the clans of Keldara kept the roads maintained, to aid fugitives from Medvara. But then the Saubral resistance to the inland paths grew stronger, and it was no longer safe."

Alicira groaned. "Because my grandfather made treaty with the Saubral to hunt down the fugitives, save for the approved river route."

She stared at the doorframe. Yes, the Saubral had betrayed Alexran through their recent alliance with Zauril. But Alexran had chosen to betray those who allied with Keldara through that treaty. Was going to Keldara such a good idea after all? What kind of bitter grudges might she encounter there?

"What Zauril would do is much worse than the most despotic thing your grandfather would ever do," Orlanden said harshly. "My lady, I spent enough time observing as diplomatic staff in Medvare-the-city during Zauril's first days. Compared to what Zauril would do, your grandfather Alexran's ambitions were like child's play. He just wanted a safe place for those of his people who survived the coup in the Empire-over-Sea. Zauril—"

"If it were possible Zauril would rule the entire world and take each of the Seven Crowned Gods as his personal patrons," Alicira said tiredly. "And that only if he couldn't ascend to Godhood."

Orlanden startled away from her, surprise widening his eyes as he signed a protective ward. It didn't activate and he scrabbled at his throat for the charm Inharise had given him. It flashed dimly, then faded.

"You jest," he muttered.

"I wish I did. You did not see it?" Hadn't he paid attention to the things she had already said? Or had his mind been elsewhere?

It is hard to believe. Yet true.

"I did not think he was *that*—" Orlanden struggled to find a word, frowning. "—foolhardy. In love with power."

"He is all of that and more." Alicira shook her head ruefully. "If not godhood through his own means, then through my child." She rested her hand on the slight curve of her belly. "He won't get it."

Shock tightened Orlanden's face momentarily before he regained control, and he stared down at his feet. "He seeks to become one of the Seven?"

"Yes," she said, throat choking down hard on the single syllable. "And to that end, he's allied with Nitel against her siblings." Determination strengthened her voice. "I will die before he can gain any such supremacy."

"That shouldn't be necessary—"

"I hope you're right." She glanced sideways at Orlanden. "Best you have my uncle renew that charm for you, if he can. It's not a magic that I have the ability to work, and we may need it later. It's served us well so far."

"I don't think it can be renewed," Orlanden said.

"I have others you can use." Alame crawled up to join them, peering past Alicira and frowning at the weather. "This fog is going to slow us down, especially as we approach the Lone Peak. Not good. We're farther away than I had hoped. We'll be lucky to reach it tonight."

"Is there any way to shorten our path?" she asked.

"Delian would know, as one of Heinmyets' riders." Alame glanced behind them. "He had the watch before Orlanden, so he may sleep longer."

"M'awake," Delian mumbled. He joined them, standing and squinting at the Lone Peak as daylight receded further. "Damn. We *are* further away than I expected."

"Any way to shorten our path from here?" Alicira repeated.

Delian frowned. "Not without dropping down into the fog sooner than I would like. It's a tradeoff. Shorter distance with the likelihood of blundering into a wandering Saubral patrol or the houndriders and Shadowwalker, or another pack of houndriders and Shadowwalkers—they'll have more out looking for us. Or ride farther and faster, be able to see better up until we drop into that last draw. I'd just as soon not run into patrols in the fog if we can help it."

The fog could be twisted against them, if they encountered a Shadowwalker strong enough to work it. Unlike storms, fog could be easily twisted and used by those dedicated to gods like Staul the Destroyer, the Saubral patron. Alicira suspected that Gegarth was one such Shadowwalker with that ability.

"Well, let's do what's needed and be on the road." Alicira stood, stretching as she straightened up, calling Narasin to let her out to forage.

Two, maybe three more days.

Then who knew what kind of greeting waited for her in Keldara? What role did Delian play in Heinmyets's service, and was it enough to provide her protection?

She needed to stop reacting and start preparing for the encounter ahead. Needed to stop brooding over the past that had brought her to this present.

But she also needed to be aware of past grievances to deal with present challenges.

Enough to think about while we're riding.

Hopefully, today's ride would be uneventful enough that she could start putting together a strategy for making her case to Heinmyets. Until now she had been locked in escape mode. Now—she needed to start thinking about survival. Her daughter stirred, and Alicira rested her hand on her belly.

One way or another I will find you a home free of your father.

And after that?

There had to be some way to stop Zauril's quest for godhood.

AFTER A QUICK GRAZE followed by a feed of oats for the horses and daybread plus meat and berry cakes for themselves, they were back on the path just before the last streaks of light faded behind them. Delian led with Orlanden by his side to consult on their path. Alicira took the lead of the mule, trailing it on her right side, away from Findel and her uncle. It was still dark, the moon not quite up yet.

The moon finally rose after they had ridden for a while. Its glow illuminated a faint wisp of fog that writhed hypnotically in front of them, seeming to maintain a consistent distance. Alicira shook her head to see if she was just tired and seeing things.

No change.

"Uncle," she said.

"Wh-what?" He sounded half-asleep.

"The fog in front of us. It's matching our pace." Narasin raised her head, ears pricked forward.

"I don't see anything unusual about it."

"Maybe I'm just imagining things. The moonlight and all."

Narasin remained wary and alert, her head going higher, ears flicking back and forth. The wisp of fog shimmered into a purplish sheen. Alicira's hands tightened on Narasin's reins. The last time she had seen that shade of purple in fog had been when Zauril had called Nitel down upon her. She pulled her bow from its case and braced it as Delian and Orlanden reined their daranvelii back to join them. Orlanden braced his bow.

"Uncle?" Her voice quavered in spite of herself.

"I see," Alame said. He and Delian drew their swords. "Let me lead. Delian, with me. Arrows, even magicked, will not work against this Goddess."

"What is it?" Delian asked, as the fog began to take form.

"Either Zauril or that Shadowwalker has invoked the Lady Nitel," Alicira whispered, as the child stirred restlessly within her and Narasin pinned her ears, projecting *danger* and the shape of houndriders.

Oh Goddess, if you were ever with me before, be even more with me now! A manifestation of Nitel plus the houndriders—*and was that a Shadowwalker with that manifestation of Nitel forming ahead of them?*

As the purple mist transformed into a humanoid shape the faint cry of houndriders echoed behind them. The child kicked frantically inside Alicira, *fear, fear, fear* radiating out and threatening to swamp Alicira's own feelings. Goddess in front of them, houndriders behind—

Goddess—

Alicira thought plaintively. She tried to think calming thoughts, imaged stroking the head of the child within her and singing a comforting song. Then the warmth she had felt before settled around the child, who calmed though *fear* still feebly pulsed out from her.

"Orlanden, the riders!" she called. "Uncle, do you need help?"

"Keep the hounds off of us!" Alame yelled. "Save your magic and stay away unless I fail! I have something Terani of Waykemin taught me! Nitel will want *you,* so stay away from me while I work the magic!"

She nodded and wheeled Narasin toward their back trail, then dropped the reins, sending the golden mare ahead at a measured, steady walk while she nocked an arrow. Should she use the same spell as before?

Wait.

That one had been too draining, and it had been meant to scatter, not kill, due to the type of shot she'd taken. Now she could shoot individual houndriders. If only she had glimmer dust in her bags—wait. Which of her saddlebags carried those small pouches she hadn't had time to investigate before leaving their shelter?

Right hand side.

She shifted her bow to her left hand and reached back to fumble open the ties to her saddlebag.

"Whoa," she breathed, as the movement became awkward. "Orlanden. One moment."

He reined Odilel toward her. "What?"

"Wait. I may have something."

She unnocked her arrow, replaced it in her quiver, and hung the bow on her saddle horn before rummaging in her saddlebag. The first small pouch held something firm and round. Not what she needed right at this moment if it was what she thought it was. The next pouch held something gooey that moved under her fingers—something else that could be of use later but not now. And the third—soft, giving way under the pressure of her fingertips like dust would. Alicira pulled that pouch out of the saddlebag and opened it.

"By the Goddess," she breathed, voice quavering as the pale blue glow of high-quality glimmer dust shone from the opening. "Dovré's tits, how did Haran find *this*?"

Orlanden moved Odilel closer. "I've never seen dust this shade."

"It is truly a royal gift," she whispered. That meant the other two pouches held— "By the Goddess," she repeated, the tone of her voice prayerful. "Haran paid dearly to obtain this. He had to. Alexran was the only one I've seen with this quality of dust." Most glimmer dust she'd seen and worked with was a darker blue. This was paler, almost the same shade as the sky when clear.

I will find a way to help you, by one means or another, Haran had said—

Just two days ago? She swallowed hard, wondering what it had cost him to find this quality of magical supplies on such short notice in Nixyin.

Dear friend, I will not squander your gift.

"Your arrows," she said.

Orlanden silently handed her his arrows, one by one. She carefully dipped the broadheads into the dust. Then she whispered the spell that made each head glow with the same pale blue hue as the dust and made it sensitive to her incantations, not worrying about her magic betraying them. No need to hide from houndriders now; not with Nitel manifesting in front of them.

Gods, will Alame be able to handle her alone?

She dipped her own arrowheads into the dust.

When she was done, she carefully closed the pouch, making certain the laces were snug before she replaced it in her saddle-bag. To her relief, the base spell did not tire her as much as that one scatter arrow had. Then Alicira picked up her bow and renocked one of the arrows, urging Narasin ahead, Orlanden riding knee-to-knee with her.

Which spell to use? She thought over her options as they returned to the steady walk toward the houndriders baying closer, Narasin's ears flattening hard against her head while her warnings intensified. Glimmer dust responded best to solitary enchantments, not combinations.

Accuracy or poison?

Both demanded a lot of power. Considering how much energy the scatter spell had taken out of her with a solitary arrow, not a choice for them shooting multiple arrows. But an incantation that would slow, then stop the houndriders in addition to any injury the arrow inflicted? One of the first battle enchantments she had learned, and used with glimmer dust this strong—yes. It wouldn't kill as quickly as poison would, but the dust would disable them with less drain on her magic. Yes. That spell.

Closer. Closer.

Orlanden flinched as the Goddess Nitel's ululating wail echoed behind them, accompanied by Alame and Delian's shouts. Alicira forced herself to focus on the oncoming danger instead of reining Narasin back to their aid. Whether it was an actual manifestation of the Goddess that Zauril had somehow managed to summon—*he couldn't do that, he doesn't have that power yet, does he?*—or whether it was just a Shadowwalker-worked hex summoning Nitel's shadow and not the Goddess herself, her uncle had to deal with it.

One magician for Nitel, one magician for the houndriders.

Narasin halted. Alicira raised her bow, waiting, waiting, even as the baying of the hounds sent chills up and down her arms.

Wait for the right moment.

Less energy needed to invoke her charm the closer they came.

Wait.

She held until she was certain of her target, then whispered her spell, Orlanden releasing mere moments after she did. New arrow, nock, fire, repeat. The pale green blood of the hounds and riders they struck flared bright, then faded, hissing as it landed on ice crystals on the ground. Without riders, the hounds circled in confusion. Without mounts, the riders grabbed at riderless hounds only to have the unbonded beasts savage them.

Before they had exhausted their arrows, they had broken the ties between the houndriders and their mounts. Four hounds lay dead, five riders were dead or dying, and three hounds wandered aimlessly around the bodies while two riders tried to struggle back up from the ground.

Orlanden unbraced his bow and drew his sword, dismounting. "I'll take care of the rest and pick up arrows. You go help *there.*"

Alicira nodded and whirled Narasin back toward Alame and Delian, nocking her next-to-last arrow as she urged Narasin into a canter. Flashes of bright purple revealed the Shadowwalker Gegarth facing off against Alame and Delian. Alame still rode Findel, the daranval using teeth and hooves against the Shadowwalker while Alame swung his sword. And Delian—

No. That didn't look right. There were two entities. Alicira squinted. Delian battled Gegarth on the ground, his daranval circling around trying to find an opening to lunge at the Shadowwalker independently of her rider. Alame fought a construct —a shade of Nitel, possibly a projection of Zauril's. As Narasin thundered closer, the construct tried to twist away from Alame and charge toward them. Alame and Findel blocked it smoothly. Then the Nitel construct swirled away like water released from a dam. Alame nearly came off as Findel rolled back to intercept it.

"Whoa," Alicira breathed to Narasin.

The mare halted sharply and stomped a forefoot, sending sparks flying. Alicira drew, taking aim at the Nitel construct, hoping that the weakening spell would slow it. As she released, Delian screamed. Alicira turned to see Delian go down. His daranval struck at Gegarth.

"NO!" she shrieked and urged Narasin ahead, grabbing her last arrow as her brother doubled over.

Gegarth raised his sword for another blow. She aimed, shot. The arrow hit his sword arm as he struck at Delian. The Shadowwalker staggered back, snarling. Alicira dropped her bow over her saddle horn and drew her sword, keening as Delian slumped on the ground, his daranval standing over him protectively. Gegarth reeled back toward his red stallion and clambered on. He was barely settled before the red stallion took off at a gallop, Gegarth clutching at his mane.

"ALICIRA!" Her uncle's warning bellow caught her short. Narasin humped up and kicked, then whirled. The Nitel visage swirled behind her, then changed form to take on Zauril's face.

"Caught!" he cackled, the shades of his orange and red personal colors flicking amongst the purple of Nitel in his distorted, larger-than-life mask-like visage. "Never fear, I've another troop of Shadowwalkers and houndriders en route to collect you."

"By the darkest fires of Staul, no!" she yelled back.

Why that God and not Dovré?

Zauril laughed even louder. "Given up your Goddess for the Destroyer? Ironic, given the Saubral dedication to him."

"I appeal to Staul the Balancer, not Staul the Destroyer," she countered, raising her sword high. "But even as the Destroyer Staul knows, my cause is just!"

"Just? From one of Alexran's brood? Do you even know what justice is, my lady Alicira?"

A tendril of orange and red light mixed with purple shot at her. Alicira used both hands on her sword to stop it. The light swirled around her blade, pushing hard to reach her.

Danger. Danger.

If the light touched her, she would be immobilized, unable to move in any direction until his minions joined them. This spell was more powerful than the one Zauril had used when he captured her. Somehow, he had gained more power since she had left Medvara.

But how? He must have taken the final steps toward dedicating himself to Nitel—

"No!" Alame charged them, waving his sword, Findel snorting defiance. Alame swung at Zauril's manifestation but his sword bounced off. Findel staggered sideways from the impact.

"What? You again?" Zauril glared at Alame and spit a fireball toward him.

"TERANI! I CALL UPON YOU!" Alame roared, raising his sword to knock the fireball aside. "In the name of our linkage, in the name of Karnoi and Cirdel who bind you and in the name of Artel who binds me, lend me your aid!"

Midnight blue light flared and the tendril of orange-red-purple magic extending toward Alicira fell. She almost dropped her sword as the pressure from Zauril's magic evaporated. Zauril's visage spun to face Alame, whose sword now glowed blue-white. Several rays of orange-red-purple lashed toward Alame and he deflected each one. But her uncle was unable to do more than defend himself.

I don't know this magic.

What magic was Alame wielding? Midnight blue was Artel, but was that a whisper of the fiery reds and magentas of Karnoi and Cirdel, the God of Battles and the Goddess of Disorder, mixed in with the lights in his sword?

Alicira choked at the memory of how those reds and magentas had tightened around her mother, and urged Narasin forward. No time to bring out the glimmer dust to treat her sword, even if she dared exert that much energy, but perhaps she could find a means to weaken Zauril. Anything to stop the battle and aid Delian—Delian. She spared a quick glance toward her brother and flinched at how still he lay, his daranval standing over him with her ears pinned and teeth bared.

Goddess, help me!

The warmth around her child pulsed but nothing more came. Perhaps she could still wrap a minor enchantment around her sword. Alicira whispered a spell and her sword glowed faintly.

Zauril's projection struck out at Alame with more tendrils. Alicira shifted her weight and raised her sword to attack one, just as an arrow whispered through the projection. It flashed bright red and orange, the purple tint wavering and fading away.

Where did it—Orlanden!

He must have finished with the houndriders. Alicira looked around to spot him as a second arrow went through the projection.

Zauril howled, all red and orange now, no purple.

"You will pay for this!" he screeched. "My curse on you for my Lady's sake!"

What remained of his fading visage feinted toward Alicira, and then a tendril struck Delian. Her brother screamed as the red and orange fog disappeared.

"Delian, Delian," Alicira moaned, shoving her sword back into its scabbard before she slid off of Narasin. "Oh Delian!"

Delian's daranval raised her muzzle to the sky and screamed, a mourning note in her cry. Alicira shoved at her to back away from Delian. The daranval stepped away, only to come back forward and nuzzle at her fallen rider, now whickering softly.

"Brother," Alicira moaned, feeling for a pulse in his neck. Then she found it, weak and thready. "Oh brother mine. Delian. No."

His eyelids flickered, opening to reveal a dull glaze that struck fear even deeper within her.

"Dark. So dark." His hands flailed frantically. Alicira took his right hand.

He's dying unless we can do something to stop it.

Light glimmered behind them. Alame used rocks and branches to brace a torch upright by Delian's head, then knelt across from her, his magic flaring briefly as he took Delian's other hand.

"He's been poisoned as well as struck," he announced after a pause while he gingerly lowered himself to the ground and eased Delian's head into his lap. "Essence of Darsnai. One of the few poisons that can be administered through a projection. That last lash from Zauril carried it."

"Can you deal with the magic?" She gently probed the bloody mess around Delian's gut, sick at heart. What little healing ability she possessed couldn't deal with *this*.

"Let me." Orlanden crowded in beside her. "I have some experience with battlefield healing."

"But this?"

Orlanden pulled up Delian's tunic, wincing at what he saw. "We need to stop the bleeding first. Alicira, get my saddlebags. Alame, what do you need to counteract the poison?"

"I think I have that," Alicira said. She raced to Narasin, fumbling in her saddlebag for the squishy sack she had rejected earlier. She tossed it to her uncle before going to Odilel and untying Orlanden's saddlebags.

Alame opened the pouch as she dropped the bags next to Orlanden.

"Alicira. By the stars of Artel, how did you find neutralizing paste?"

"Ask how Haran found it in Nixyin, along with the purest glimmer dust I've seen since Grandfather's private store." She knelt next to Delian and took his hand again.

Orlanden shook his head as he pressed a wad of bandages against Delian's middle. "I've never understood Haran's ability to find obscure and hidden things." He looked up at Alicira. "He told me exactly where to find you in Medvare-the-city."

Alame delicately dipped a finger in the pouch, scooping up a dab of dark paste that he pushed into Delian's mouth. "It is a talent indeed. Alicira. Stand watch. We should stay here to give him a chance to survive his injuries but we can't. Not if Zauril has more Shadowwalkers in pursuit. Let us get Delian in what shape we can to travel. If there is any more you can do to banish *him*—"

She nodded, understanding what he meant, and rose.

Orlanden pulled off his bow case and tossed it toward her. "Your arrows are in there. I retrieved all but two, and those were broken."

"Thank you." She separated out her arrows from Orlanden's, identifying them by the feel of the small crests carved into each shaft, and put them in her case.

Then she walked to the edge of the small circle of light cast by the torch, staring out into the darkness. Her throat tightened as she felt the all-too-familiar desire to collapse, sob, scream, and rend the earth around her that had haunted her over the past few months.

Delian was dying. Her brother. Last of her close family. That would leave her as Richenax's last child, Alexran's last grandchild. Just her, Alame, and her unborn child left of the Miteal.

She choked back sobs. Not now. Not time to mourn. Not when there was work to do.

Narasin joined her, gently nuzzling Alicira's hand. She leaned on her daranval, extending her awareness to brush against Narasin's, wordlessly trying to convey the need to watch.

Narasin sent back soothing images of herself nuzzling Alicira, then nuzzling an image that varied between human infant and young red foal, then more of the same warmth.

Alicira queried further, projecting Gegarth's appearance.

Narasin returned a picture of Gegarth riding away hard, collapsing on the neck of his horse. For now, they were safe from him. She had executed fortunate shots each time they encountered each other. But would that continue, or would her magic fail her the next time they battled Gegarth?

Alicira slid her arm over Narasin's neck and risked a moment to bury her head in the golden mare's mane. Narasin nuzzled her hip, then carefully raised her head, continuing to send reassurance to Alicira as well as pictures of herself on alert, no danger nearby.

Alicira didn't cry as she rested her head on Narasin, much as she wanted to. Instead, after a few stifled gulps and shudders, she wiped her eyes and straightened up.

Now more than ever she was determined to stay free from Zauril's grasp.

"You will pay for this," she whispered into the night, reaching for the little bit of magic she had that was still tied to Medvara, that last tiny piece she had clung to in order to keep control of her powers. "*In Dovré's name, you will pay.*"

Then she closed her eyes, visualized a sharp knife, and used that blade to sever any further ties between herself and Medvara, ignoring the deep wail of loss building up deep inside.

Medvara is gone to me.

A whirling vortex of emotions raged through her as her magic roiled, losing that last connection to the land that had once given her power. Alicira's fingers curled into fists in Narasin's mane, and she breathed deeply, calling the emotions to her and ruthlessly centering them within herself, within the child who now struggled and kicked at the sudden onslaught of magic.

I am sorry, my daughter. But this is our only hope of surviving free from Zauril.

She extended her awareness to tame the raging spiral. Unexpected assistance from Narasin's awareness helped Alicira provide a foundation for her magic and calm the child. That done, she unclenched her hands and stepped back from Narasin, taking a deep breath. Then she raised her hands high and began to chant, the magic forming the words of its own volition as she shaped this last curse she could throw at her usurper.

Her body shook as the power responded to her call, vibrating deep within her.

"And with this, oh Zauril, I issue my final curse!" she

shrieked into the sky above, and tossed the gathering magic between her hands in the general direction of Medvara.

She screamed as the last pieces of Medvara ripped away from her, her power ebbing as the blessing of Medvara faded from her, broadening that wound deep within. Alicira sagged against Narasin as the magic faded and the world around her settled, drawing ragged, hard breaths, not yet daring to investigate her senses to see what, if any magic remained to her.

Not that I would have it for much longer anyway, at least not until the child is born.

At last she straightened. Narasin turned her head, the sense of her presence nearly as strong as before. Alicira blinked. She took her scarf in both hands and tried to raise her othersight. For a moment she thought it was gone, faded away, but then it responded, not as strong as before but still present.

But the gaping hole where her magical awareness was located had doubled in size.

That will need to be mended once my daughter is born.

For now, though, it was gone, a deep emptiness echoing at her core. Narasin nuzzled Alicira's hand and she felt the daranval's awareness spilling into hers, smoothing out the rough edges of that deep breach and modulating the ache in her heart.

NarasinandAlicira. NarasinandAliciraandyoungling.

Alicira dared to touch Narasin's mind with her own. Faint prickles radiated from her gut as the child brushed against both of their awarenesses. Then, abruptly, the channel to the child was cut off.

NarasinandAlicira.

NarasinandAlicira?

NarasinandAlicira!

This time Narasin's thoughts were more impatient and intense. Was this the bonding that Alame had spoken of? In any case, the mare had not led her wrong yet.

NarasinandAlicira.

Alicira answered, accepting.

In return, a wave of joy broke over the two of them. Alicira reeled momentarily, then blinked as the magic world settled around her. Now she was more aware of Narasin's presence. The magic available to her lacked the high, intensive jangle of the land connection to Medvara's magic. But, wonder of wonders, the connection with Narasin substituted for the Medvaran link. The loose ends of her severed magic settled. Not as powerful. Not as far-reaching.

A hole still existed in her magical senses that she would need to patch after the child was born and—hopefully—she had a land tie to substitute for her linkage to Medvara. But there was a faint presence inside her mind that emanated from the golden mare. If she focused on it, she was aware that she was also present within Narasin. A shared magic. Narasin couldn't provide the magical foundation that even that one tiny link with Medvara could—but it was still strong enough to allow Alicira to work most of her magic safely, without the worry of being taken by the magic currents themselves. Even better, she doubted that this magic would draw her to Zauril's attention.

Was this what Alame meant by finding other ways?

She doubted that. The power he had called upon to banish Zauril's link to Nitel was nothing she recognized, and certainly not the same as this linkage she had with Narasin. He'd called on Terani—of Waykemin?

She experimented with this newer magic to reach to Delian,

to gently send the feeling that *I am here, I am with you.* In return, she got the faintest stir of recognition. He still lived, but barely. She withdrew and turned her attention back to watching for danger, maintaining the lightest of links with Narasin. Together, they watched as the sense of Gegarth's presence gradually faded away.

"It's done," her uncle said grimly from behind her. "Poison is cleared. Orlanden's almost finished doing what he can. We should be leaving soon."

"Can Delian travel?"

"Does it matter? We can't stay here, not with Zauril's knowledge of our location. If we can get Delian to Hein-myets's people, perhaps there's a healer there who can help him."

"If he survives the ride." She hung her bow back on the saddle horn. "Is there any means we can use to make the travel easier?"

"Not at the speed we need to go." Alame raised his hands. "Alicira. At this point his survival is in the Gods' hands."

And they are proving fickle.

She changed the subject since she had no counter. "I cut the last tie," she said, voice flat.

"I felt it." His hand rested on her shoulder. "But you're not severed completely from magical control. How did you ground your magic if you don't have the land to draw on?"

"Narasin."

"Ah. I didn't have Findel when I was cursed. It's also different if you sever the link yourself—may I check?"

That allowed for a deeper probe into her mind than she had ever allowed anyone else to do. But her uncle was the only other one who would know what she had gone through.

Alicira nodded. Alame took her hand, then leaned his forehead to hers. His touch in and around her magic was quick and deft, nothing like Zauril's ham-fisted hammering at her shields in an attempt to force submission. Then he slipped out, and straightened up.

"It's not perfect. You still have loose attachments and those will need to be dealt with."

"But not until I have a reliable connection to a land of some sort or another," she said. "And that takes time I don't have, before I lose my magic temporarily. The daranval magic isn't enough. However, it will work until the child is born."

"Agreed." He stepped back. "Back to Delian. One of us will need to ride with him. Probably Orlanden, since that'll give us one archer and one sword should we be attacked."

"No," she said. "Me. Put him up before me on Narasin."

"Alicira! In your condition—"

"I'm his sister. It's my duty. If he dies on the way, let it be in my arms."

"But your health, the child, your magic—" Alame gestured with both hands, frowning in frustration. "We need to take care of you!"

"What better way to take care of both of us than to have me handling Delian? Uncle." Her voice caught. "He's my last remaining close family. My last sibling. No. Me. Please."

"Alicira. Stubborn as ever."

"Sister's right. Sister's duty. Sister's honor. Richenax's son, Richenax's daughter. It is only fair."

"Will you be able to handle it?"

"I'll have to. Heinmyets is supposed to meet us at the Lone Peak?"

"His riders, at least. I know Delian had sent messages by his daranval, in case Haran wasn't able."

"Can we advise them of our current situation?"

Alame shook his head. "Not unless one of us could speak through Delian's daranval. It would sap what strength he has for him to do it. Findel does not have a connection to any of Heinmyets's daranvelii, and while Narasin might know the daranvelii with Heinmyets, we don't know the people who would be riding with that group."

"I'll ask Narasin." She awkwardly tried to picture *communicating with distant daranvelii, talking to Delian's daranval.* Narasin came back with blurred images, and then sadness. Apparently she couldn't. "I don't think so."

"It would take more experience with your daranval to do it." Alame's voice went very quiet, and he looked down. "Findel does not talk well over the distances, or I'd try." Abruptly, he turned back toward the torch and Delian. Alicira followed him.

She knelt beside Delian. "Brother?"

His eyes flickered. "Sister." His hand fumbled for hers and she took it tight.

"We have to ride. We can't stay. I'm sorry."

"Leave me," he husked. "Save yourself."

"No. I won't leave you to the houndriders."

"Slow you down."

"I won't leave you," she repeated. "You'll ride in front of me on Narasin." Her hand tightened even more on his. "You'll ride with me. We'll get you to Heinmyets's people. They'll have a healer."

He smiled feebly. "You'll keep me alive through sheer will."

"If that's what it takes."

He squeezed her hand. They sat quietly until Orlanden led Narasin up. Alicira and Alame helped him sit, and the three of them got him to his feet. They worked together to ease Delian up on Narasin. Then, while Orlanden steadied Delian, Alame boosted Alicira up so that she straddled the mare behind the saddle, sitting on top of the saddlebags. Once they were settled, Orlanden took the lead while Alame followed. Alicira concentrated on keeping Delian upright.

"Lean on me," she whispered to him at one point.

"I'm afraid to let go," he gasped.

She used what little magic she dared to help ease his pain

without overwhelming herself. Her focus grew ever inward, one part monitoring Narasin's awareness for Shadowwalkers and houndriders near them, the other taking on what she could of Delian's pain.

Delian slowly sagged against her, becoming limper in her arms as they traveled. Alicira dropped Narasin's reins to wrap her arms tighter around her brother, trusting the mare to stay with the others. Her magic told her that he was fading more and more. One part of her wanted to rouse Delian, shake him to keep fighting. But the part of her that was aware of how badly injured he was held back.

Oh gods, the pain he'll suffer—is suffering.

Their uncle rode close, now riding knee-to-knee with them. He reached over and took Delian by the shoulder to help steady him when the trail allowed. She sensed his magic flaring, then running quiet before withdrawing. Alame's face sagged and he shook his head.

Delian's breathing slowed while they navigated up a steep hillside deep in the fog.

No. Brother, stay with me!

She broke her earlier decision not to rouse him. She shook him a little.

"Ciren," he moaned. "Oh gods, Ciren, dear heart."

Ciren? She didn't know of any Ciren, much less one that her brother would call *dear heart.*

"Who is Ciren?" she asked.

Nothing came from Delian but another groan. His thoughts were distant, so distant. Then his awareness was almost gone, a little flicker of himself remaining.

Alame rode close again as they climbed out of the draw. He patted Alicira's shoulder before placing his hand on Delian, helping steady him, falling back only when they dropped down into the last draw. She could tell from the growing lighter color of gray that it was almost daylight. Would they ever be free from this fog? Perhaps if its dank chill didn't pull so much at Delian, if they could ride in the sunlight, he could regroup.

Just one ray of sunlight.

Delian exhaled one long final breath as they climbed out of the last draw into the early morning sunlight at the foot of the Lone Peak, that flicker of his self fading to nothing before the sun touched him. Alicira held him even tighter when no more breathing came, tears silently forcing their way out of her eyes to freeze on her cheeks as an east wind stirred around them.

Alame rode close, taking Narasin's reins. She allowed herself more tears, losing track of where they were, where they were going, her only world herself and her dead brother. It was a perfect moment for Zauril to strike at them, but right now she didn't care.

Delian was gone. Melaraen was gone. She was the only surviving child of Richenax and Melara.

Narasin halted, and she became aware of voices she didn't recognize speaking to Orlanden and Alame. She didn't try to make out the words but clung to Delian. Alone. Not just orphaned but alone. No siblings, no parents. Only her uncle.

"Lady Alicira?" A deep, warm, welcoming voice.

She raised her head to look down at the man and woman standing next to Narasin. The man gave her a small smile, fading quickly into a sorrow-laden frown. His gold-flecked brown eyes drew her in, welcomed her. The faintest touch of magic kept carefully under wraps emanated from him. Broad shoulders, tall and stocky, dark hair in two braids under a fur cap, curly dark beard against dark brown skin the shade of wet earth. The same man on the black daranval that the Goddess had shown her a few days ago.

Heinmyets.

The woman next to him also stood straight and tall, broad-shouldered with dark hair bound into a single braid, her face long and elegant with high cheekbones and skin the shade of redbark pine, her full lips pressed together tightly in sorrow. Power radiated from her as well.

She must be Inharise.

"Yes?" Alicira croaked.

"I am Heinmyets," he said, voice rumbling and soothing, a practiced magic shaping his tone to calm her. "Delian has left us?"

She blinked back more tears and nodded.

"I owe him deathright obligation. He was sworn to my service." He gestured to the woman. "This is Inharise. May we help you with him?"

She didn't want to release him. That would mean Delian was truly gone. Heinmyets showed no impatience but waited, letting her think.

"He is the last of my family, save for my uncle," she finally whispered through the thickness of sorrow that muddled her thoughts.

Inharise laid a graceful long-fingered hand on her back. "When you are ready we will help. We can wait. When it is time we will honor you both." Her voice carried even more power than Heinmyets's did, a magic Alicira didn't recognize.

So this is Heinmyets's Clendan woman.

She could like this woman, already did like her even without knowing why given that her presence meant the haven she had hoped for here was unlikely. She buried her head in Delian's shoulder one last time. He'd given up his life here to come back to Medvara and help her escape. He hadn't needed to do that.

"Oh brother," she whispered. "How will I ever repay the debt I owe you?"

"He loved you dearly," Heinmyets said. "When the news came of Zauril's attempt to force a marriage he knew he had to return to Medvara. I would have come—"

"*We* would have come with Delian," Inharise interjected. "But he would not have us do that."

"He wouldn't have wanted the help," she gulped. "And it was probably best you didn't come with him, but oh gods, gods, to lose him like this." Tears blurred her eyes further.

"Come rest," Heinmyets said. "We have a tent ready, and we will give Delian honor. You cared for him at the end. Now it is time for you to be cared for."

Alicira shuddered, hearing the reason and persuasion in his words and finally yielding to it. "All right."

"Yamits. Mohanit. Jetan." As Heinmyets spoke, three men came forward. Heinmyets eased her arms from around Delian and gently guided him off of Narasin and into their grasp. Alicira swayed in the saddle. She would have fallen except that Inharise held her steady. Then together Inharise and Heinmyets drew her off of Narasin, Heinmyets taking her firmly into his arms.

"Rest, my lady, rest," Heinmyets said, holding her close. "You are safe with us."

She needed to negotiate what her position could be with these people as soon as possible. But at this moment her greatest desire was to sleep, free from dreams, free from the ache that gnawed at her.

Brother, oh brother.

They had been so close to safety. So close.

Heinmyets and Inharise took her into a small circular tent. A fire burned in the center, smoke drifting through a narrow gap between the tent poles at the top. He knelt and placed her on a pile of furs that she realized was a low bed, padded with furs and boughs underneath.

"A place to sleep," Inharise said.

Alicira nodded, and sat up to fumble with her boots.

"Let me." Heinmyets bent to slide them off while Inharise helped Alicira with her jacket. Then Inharise pulled back the heavy furs covering the bed. Alicira crawled inside.

"If only I wouldn't dream," she whispered.

Inharise patted her hand. "I will be here. Myets."

"Yes?" Heinmyets said from the other side of the tent.

"Bring the smudge if it's ready."

He didn't say anything but brought over a long smoldering bundle of juniper, sage, and other herbs all tied together. The mixture of scent was unfamiliar. Inharise tied the bundle to a holder fastened to one of the tent poles. Then she took some ash from the smudge's tip and brushed a circle on Alicira's forehead.

"There," she said. "That will help."

Alicira nodded. She turned onto her side and closed her eyes. Exhaustion drew her quickly into sleep.

CHAPTER 6

Alicira woke warmer than she had felt for ages. The half-light of dusk dominated the tent, so she must have slept the day away. Fatigue still pulled at her, but she was rested enough to be hungry and wonder briefly why she was here.

Then memory crashed over her.

Delian dead.

They had met with Heinmyets too late to save him. Heinmyets and Inharise had put her to bed here, or was she dreaming that?

Her nostrils flared to catch the enticing scent of warm broth.

"I expect you'll be a bit hungry." Inharise, leaning against a tripod back support next to the bed, looked up from her knitting.

Alicira slowly pushed herself up, staring as Inharise finished her stitch.

She was working a type of magical yarn.

"You—you knit?" she whispered. "You knit the magic yarn?" She half-reached to touch the yarn, then pulled back. "May I see?"

"It is not quite what you Miteal do." Inharise handed the cap she was knitting to Alicira. "But years ago, one of your people brought a few of the magic-bred sheep to Keldara and thus to Clenda. My grandfather traded with Thenil of Keldara for a young ram, a runt they had no use for." A faint smile touched her lips, then faded. "That runt's get crossed with our sheep nicely. We do not spin the yarn of your power, but it holds our magic quite effectively."

"The sheep I sent—"

"Are young yet and not ready to be sheared. But they are safe. We will have more magic and power from their wool, soon."

The spells in Alicira's scarf stirred. She quieted them, wanting to feel this other magic. The power pulsing through the nearly-finished cap was most definitely not of Miteal origin, not even Aireii. But as Alicira fingered the neat stitches, the yarn, she got a sense of its pattern. Not that different from the enchantments she had learned to spin as part of the leadership of Medvara in form, but the magic's substance moved in a different way.

An earthier mix than that of the Goddess's magic, as wrapped in sky and stone as that was. She could almost smell grassy highlands with tall redbark pines stirring in this sorcery, see the deep river canyons that scored those highlands, feel the warmth of a summer's day contrasting with the cool swift river water.

This different magic called to her skill in the same manner as her own magic as she followed the way with which it fit in the wool. It might take her some time to learn all of its paths, but she could trace how the spells wound within the yarn.

Longevity and warmth were the primary spells in this cap.

Most importantly, she could spin this yarn once she was grounded to this land's magic.

"The place I feel, the magic ground. Is it Keldara or Clenda?"

Inharise smiled, then grew solemn again. "Clenda. No one

spins the magic of Keldara. It refuses to be bound. No one has that control, though Heinmyets tries. We have tried spinning Clenda and Keldara together, thinking the combination might work, but something is missing."

Alicira handed the cap back to Inharise, strangely reluctant to let it go. She unwrapped the scarf from her neck.

"This is my spinning and knitting."

Inharise put the cap down and took the scarf. She puckered her lips thoughtfully as she fingered it.

"Fine work." She picked up the cap and held the two together, her smile slowly returning. "They complement each other. Feel."

She held them out to Alicira. She took a finger's grip of each one together, careful not to grasp too much of either item.

"They do indeed," she whispered. "Then there are possibilities for me here?"

"Oh my dear, most definitely so." Inharise handed the scarf back to Alicira, then tucked away the cap. "But now is not the time to speak of these likelihoods, not until Heinmyets can join us. At this moment, though, you must be hungry." She got up and ladled some broth into a wooden cup from a small pot hanging over the fire. "Your uncle prepared this for you to drink."

"Thank you." Alicira took the cup with both hands, letting the warmth soak into them as she inhaled the steam. She recognized the strengthening and soothing herbs Alame used. "What is to be done with my brother?"

"He will have a fire tonight," Inharise said. "Would that we could have given him longer honors, but after what Alame told us, we dare not linger. We're still in Saubral territory. We honor him, then ride. We are still a day's difficult travel from the Keldaran border, and would have not remained here save for the messages from Haran warning us that you rode hard with pursuit following."

"So Haran is well?" Alicira took a careful sip from her cup. Still hot, but the flavor spread through her, soothing her restless gut and providing the smallest bit of strength.

"He was when he sent word."

"From Nixyin?"

"No, the bird flew from Lananil," Inharise said, naming a ferry town upriver from Nixyin on the Larij side of the Chellana.

Alicira heaved a sigh of relief. Haran had gotten away. She tried more of the broth. Slightly cooler. She drank more. A child cried out, and Inharise crossed to the other side of the tent, making soothing noises. As Alicira drank the rest of the broth, Inharise dealt with the child, bringing it over to Alicira. She undid her tunic and put the child to her breast. The young one suckled enthusiastically and Inharise smiled down at it.

"A strong boy," she said, pride echoing in her voice.

Alicira's heart fell and her gut roiled. So that option was closed to her. "Heinmyets's child?" she asked.

"Yes." Inharise said. "His name is Cenarth. That means "conqueror" in my language."

"Then you two are wed." Her voice went flat.

"What?" Inharise looked back up at Alicira, startled. "Yes, but —we have a simple commitment. My Goddess Terat told me two years ago that we needed a third to help us spin Keldara and Clenda together."

"A third to spin Keldara and Clenda together?" Alicira's voice wavered.

"Yes. The two of us cannot contain all the tendrils of magic, try as we will. Heinmyets's grandmother Jeinyet said it was possible within a threefold marriage."

"If I spin and weave with you—" Her voice cracked and she had to rein back the excitement.

"Given the feel of your weaving, you may well be the one Jeinyet prophesied." Inharise looked back down at Cenarth, then up again to meet Alicira's eyes. "If the three of us can spin yarn and weave the pattern of magic together, then the Two Nations remain shielded and safe."

"You would not mind?" She had been willing enough to consider what pattern she might need to adopt with Haran and Orlanden had she married them, despite what her family might think.

But with Inharise and Heinmyets? Haran and Orlanden did not spin. This would be different. Melding their abilities to spin would require a deeper intimacy with Heinmyets and Inharise than would have been possible with magicless Haran and Orlanden.

What power could we wield?

"We have both felt there was a piece of us missing. If we can spin together—but not now! This is not the place or the time."

"I understand." Her mind raced.

The Great Pattern. A Tapestry. Alexran had controlled magic so tightly in Medvara, breaking even the grandest ceremony into smaller chunks that he dominated, that she had never seriously contemplated the likelihood of weaving the great magical pattern mix of magic and magical yarn that shielded the land of those who created it. No partners had been available to practice it. Her tutors had sworn the memory of how to weave that pattern was lost, that Alexran's indoctrination into it either had never happened in Daran or was broken by Etikar's actions when he deposed Elithtra back in Daran.

But Inharise spoke so casually of weaving the pattern. Had someone amongst the Aireii diaspora to Keldara carried that knowledge, unbeknownst to her grandfather?

Or was this a new revelation of the Goddess?

No matter. Now was not the time to speak of it, not while they still traveled Saubral territory and Delian lay unhonored.

Once Delian had been safely honored and his spirit given no

reason to haunt them, once they were safely within Keldara, they would speak of this.

"Would you like to hold Cenarth?" Inharise asked. Alicira startled, guiltily realizing she had been absorbed in thought and not paying attention.

"Yes," she said, reaching for the boy almost before she finished speaking. Inharise settled Cenarth into her arms and Alicira pulled him close, gazing at the curly brown hair, the brown button nose, the long black eyelashes so like his father's.

In a few months I will be holding my daughter.

Holding Cenarth brought that reality starkly close. Alicira stared down at the child, wondering what her daughter would look like. Would she have Zauril's reddish-brown hair or her own silver-streaked gold? Or would her daughter have the straight dark hair of her grandfather Richenax and great-grandfather Alexran? Until now Alicira hadn't considered the possibilities.

The rustle of the tent flap opening made her look up. Heinmyets stood in the doorway.

"Good. You're awake," he said, smiling at Alicira.

"Myets. She spins. Feel her scarf." Inharise turned to Alicira. "May I?"

"Yes." Alicira let Inharise gently ease the scarf from around her neck and hand it to Heinmyets.

"You knit this?" he asked Alicira as he held the scarf in both hands, holding it up to study the pattern.

"I spun and knit that yarn when I was tied to Medvara," she said.

"You no longer have any link to the land?"

Alicira shook her head, swallowing hard as dampness blurred her vision. "I cut the final ties to Medvara to try to save Delian and curse Zauril," she whispered.

Delian. Brother. Gods.

Cenarth squirmed and whimpered as her arms tightened on

him. Someone took the child away and Alicira buried her head in her hands.

Large warm hands covered hers. "Shh. Shh. All will be well."

"He didn't have to save me," she breathed through her fingers. "He could have stayed here."

"And let Zauril grow in power at the cost of his beloved sister? No, he could not. Would not." Heinmyets spoke softly but firmly. "Listen to me and do not blame yourself. We spoke of his choices once he learned what had happened in Medvara. When he determined that he needed to rescue you, he would hear of no other way but to go himself, alone, not even taking Ciren with him, much as she begged to join."

"Ciren?"

"My sister. They were promised."

Alicira raised her head, staring at Heinmyets. "I did not know. He didn't tell me during our flight. Oh Gods. How she must feel!"

Now things were coming clear, including Delian's last words. No wonder he had been so confident of her reception in Keldara, since he was sworn to marry Heinmyets's sister. But why hadn't he told her about Ciren?

Heinmyets kept hold of her hands as she lowered them to her lap. "She sits vigil with him now."

She looked down at their hands, shaking her head. "How can I face her?"

Heinmyets's hands tightened on hers. "Do not blame yourself, especially for Ciren's sake! We also would have followed him to Larij and Medvare in spite of his protests, save that the Council of Keldara refused permission, fearing to take action against Zauril."

"So what happens when Zauril goes to the Council and demands my return?" She could barely form the words as she looked up into Heinmyets's eyes.

"I made a vow to Delian as a shield brother and bond

brother-to-be that I would protect you," Heinmyets said. "And we will talk details once we are safely in the village of Wickmasa, in Keldara. This is not a good place for that talk. I would be on my own ground, my own land when I risk invoking Zauril's minions by what needs to be said! For now, if you can move and be ready, we will pack and be on our way, once Delian is honored."

Alicira blinked back more tears. "I would sit with Delian, but that would leave the rest of you to do the packing."

"You are his sister and should sit vigil with Ciren. There will be time for you to do other things like packing! Come, I will take you to Ciren and Delian." He rose.

Alicira fumbled for her boots and pulled them on. Her jacket hung on a tripod by the bed. She stood and pulled it on, then wrapped her scarf around her head and neck, folding it in the form of *she who mourns*, wrapping it to cover her head as well as her neck.

"Come." Heinmyets took her hand with a delicate grace unexpected given his size. He led her out of the tent. She stood still for a moment once outside, blinking at the fading afternoon light that still seemed far too bright, wobbling slightly as fatigue and aches suddenly made themselves aware.

Used too much magic for my current condition, combined with not enough sleep.

The encampment was bigger than she recalled from the morning, with five tents, a small herd of horses and daranvelii grazing nearby, several small fires in front of the tents as well as a cook fire, and—

Delian's body lay on a pile of boughs and cordwood about one hundred paces from the nearest tent. A dark-haired woman sat on a stump next to him.

Ciren.

A soft rumbling nicker distracted her. Narasin gently nudged Alicira. She pulled away from Heinmyets and wrapped her arms around the daranval's neck. Soothing emotions came from Narasin as she brought her head around, enfolding Alicira between head and neck. They stood like that for a few moments. Then Heinmyets put his hand on her shoulder.

"It is good to see the bond between you and your daranval," he said.

Alicira straightened up, sending grateful thoughts back to Narasin. "Thank you for the gift of her."

"She has gone long without a human partner," Heinmyets said.

"Thank you," Alicira repeated, stroking Narasin's neck. She drew a deep breath. "Now. Please introduce me to your sister."

Oh Delian, why didn't you say anything about her? I would have loved to know that you had found a mate.

The woman—*Ciren*—rose at their approach. She stood as tall as her brother, long dark hair plaited into a single braid with curly tendrils popping free around her face. Her face was lean compared to Heinmyets's rounder shape and her skin had a redder tint, not as bright as Inharise's redbark shade but in between the two.

More like Cenarth.

But her shoulders were nearly as broad as Heinmyets's, though her build was slimmer and lankier than his.

"Lady Alicira, the Lady Ciren. Ciren, the Lady Alicira," Heinmyets said.

Alicira bowed first, low and deep. "My regards to my brother's love," she said when she straightened. "It is my regret, I must say, that he did not speak of you. I wish we had. It would have given me much pleasure to have known that he loved and was loved before his death."

Ciren's bow was equal in depth to Alicira's. "Delian was very private about our relationship, for fear the Council might object. We had no time to consult with the Council before he left to save you." She looked down at her hands and then back up. "We agreed to keep our promise quiet until his return."

"I am so sorry. He should have stayed with you and not come for me," she said.

"And what honor would that have served? I would not have him regretting that you suffered while he chose happiness." Ciren took Alicira's hand. "I wish he had not been so adamant about my staying behind, else I would have come with him, no matter what the Council would say about my choice."

"My brother often kept his own council." Alicira sighed. "Once he had determined his path there was little moving him. But there were hints, and if I had been less wrapped in my own problems, I would have known enough to ask him directly if he had a love. Does my uncle also know about you and Delian?"

"Yes, we spoke earlier, while you were resting."

"Here." Heinmyets rolled a round of cordwood over to them. "A place for you to sit, Alicira."

"Thank you." She smiled at him, grateful for the small kindness.

Whatever her future with this man, this friend of her brother's, at least he appeared to be thoughtful. He patted her shoulder gently, then left them, striding toward the tents, picking up a bag outside of a tent next to the one she had been in and carrying it to a wagon she just now noticed.

Unaccountably, relief flowed over her at the sight of the wagon. They'd be traveling more slowly with it, but as part of a larger group. Numbers provided some protection, even against magical attack. Given what she had seen of the magic present between Heinmyets and Inharise, perhaps it would be enough to keep the Saubral Shadowwalkers and any shade sent by Zauril at bay.

And if the three of us can link our powers together—

Ciren perched on the stump. "Can you tell me more about what happened? Both Orlanden and Alame have been stingy with description, hoping to spare me the details of his death, I suspect. Will you tell me about how he rescued you, and how he died?" Tears shimmered at the corner of her brown eyes.

Alicira blinked and swallowed hard. "I will try."

"Just to know would help." Ciren brushed her eyes with the back of her hand. "Tell me what you can."

"Then I will do my best." Alicira settled on her stump.

Where to begin? At last slowly, haltingly, she described how Orlanden and Delian had discovered a hole in the spells that had confined her, with the help of secret sympathizers in Medvare. Before long the words came easily.

CHAPTER 7

THE SINGLE WAGON AND FOUR MULES BESIDES THEIR OWN WERE loaded by the time dusk settled over their camp. Once everything was packed, both Heinmyets and Alame joined Alicira and Ciren, both men bringing unlit torches that they planted firmly in the snow. Alicira had finished recounting the events of the trip to Ciren and they sat in silence. She expected the quiet to continue.

Instead, Heinmyets cleared his throat. "Ciren. Do you remember when Delian hid that squirrel in old Jeralte's bags?"

"Oh. Oh!" She laughed. "The fool had it coming, but it was funny. You see," she explained to Alicira and Alame, "Jeralte was a braggart about his fishing and hunting skills. He'd claim to have a full bag of the biggest fish ever or the most premium skin off of a beaver. But when he'd bring it out the fish was spoiled or the hide had shrunk! One day Delian snuck a dead squirrel into the furs Jeralte turned over to trade. Only it wasn't dead. I never was sure if he knew it wasn't dead!"

Alicira snickered. "Delian did love his pranks. When we were small one of our playmates liked to torment our younger sister by hiding worms in her gloves. Delian hid slugs in Parkon's socks. He never teased Melaraen again!"

That broke the tension. They continued telling stories about Delian and his pranks, Delian and his dislike of bullies, Delian's love of music, until the last rays of sunset faded. Silence fell amongst the four of them as the sun set, a faint green flash shining from the horizon before it was gone. Alicira choked back a sob.

Even the Goddess shows Delian honor.

Heinmyets rose. "It is time," he pronounced in a deep, rolling tone. Inharise, Orlanden, and the rest of the riders gathered by the fire. Inharise lit a torch, then Orlanden. They led the riders toward the small family group. She handed it to Heinmyets and stood on his right side. Heinmyets gestured for Alicira to stand on his left, then took Orlanden's torch before he turned to face Delian's body.

"We gather together, members of my troop, those nearest and beloved, to give honor to our friend, rider, and family member Delian," he said. He lit the first torch, the one he had carried over. "I light this torch as Delian's Leader. In the five years he rode with me, he served Keldara faithfully and with his whole heart. Let this light carry him safely to the Goddess's Heart!"

"Let this light carry him safely to the Goddess's Heart!" they echoed.

Tears filled Alicira's eyes as she repeated the words with the others. Of her dead, Delian was the only one to be honored. Zauril and his followers had burned her family without ceremony and with many curses.

Oh Goddess, may this serve as the honoring for my parents and grandfather, for Melaraen.

Heinmyets handed Alicira the torch. Her eyes met his and he nodded as if he had heard her wish to the Goddess. She took the torch firmly in both hands, bracing it against the ground.

"I give this to she who is closest to our honored one by blood to hold, she who has lost so many and stands here in honor of her entire family, not just her brother," he said.

Heinmyets handed the other torch to Ciren. She stepped forward and lit the other standing torch. "I light this as Delian's promised, in memory of his devotion and of his determination to do what was right no matter what others thought. Let this light carry him safely to the Goddess's Heart!" After she lit the torch she stood next to Inharise. They turned to face the others again.

"Those of us closest to Delian have spoken. Now it is time for others to speak," Heinmyets said.

One by one, as each member of Heinmyets's troop came forward to speak a few words about their lives with Delian as a rider with Heinmyets.

Tears blurred Alicira's eyes as she listened to them. Her brother had been liked and honored amongst Heinmyets's riders, more than he ever had been at home. Here he had been accepted, his lack of magic despite his Miteal birth unremarkable.

After all had spoken, Heinmyets began the funeral chant, calling upon the god Artel. Alame joined him, then Ciren brought up Dovré's part. Alicira joined Ciren, followed by Inharise with the goddess Terat's part, and they sang the funeral chant. After the last shout consigning Delian to walk amongst the stars, Heinmyets stepped forward, knife in hand. He handed it to Alicira.

"Now it is time to cut hair. I would be honored to have you cut my hair." He gestured to Orlanden. "Take her torch."

"How much?" she whispered.

"This braid," he said, twitching his right braid.

She took it firmly and cut it close to his scalp. He took braid and knife from her and threw the braid onto Delian's body. Then he went to Ciren and cut her single braid. Ciren handed him her torch, took knife and braid, and threw her braid onto Delian. As Ciren approached her, Alicira hastily tried to gather her short hair into a tail, at least. She had cut hair for her family against Zauril's orders, which now left little hair to honor Delian.

"Don't worry," Ciren murmured. She cut a small chunk next to Alicira's face. Alicira took the scattered strands and laid them on Delian, throat tightening as Alame and then Inharise cut hair for Delian.

Heinmyets returned Ciren's torch and indicated that Orlanden should return Alicira's. Then he and Inharise took the two torches that had been planted in the snow.

"Now we send our friend to his rest." Together, the four of them lit Delian's pyre.

Once the fires burned steadily, Ciren threw a handful of dust on the flames. Alicira drew back as tongues of flame licked toward her, surprised that no heat radiated from the blaze as it leapt to three times her height with the dust's addition, then faded, leaving only ash.

"What is that?" Alicira turned to Ciren.

"Dovré's cold fire," Ciren answered. "It is a magic of Clenda that the healers mastered to dispose of bodies quickly, after the last plague swept through."

"I have never seen this before. I would learn more of it."

"I will show you," Ciren promised. One of the riders brought her a bag. "Come. The first step is to gather what we can of his ash for further consecration in the hall of memory."

Alicira joined her, questions brimming along with sorrow. It did not take long to gather the ash, already cool to the touch. The Goddess's touch was clear as she handled the ash.

Once they had finished, they rejoined the others. The riders lit five more torches before putting out the campfire. Then they mounted, except for two riders who clambered onto the front of the wagon to drive the two mules pulling it. Alicira joined

Alame and Orlanden in the first rank following the wagon as the others fell into places around them, clearly falling into an established order with Heinmyets and the rider Mohanit bearing torches in the lead in front of the wagon and Inharise with the rider Yanara at the rear. One of the other riders handed Orlanden the remaining torch.

"Let us ride," Heinmyets said, urging his black daranval stallion on. Before long they were trotting along the road.

"How long until we reach Wickmasa?" Alicira asked the rider next to Alame.

"With the wagon, by midnight tomorrow. We could go faster without it and in daylight, but best to remain together and travel at night in Saubral country," she answered. "Though we will stop within Keldara by morning, it's still close enough to the border to be a worry."

Another night out, at least two more before she knew more about what awaited her in Keldara. Alicira settled in to ride, resigned to wait two more days.

At least she had a comfortable bed in a tent. Even that little change provided some relief.

AT DAYLIGHT they stopped in a high mountain clearing in the redbark pines. Snow lay in patches around the camp, in places deep enough to come up to Alicira's ankles. Heinmyets's troop fell into what clearly was a practiced routine for setting up camp quickly. Having the wagon along allowed for carrying some split cordwood and handsaw-cut rounds for cook fires, as well as larger tent-warming fires.

Two riders headed out to hunt. One group unloaded the wagon and the mules. Orlanden hauled wood and started the main fire while Alame helped tend the animals. Alicira joined Inharise and Ciren in setting up the tents, though her role was more that of fetch and carry as the two women directed since she was not familiar with this mode of tent pitching. Cenarth watched them from his carrier that now leaned against a tree, a cradleboard with a deerskin wrap that held him snug and hung from the horn of Inharise's saddle when she rode.

But soon the tents were set up and bedrolls laid out in each tent.

"Only three tents," Inharise said when they were finished, surveying how tightly packed each tent was, with six beds in each. "A close fit, but just to sleep for today. We could have done without, but I for one will rest better inside during this season. I've done enough sleeping out in the cold, and with a child tents are better."

"Agreed." Alicira groaned and dropped onto her bedroll, fatigue and sorrow catching up to her.

Ciren sat on the bedroll next to Alicira. "Are you going to be all right?"

"Ciren, she's pregnant. She's tired." Inharise extracted Cenarth from his cradleboard. She changed out the lining in his underpants for fresh, wiping him clean with extra down from the same bag that she used to refill his underwear. "Of course she's going to be all right. You remember how I was when carrying Cenarth!"

"I'm not as tired as I have been the other travel days. I didn't need to use magic during our travels last night," Alicira murmured. Gods, she wanted to crawl under the covers and go to sleep. But it would be best to eat first.

"We should be in Wickmasa tonight," Ciren said. "Heinmyets sent Yahnek ahead to let them know."

"If we are so close, why not push on?" Alicira asked.

"The wagon mules are played out after a night's drive, for one," Inharise said, putting Cenarth to her breast. "And it will be well into the middle of the night by the time we reach Wickmasa. If all of us were fresh, traveling that distance would be one thing. But with the three of you staggering in your steps—the road from here is difficult even in daylight. Better you be rested."

"And Saubral? What about that troop Zauril's supposed to be sending after me?"

"We *should* be able to detect them before they come upon us. Between your Narasin and Heinmyets's Elantai, we will know should a Shadowwalker draw near."

"That's practically on top of us," Alicira pointed out. "I don't know about Elantai's ability to notice Shadowwalkers, but they have to be pretty close for Narasin to sense them."

"True. But if the Shadowwalkers cross the border, Heinmyets should know," Inharise said.

"Know?" Alicira winced.

All these questions make me feel stupid. I'm certain that children not much older than Cenarth already know this!

"We do not have the strength to safeguard the border. Not yet, from what we can discover," Inharise said slowly, thoughtfully. "My magic is still slow to return after Cenarth's birth, but I can sense Clenda. Heinmyets will know if the Saubral cross the border in Keldara."

Alicira pushed herself upright. "You can feel your borders?"

Another lost gift that she had learned about in her studies. Her teachers had been convinced that it hadn't survived the passage from Daran. Gods, what other vanished skills did they have here?

"It is—" Inharise paused. "It is something new that has come to us." She looked up from gazing down at Cenarth. "When Delian left to rescue you."

"Then we're all right."

Inharise shook her head. "No. We do not know if the intruders are just a solitary wanderer, a family group, or Shadowwalkers with houndriders. Nor do we know where they cross into our lands. We just know they're there."

"So you just woke up with this ability?"

"More or less." Inharise frowned. She bit her lip, then continued. "I have an affinity with the goddess Terat, because I always caught fish and could sometimes call the rain. The day after Delian left us, I woke from a dream that felt like the ones that Terat sends. Then I found that I could not only picture the borders of Clenda, I could sense a layer of protection around them as well. Heinmyets reported a similar dream from Artel. A few days later, a small party of Saubral wandered over the borders of Keldara. Heinmyets sent messages by daranval to watch, and a few days later one of his patrols chased them out. But he couldn't pinpoint where they were."

"Border spells are difficult," Alicira mused. "Or so I've been told."

Inharise studied Alicira for a moment. "You know this magic?"

"Not the magic itself, no. I've never worked it. But I was taught about it. It used to be a Miteal gift."

"Interesting," Inharise said. "We will have much to talk about when we get to Wickmasa."

Won't we indeed.

Alicira lay back on her bedroll. Her magical training was seriously lacking when it came to magic wielded by magicians other than Aireii-born. What next?

Heinmyets joined them. "I have sent a message to Wickmasa using Elantai, and kept Yahnek here," he said. "Keep up our numbers just in case. We are within the normal range for any daranval to speak to daranval. The daranval belonging to Wickmasa's healer Siljaren is Elantai's sister, a year younger and strongly connected to her brother. Wickmasa has a young priest of Staul who is very strong in the ways of the Balancer. It will be best to have him ride out to meet us, should the Saubral come upon us quickly."

"By himself?" Alicira asked, sitting back up.

"No. He will bring others, to help us defend ourselves against both houndriders and Shadowwalkers. The border villages like Wickmasa are skilled in dealing with both."

Staul the Balancer. Alicira shuddered. At least that priest was dedicated to that part of the God with Two Faces, not Staul the Destroyer.

"But will he be able to hold against those who carry his god's other aspect?"

"Metkyi is very strong," Heinmyets said. "And his presence will require the Saubral to hold true to *all* of Staul's nature, not be influenced by Zauril's leaning toward the Destroyer, as well as their own preferences."

"I would prefer not to be noticed by any pledged to Staul," Alicira whispered.

Early in her captivity, she had wondered why Zauril had chosen to follow Nitel instead of Staul. Then she had decided it was because the Balance flowed even into those dedicated to the Destroyer, like the Saubral.

Or perhaps it is because Zauril does not want to be subject to the same God as the Saubral, with a token constraint of the Balance.

That thought had not occurred to her before. Unlike Staul, Nitel was not committed to a balance, not tied to any desire save her own search for dominance over her divine siblings. Staul might have the darker reputation, but after six months with Zauril, Alicira feared Nitel more than Staul.

Inharise took her hand in both of hers. Only then did Alicira realize how cold she was, in comparison to Inharise's warmth.

"Metkyi is truly of the Balance," she said, taking Alicira's other hand and holding both of them between hers, rubbing gently. "And now we should eat and rest. Even with Metkyi bringing aid, should the Saubral cross the border, we will need every bit of strength we can summon, magical and non-magical alike. Meantime, *you* should crawl under covers and get warm. I remember these times from carrying Cenarth. Best you not chill."

The firmness in Inharise's voice was enough to keep Alicira from objecting. She slipped into her bed and Inharise tossed an additional fur over her as well. She had almost fallen asleep when Alame and Heinmyets brought them bread, meat, and cold root vegetables. After sitting up in bed to eat, she curled back into her blankets as the others settled into their beds.

Tomorrow I will be in Wickmasa.

Even the worry about what that might bring was not enough to keep sleep from her. Though, by all the Seven Crowned Gods, she was more than ready to be done with this daily traveling.

And yet, it is better than even the best day in Zauril's captivity.

All the same, she hoped her life would settle soon.

CHAPTER 8

ALICIRA DIDN'T KNOW WHAT WOKE HER FIRST, AN OVERWHELMING sense of *wrongness* from Narasin or Heinmyets's yell. She sat up, fumbling for bow and arrows and sword, heart pounding, the child within her kicking and thrashing.

"Wait." Inharise grabbed Alicira's wrists to stop her as she tumbled out of her bedroll, staggering toward the door.

"Can't you feel it? The Shadowwalkers are coming!" she screamed back, Heinmyets's bellows amplifying Narasin's *danger. Danger. Danger.*

"Stop it!" Alame yelled. "Alicira, control and channel your power!" He took both of Heinmyets's hands. "He doesn't have control of the magic, and your reaction makes it worse. You need to channel Narasin!"

Danger almost drove her to try to break through Inharise's restraint, run to Narasin to defend against the Shadowwalkers. But there was something else, a sense of waters flowing around Alicira as she met the other woman's eyes.

"You have to control Narasin," Inharise breathed. "She's projecting so strongly that it's overwhelming him. Elantai can't reach him. It's an effect of both yours and Narasin's magics.

133

Heinmyets wasn't like this when the Saubral came through the border before."

"How do I control her?" she asked.

Inharise's face wrinkled in puzzlement. "You've not been taught?"

"I've never had a daranval, not until I fled Medvara."

"Close your eyes. Reach for her, and tell her it's all right. You're here."

Alicira followed Inharise's directions, reaching out to Narasin.

It's all right. I'm here. I understand.

As she kept projecting soothing thoughts, they kept being interrupted by the roiling of her daughter's fear.

Both her horse and her child were feeding their worries into her, then. Alicira took a deep breath, reaching to her daughter's consciousness, thinking soothing thoughts. The child's panicked thrashing settled, though she still moved restlessly within. And Narasin—

The golden mare's nose poked through the tent flap.

"I'd better go to her." Alicira hurried to the mare.

She stroked Narasin's neck as the mare nuzzled her. Calmness slowly descended over them, though Narasin still projected a warning. Behind her, Heinmyets stopped shouting, Alame speaking to him softly.

Another horse shoved his head through the tent flap, shouldering Narasin aside—Elantai, Heinmyets's black daranval stallion. Heinmyets staggered over to his horse, murmuring to him. Alicira leaned her head on Narasin, trying to picture where the Shadowwalkers were, but the location and number of the Shadowwalkers was confusing and blurred.

Heinmyets drew a ragged breath. "No Metkyi yet? Then we must prepare. Alame, get the others to build up the fire and look for logs to help build a physical cordon around the camp. Inharise, Alicira—we must combine our magic, to see if we can create a magical barrier to supplement any walls we can build." He clucked to urge both Elantai and Narasin out of the tent. "I felt the intrusion so very strongly but I think you made my awareness happen," he said to Alicira. "I could feel a new magic in the flow of magic around me." He took her hand. Alicira sensed *his* magic, *his* strength, that came from the earth itself, more than just the land's power but a personification of earth and growing things. "Yes. I sense it now. It was you. You make me feel things more strongly. I feel fire when I touch your magic, and that's new."

"And I feel the land," she said. "But it's not just me. The child and Narasin both run through me. They fed on each other—"

"And either you or Narasin projected to Elantai."

Inharise took both of their hands, the sense of water flowing through them becoming stronger than before. Within herself, Alicira sensed the growth of a flame she had only briefly touched in the past. Her magic expanded, melding with that of Inharise and then Heinmyets, their three powers first circling, then joining to build something greater than themselves.

Her child stirred in dismay.

Be still, little one. Goddess, if you could—

Like this.

Inharise thought at her, showing Alicira a pattern etched in green flame. Alicira followed her design, tracing the lines to magically weave a protection of water and fire that settled around the child.

It was what I did to protect Cenarth, before my magic faded while carrying him.

Thank you.

Alicira extended her magical self and tucked the memory of that weave away. This was magic she should have known—but why would she? Her tutors had been male and both her mother and sister lacked magic. None of them had any idea of how a woman carrying magic should handle pregnancy.

Still, I should have known. Should have studied.

Inharise squeezed her hand and brought Alicira's thoughts back. With the child's emotions dampened, she found that she could braid the fiery flow of her magic with Inharise's water and Heinmyets's earth more smoothly. Her awareness shifted, and she visualized a spindle to spin their magics together. Alicira deftly mixed their skills to form a strong, tight spell thread that expanded and grew with little effort. Inharise caught the thread, and with Heinmyets's assistance wove the threads Alicira created into a protective configuration. Alicira spun pure magic while Inharise and Heinmyets wove until the pattern grew too large to contain within the tent.

Inharise took the pattern and cast it out. Alicira *felt* it expand to cover the entire camp.

She sank onto a bedroll, weak-legged after spinning so much magic. Inharise and Heinmyets joined her, Heinmyets on her right, Inharise on her left, all three of them panting with the exertion.

"I have never performed a working of such power," Inharise breathed. "With you in the mix, with your spinning, Alicira—"

"She is the piece we needed in our spinning and weaving," Heinmyets said.

"Will it be enough protection against the Shadowwalkers?" The dread warning from Narasin still tightened Alicira's gut.

"It will slow them," Heinmyets said grimly. He pushed himself back up and extended a hand to help Alicira to her feet.

"Come. Let us go back outside to eat. Stand our ground and set our defenses rather than be caught on the run."

She took his hand and let him pull her up. "Why not run instead of taking a stand?"

Her stomach rumbled loudly and for the first time in days she felt as if she could eat.

"This is a defensible site, especially if we have the time to construct protections. It's a safer risk than taking the chance that they would come upon us while traveling. The road over the Wickmasa Pass is rough and difficult at night. I would not choose to be caught on it by a foe, if I can avoid that prospect."

Alicira nodded, not knowing what to say in response, and they went out. The campsite glowed golden under the protective barrier they had woven, the light shining through it brighter than the midafternoon sun.

Alame left the cordon that was starting to be built around the edge of the magical barrier. "You worked this?" he asked Alicira, frowning.

"All three of us worked it," she said.

Alame's eyes widened. "The three of you? Niece, that is uncommon. I haven't seen magic like this since—" He shook his head. "I don't think I've ever seen a working like this."

"She spun while we wove," Inharise said. "Our magics fit together, as if they were made to do so."

"It is well done." Alame eyed them. "And if the three of you can spin and weave the magic wool like you do pure magic," he gestured at the barrier, "then Clenda and Keldara will be stronger than Medvara at its height. Magic without the wool is always lesser."

"We will remedy that as quickly as we can," Heinmyets said. "But now, food. Magic is hungry work."

"Ciren has prepared a meal," Alame said.

They joined Ciren at the wagon. She had sliced biscuits in half and inserted slabs of the deer meat from their earlier meal.

Alicira gobbled down her biscuit, the fresh bread and meat settling in her stomach better than the waybread and dried meat pounded together with berries had. Ciren also handed her a small wooden mug of milk, bluish-white and faintly shimmering.

"Daranval milk," she said. "Paran's mare just weaned a foal, and—well, I have heard that it is good for a pregnant magician to drink this milk." Ciren grimaced. "It is strong-flavored."

"If you can tolerate the taste, it will help calm your child," Inharise added. "Drinking daranval milk allowed me to keep using my magic for at least a moon longer than the healers thought was possible."

If it will help....

Alicira sniffed at the mug, wrinkling her nose. But she gulped the milk as quickly as possible to avoid the sour flavor, grateful when Inharise refilled the cup with water. A tingling sensation radiated from her stomach and she felt steadier, more grounded.

"I think it may have helped," she said, surprised.

"Good." Heinmyets frowned in concentration as he studied the earth about them. He knelt, poking at the soil with his right forefinger. "We have more magic to work. I want to see just how close those Shadowwalkers are. I think there is a vein of earth's power here." He flattened his hand. "Yes. I can barely access it, but it's here. Alicira. Inharise. We can use this channel to discover how far away the Shadowwalkers are by working our magics together again. If you could lend me some strength?"

They knelt beside him. "How?" Alicira asked.

"Just put your hands on mine." His voice was distant as he stared at the ground. "I can almost see where the Shadowwalkers are, so if we can seize that vein, then we will know. The line of power is deep within the earth, almost too far for me to reach. I can nearly grab it, but then it wiggles and won't come clear. I just need a small bit more strength!" Frustration tinged his voice, a frustration Alicira recognized from her own wrestling with magic's limitations.

Alicira put her hand on top of Heinmyets's, and Inharise on top of hers. Their joined hands seemed to sink into the earth. She sensed the magic Heinmyets was trying to seize, a silvery flowing heat thread that squirmed away until their stacked hands closed on it and pulled it to the surface.

An image shimmered into her mind, and she caught her breath at its clarity as details of the landscape came into focus. She had never worked farseeing magic that came this clear!

Then she shuddered as she saw the three Shadowwalkers, one of them Gegarth. They rode single file down a narrow trail which snaked along midslope on a steep river canyon wall with rock outcroppings and no trees. Houndriders swarmed around the Shadowwalkers as surefooted as if they were on flat ground, six upslope from the Shadowwalkers, four downslope. Ten regular Saubral riders followed the Shadowwalkers. A heavy presence loomed over the group, as if they carried a God's manifestation with them. She would have flinched away in dismay, but the combined presence of Heinmyets and Inharise calmed her.

Heinmyets mindspoke.

They're near Sintel's High Pass. Inharise, do you agree?

Yes. They can't be here until around dark—Myets, that was a powerful sensing! Farther away than before.

Heinmyets nodded.

> The three of us together changes things. Nonetheless, this range gives us time to prepare, better than I had hoped. Good. I am going to try to speak to Twana, if you can tolerate the drain on your strength for that long, Alicira.

> I can.

Inharise echoed her answer.

With a change so swift it made Alicira momentarily dizzy, their focus changed to a village in a small valley, with long-houses made of reed mats and smaller lodges of hide sewn together or woven cloth. A young woman packing folded clothing into hide panniers to be lifted onto a waiting mule's packsaddle startled, then appeared to look directly at them.

> Twana.

Her jaw dropped open as her eyes widened and she dropped the clothing she held. "Heinmyets? What is wrong, that you use the earth's channel with such urgency?"

> New power has come to us but with it has come great need. Three Shadowwalkers with ten houndriders and ten Saubral have crossed the Sintel into Keldara, to be here near nightfall, close to Metkyi's arrival. They seek the lady Alicira at the behest of Zauril. Cloaked power rides with them, quite possibly Staul the Destroyer.

At that, Twana shook herself. "W-what should I do?"

> Go to Imnari. Tell her to send at least ten more riders after Metkyi. You need to come with them. Bring Siljaren in case they have invoked the Destroyer. Tell them to ride fast and hard!

"I will." Twana walked away from them.

Heinmyets released the molten silvery ribbon along with their hands. The thread burrowed back deep into the earth, so far that Alicira could not sense it.

"Won't be riding *that* channel for a while," he muttered.

Alicira stared at her hand as she rocked back on her heels.

Earth magic. I worked earth magic with Heinmyets and Inharise.

Earth magic, the most powerful of all magics. She looked up to see her bewilderment mirrored on Inharise and Heinmyets's faces as they knelt next to her.

"I have never found as much power by myself as what we have woven together this morning," Inharise said.

"Nor I," Heinmyets added.

"Me neither." Alicira's voice trembled. "How?"

"The Gods are moving and changing the world around us," Heinmyets said. "That has to be it. Delian foresaw this possibility, and kept suggesting that we consider a threefold marriage." He shook his head. "He knew."

"But Delian had no magic," Alicira said. "I was the only one of my siblings born to magic."

He did not say anything about the threefold to me.

Then again, after enduring six months under Zauril, would she have listened?

Alame joined them. "Visionaries don't always need magical talent, niece. Delian was one such."

"He may not have been born to magic but he was a good observer," Heinmyets said. "He then put together the pieces together to project what might happen based on those observations. We talked often about your magic, Alicira." He glanced at Inharise. "And then Inharise and I talked, planning what we might discover if you were able to get free. But still—this."

"Will it be enough to stop Zauril if those Shadowwalkers invoke him?" Alicira asked, throat tight.

"It depends," Inharise said. "But it will be good to have

Twana and Siljaren as well as Metkyi here. If the Gods are with us, they'll reach us before the Shadowwalkers."

"And if not?" Alicira's fingers tightened into fists.

"If not," Heinmyets said slowly, "then we will do our best to delay and obscure Zauril's purposes until Twana and Siljaren as well as Metkyi are here." He glanced at the sky. "We must prepare so that we may hold here for a protracted battle. My suspicion is that we will not rid ourselves of these Saubral so very easily, especially if Zauril's purposes drive them. We will need to hold strong until further support comes from Wickmasa."

"Perimeter charms," Inharise said. "Scatter them through the woods to be triggered by the Saubral." She glanced at Alicira. "Do you know how to devise those?"

"I do not, but I am willing to learn."

"That will be good." Heinmyets frowned. "Alame. You and I need to assist in building barricades. A little magic to aid in reinforcing those structures won't hurt."

Narasin sent Alicira an image of riders coming as Elantai trumpeted an alert. Alicira tensed but Heinmyets smiled.

"Good news. Metkyi has arrived! More hands to prepare!" He strode toward Elantai, now staring toward the east. Inharise started to follow him, then hesitated as Alicira stood.

"Come. You need to meet Metkyi." Inharise took her hand, squeezing it gently before hurrying Alicira along to join Heinmyets.

A group of seven riders trotted down the trail, headed up by a neatly dressed young man whose attire would not have been out of place at the Medvaran court. The other riders with him were more roughly dressed.

"Metkyi." Heinmyets strode forward as the lead rider dismounted. "Your timing could not be any better. We have but a short time to prepare before the Shadowwalkers are upon us."

"We rode as quickly as we could. How many, do you think?"

"With the lady Alicira's help, we were able to spy their presence," Heinmyets said, turning to Alicira and bringing her forward. Metkyi bowed to her, not as deep a bow as she would expect from a courtier in Medvara but still within the bounds of respect. "They will arrive around nightfall. Three Shadowwalkers, ten houndriders, ten regular riders."

Metkyi frowned. "Those numbers are too close to what you have here for my comfort."

"Mine as well. But we mindspoke to Twana. She and Siljaren are leading another group from Wickmasa to lend further aid."

"Mindspoke to Twana?" Metkyi eyed Alicira, raising a brow questioningly. "You must be a powerful Aireii magician indeed."

"Not that much power," Alicira dissembled. "Just enough to join with Heinmyets and Inharise so that Heinmyets could work earth magic."

Metkyi's eyes widened.

"We tapped a ground flow," Heinmyets added, before Metkyi could speak. "The three of us together might well be able to spin the magic of Keldara, Metkyi."

"That would be power indeed," Metkyi said.

"And meanwhile, your help is much needed in setting up barricades," Heinmyets said.

"And we need to be making perimeter charms." Inharise nudged Alicira. "Let's see what we can find around camp."

Alicira followed Inharise into the stand of redbark pine. The snow here was less patchy than the clearing but it had melted away from the base of some of the larger pines. Inharise knelt by one of the larger pines. She traced a sigil on one of the large, scaly plates of the pine's bark. Then she pulled a blue scarf made of a shiny material out of the pouch fastened to her belt, along with a stone knife. Alicira went to her knees as well and tentatively held her hand over the scarf. No magic flowed from it.

"I have to use non-magicked materials for my charms," Inharise said, gently using the tip of the stone knife to pry the bark plate free from the tree. "Not just the knife I harvest the materials with, but anything that comes in contact with what I'll be using."

Alicira nodded, familiar with the technique. "I have done this with my own charms. Just different materials."

"Good." Inharise finished her cut. "Now if you would catch this plate—" Her voice trailed off as the plate came free in one whole piece. The whole peeling fell gently into Alicira's hand.

"Put it on the scarf?"

"Yes." Inharise rocked back on her heels, frowning. "This season is challenging—ah. There." She rose and gathered long-needled branch tips that had blown off in a recent storm, the needles still green. "Bark and needles. Now if I can find some cones—" She wandered in a spiraling circle around Alicira, stooping occasionally to pick up cones until her hands were full. Then she returned to drop the cones on the scarf. She frowned down at the pile, tapping her chin with a forefinger.

Alicira waited as Inharise contemplated. Bark, needles, and cones. She wondered if Inharise used direct magic or a carrier substance such as glimmer dust to enchant the charms.

It must be something I can either do or use.

She knew of perimeter charms, but the ones she had worked with were made with constructed materials and required a potion to pour over them as well as a chant to aid with quick drying. She didn't *think* Inharise would be carrying *that* potion, as volatile as it was. Those concoctions were best created in a workshop and used quickly.

But there were other charms that used glimmer dust instead.

"All right," Inharise said. She returned to the base of the tree she had taken the bark from. "Alicira. We both need to gather dust."

"Gather the dust?" Alicira knelt beside Inharise, watching carefully as Inharise scraped small pinches of dust and fine back particles right where the tree's bark met the earth. She sifted each pinch into her palm.

"Yes. Work around the tree in the same direction I am going until we have gone all the way around it." Inharise moved to her right, closer to Alicira. Alicira moved over.

"Are we breaking the particles down for fineness or are we cleaning the dust?" Alicira gathered her first pinch.

"Making it fine."

Alicira nodded. They worked silently until they had made their way all around the tree trunk. By this point she had a palmful of finely sifted dust and bark particles. Inharise looked over to inspect Alicira's collection, holding her hand next to Alicira's to compare the two.

"Alike. Good. Now, we stand and say a spell over the dust, then spread the dust over the bark, needles, and cones."

"No glimmer dust? I have some, of very good quality."

"I've not worked with it," Inharise said. "You don't think glimmer dust would conflict with my spell?"

Alicira shrugged. "I've never spelled ordinary dust. I wouldn't think it would be a problem. Let me get it. You should be able to tell from the feel of it, don't you think?"

"If glimmer dust will work with my spells it would be easier," Inharise said. "Less energy expended." She pulled out another scarf and dumped her dust on it.

Alicira tipped her hand to spill her dust to join Inharise's, then hurried back to their tent. As she passed through an opening in the cordon, Narasin met her, following close on her heels until Alicira went inside the tent. Narasin stuck her head through the flap and watched Alicira as she grabbed the pouch of glimmer dust out of her saddlebags. When Alicira came out, clucking at Narasin to back out of her way, she saw how Metkyi, Heinmyets, and Alame were using magic to move large tree trunks to form a barricade around their camp.

Hope they don't overdo.

At that thought, she paused, then went to Heinmyets, Narasin following closely behind her.

"Would some glimmer dust help with your magics?" she asked. "It might allow the three of you to conserve your strength for later."

Heinmyets shook his head. "Metkyi has prepared charms that we are using. They don't require a lot of extra magical or physical energy." He smiled at her. "But thank you. The perimeter charms going well?"

"We're enchanting them next."

"Good. We'll leave you an opening right there." He pointed to where two sticks pounded into the ground marked a space just wide enough for one person to pass through. "Don't linger. Those Shadowwalkers will be here soon. I'll feel better when you're both inside the barricade." He scowled. "Would you take Narasin with you? I'd prefer the two of you have a warning."

"I will."

His scowl changed to a weary smile. "Be careful. Please." He cupped her cheek in his right hand, his touch gentle but still prickling her skin with cloaked power. She found herself smiling back at him as he studied her. His face softened even more. "We make a good team, the three of us. I would not risk either Inharise or you."

Was that a quaver in his voice on those last words?

"We will keep ourselves safe," she promised him.

"Good." Before she could respond, he leaned over and kissed her forehead. "I will not be like Zauril," he whispered.

Heinmyets stroked her cheek once more, then turned away, hurrying to help two Wickmasa riders wrestling with a heavy log. She paused to watch as he murmured a few words, flicked his fingers, and the log lifted from the riders' arms, floating gently as they guided it to its place. Then she shook herself, and hurried out the entrance, Narasin so close behind her that she could feel the mare's breath on her neck.

Alicira held the pouch out to Inharise. "I stopped to offer some to Heinmyets, but he said they are using Metkyi's charms. I hope they don't tire themselves out!"

"I do as well. Metkyi's charms? He doesn't devise them often, but when he does, young as he is—he does well." Inharise eased open the pouch strings and fingered the dust, sifting a pinch through thumb and forefinger. "I don't think this will resist my spells. Perhaps if we use the plain dust first, then this on top of that spell—you have a spell to use the dust for a perimeter charm, right?"

"Yes, and that combination sounds like a good idea." Stacking spells was better than blending them, especially when spellcasters lacked the time to check the compatibility of their magics.

Inharise brushed off her fingertips and snugged the pouch strings tight, handing it back to Alicira. "Then let us do it."

Alicira tied the glimmer pouch to her belt to get it out of the way of the first spell. "Where do we start?"

"We say a chant four times." Inharise knelt and gathered up the scarf with the dust on it. "You take some dust in your hands, I take some in mine. Then we say *Innocent dreams, innocent dust. Innocent dreams, innocent dust. Hide and protect, guard and beguile. Innocent dreams, innocent dust. Innocent dreams, innocent dust.*"

Alicira repeated the spell. Then she nodded, and Inharise poured half the dust into her cupped hands. She waited until Inharise held the rest of the dust. Then, together, eyes locked, they repeated the spell four times.

Innocent dreams, innocent dust. Innocent dreams, innocent dust. Hide and protect, guard and beguile. Innocent dreams, innocent dust. Innocent dreams, innocent dust.

With each repetition Alicira felt sorcerous power that was not her own but Inharise's slither through the dust, as if a small worm or snake had come to life in it. The spell roiled and stirred the dust in her hands as they finished the fourth repetition. Inharise knelt next to the gathered bark, branch tips, and cones, and sifted the churning dust over all of it. Alicira copied her movements, down to the final dusting off of hands. When they had finished, the needle tips quivered as if they were still on the tree in a light breeze.

"It's a good working," Inharise said. "And now the glimmer dust?"

Alicira retrieved the pouch from her belt. "Hold out your hand." She placed a pinch of the dust in Inharise's palm. "We sprinkle the dust first. Then we chant *Watch and defend, protect and shield.* Three times."

They scattered the dust and chanted. The pile flashed bright blue, then faded. Alicira delicately held her hand over it, careful not to touch the cones on the top, to measure the magic radiating off of it.

"Powerful magic," she said. "How do we set these charms?"

"Scatter as we walk around the cordon." Inharise began to separate the cones into two piles on the scarf that had held the dust.

"No activating words?"

Inharise shook her head as she sorted branch tips. "Not with mine. Does your spell require more?"

"It would be best to say *Watch* as you scatter your charms."

Inharise broke the bark plate into smaller chips. "Then I will do that." When she had finished with the bark she moved one pile onto the now-empty scarf and picked it up.

Narasin nudged Alicira, projecting worried feelings.

"Inharise! Alicira! How much longer?" Heinmyets called from the opening in the cordon. "They come closer. Alicira, do you not feel anything from Narasin?"

"I—" Alicira hesitated, then realized that a low-level feeling of danger had been pushing at the back of her thoughts that she hadn't noticed until Narasin nuzzled her. "I think I've been so focused on the charms that I didn't feel it."

"They are near. Hurry!"

"Here." Inharise took Alicira's bag. "Get up on your horse. You'll be able to work more quickly."

"What about you?"

"I'm not the one they're after!"

Alicira eyed Narasin's bare back, then leapt so that she lay across Narasin's back. The golden mare stood still as Alicira swung her right leg over and sat up. She reached for the bag Inharise handed up to her.

"Together or separately?" she asked Inharise.

"You go right, I'll go left. When you finish, go on inside!"

"No. I'll wait for you."

"You're the one they want," Inharise repeated.

"And they won't grab you? Besides, you'll need to know where I leave off!"

"True," Inharise conceded. She turned and began to walk around the cordon to their left, scattering bark and cones and needles every few strides. Alicira shifted her weight and Narasin turned right. She scattered pieces carefully around the perimeter, murmuring *Watch* as she worked. At last her scarf was empty, and she shook out the last of the dust, waiting for Inharise. She spun Narasin to face out from the cordon, watching and wishing she had her bow at least with her.

Inharise came around the corner, face fixed in focus on the charm. She shook out her scarf near where Alicira had.

"Done."

Narasin snorted, then pinned her ears, an all-too-familiar sense of dread pouring through Alicira.

"They're here," Alicira said. Reflexively her fingers tightened on Narasin's silver mane.

Zauril would not find her so easy a target this time.

CHAPTER 9

"ALICIRA! INHARISE!" HEINMYETS CALLED. "GET IN HERE! THE Shadowwalkers have arrived!"

"We know!" Alicira shouted back. "Can you get up behind me?" she asked Inharise.

Inharise nodded. Alicira slid forward as far as she dared. Inharise grabbed Narasin's mane, then with a swift running leap landed astride Narasin as the mare startled forward. Inharise lightly balanced herself against Alicira's back. They rounded the corner near the entrance. Narasin skidded to a high-headed stop as houndriders burst out of the trees, baying at them. Alicira grabbed mane as hard as she could as Narasin half-reared, beginning to turn midair to run away. Inharise somehow maintained her balance.

No. The opening.

Alicira thought hard at Narasin as she used leg pressure to turn the mare back to face the houndriders. She kept one hand tangled in the mane as she untied the bag of glimmer dust from her belt and shoved it into Inharise's hand.

"Throw a handful of dust at them if they get too close!" she yelled.

"And then what?"

"I'll think of something!" Gods, too bad she didn't know a shapechanging spell. Not that it would work on houndriders or Shadowwalkers, but perhaps the hounds might be affected by it.

Narasin thundered ahead, ears pinned flat against her head as she raced for the opening. The houndriders charged toward them.

"How close is too close?"

"Get a handful out now!" Alicira answered. "When I say now—"

One of the perimeter charms exploded as the lead houndrider crossed it. The other houndriders flinched back, hesitating just long enough for Narasin to gallop past them, heading for the opening. The houndriders bolted toward them but not fast enough to cut Narasin off.

She felt Inharise turn to look behind them. "Getting closer!"

What charm? BLIND.

It wouldn't last very long, just long enough for them to get to safety.

"NOW!"

As Inharise threw the glimmer dust, Alicira whispered the blinding charm. The baying of the hounds changed to whimpers. Narasin extended her stride. They reached the opening and darted through, now safely within the protective spell they had cast earlier. Metkyi and Alame braced logs against the opening.

"CLOSE!" Heinmyets bellowed, and the logs shifted to form a tight barricade. He frowned at Alicira and Inharise. "That was too close. It's a good thing Narasin was with you."

Alicira nodded as Inharise slid off of Narasin. She leaned forward and patted Narasin's neck, taking a moment to wrap her arms around the mare to hide the sudden fit of trembling overtaking her. The Shadowwalkers had come down upon them *so quickly.*

Heinmyets rested his hand on her thigh. "Are you all right?"

She drew a deep breath and sat up as the tremors eased. "Just —they came so fast. I didn't quite expect that."

Until this flight, she'd never needed to think about the speed of houndriders.

You were never a fugitive until now.

"The hounds are quicker than you realize," Heinmyets said grimly. "I've seen it too many times."

A Shadowwalker screeched just outside of the opening. Alicira shivered again as an arrow smacked against the protective spell. It remained in place, gray spreading across the gold until a circle the width of two hands formed. She pressed her lips together resolutely.

"We'd better get ready to fight." She slid off of Narasin. "What should we do now?"

Heinmyets eyed the gray circle as more arrows peppered the spell's reach, dotting the gold with gray.

"I don't think the shield will last for much longer," he said. "We need to speak to them."

"Well, I guess I had best be the one to start the parley." She straightened her shoulders. "After all, I'm the one they want."

"Not alone," Heinmyets said.

"We are with you," Inharise said.

"All of us," Alame added. He waved Metkyi forward.

Heinmyets took her left hand and Inharise her right. Alame and Metkyi joined them, Alame and Inharise joining hands while Metkyi and Heinmyets did the same. Power jolted through Alicira's hands and she felt the flow of the four other magicians. She closed her eyes and pictured a weaving of their very different abilities. It braided in and around them, linking their magics together. Then she opened her eyes.

"Let's parley."

Hand-in-hand they marched toward the opening. Orlanden and the other riders took up positions flanking them. Two riders darted forward to slide the logs away from the opening after Heinmyets growled "Open."

"I'm not going out there unless we have to," Alicira said. "But I want to stand in the center of the opening."

No one answered her but they followed her lead as she slowly processed to the opening. Alicira coughed and swallowed hard, squeezing Inharise and Heinmyets's hands.

"Shadowwalkers!" she called, projecting as boldly as she was capable of doing. "I am Alicira ea Miteal. What do you want with us?"

Gegarth rode up to the opening. "I want *you*, runaway and betrayer of your bonded one. Zauril wants you back."

Was it her imagination or was that a gray shadow hovering behind him?

"The bond never happened," she retorted. "Zauril retained me against my will and tried to force a bond. I will never return to his not-so-tender mercies."

Gegarth raised his hand. The gray shadow expanded. "Your wishes are immaterial," he rumbled.

"Stop." Metkyi pushed past her, his link to their magic fading slightly as he released Heinmyets's hand. As he strode out the opening toward the Shadowwalker his shape seemed to shimmer, then transform from the neatly attired young man to a disheveled wild man. "You will not use that form of Staul to serve Zauril's ends!"

Gegarth growled at Metkyi and Metkyi snarled back, looming larger than he had before, rumbling deep in his chest. Then the Shadowwalker drew a sword and charged toward Metkyi, the gray shadow clinging to his back.

He needs our help physically as well as magically. I'm not letting him get cut down by himself!

Alicira burst through the opening, Heinmyets, Alame, and

Inharise keeping pace with her.

Metkyi raised his hands and began to chant in deep, sonorous tones. The sense of *presence* suddenly became stronger, threatening to overwhelm their magical bonds so that Alicira hesitated, concentrating on managing the flow of Metkyi's magic into their links. Metkyi's form appeared to change yet again, back to the neatly dressed man—but this man was taller, skin dark as a moonless night, a scepter in his right hand.

Staul the Balancer.

Even though she never had encountered this aspect of the God, Alicira recognized his presence as it blasted into their connections. She closed her eyes to focus on tightening her shielding so that Staul's presence would not overwhelm their links. When she opened her eyes again, Gegarth's horse had stopped two horse lengths from Metkyi-as-Staul. Gegarth lowered his sword as Metkyi-as-Staul strode toward him, forefinger pointed accusingly at the gray shadow that clung to the Shadowwalker. He stopped a horse's length's away from Gegarth.

That shadow is why they call them Shadowwalkers.

She had never seen it on a Shadowwalker before, but now she understood. The shadow of Staul the Destroyer rode them in various forms. So what would it do when faced by Staul the Balancer? And was that gray shadow as strong as the Balancer, divided as it was amongst the Shadowwalkers?

I need to learn more about the Shadowwalkers.

"Leave him," the God commanded.

The shadow slipped away from Gegarth who stared, defiant, at his God. The shadow drifted into Staul's shape and Alicira felt the change within the God, the Balancer swaying toward the Destroyer. Gods, she hoped Metkyi was strong enough to manage both aspects of his God at once!

Gegarth struck his chest with the clenched fist that held his stallion's reins, the gesture as much defiance as it was reaffirming his loyalty.

"My Lord, you made an agreement with Zauril!"

"*Did* I?" A mocking tone slipped into Metkyi-as-Staul's voice. "I do not remember Zauril as being pledged as one of My Own whose wishes I particularly need to respect. Or has he changed his affiliation to me from my sister Nitel?"

"He—has not changed his allegiance," Gegarth said reluctantly. "But he did enter binding oaths with you, my Lord!"

Metkyi-as-Staul cocked his head to one side. "With my divided aspect as the Destroyer, to one of my shadows and not my full Destroyer. Neither you nor Zauril have sworn oaths to *me*, to both my selves. Not like this one I wear has."

"The oaths were still sworn."

"True," Metkyi-as-Staul conceded. "But tell me. Why does one of the Saubral serve the needs of Zauril of Medvara? Has your Hidden One decided to take allies after all?"

"The Hidden One does not speak for all of us!" The other two Shadowwalkers rode up beside Gegarth. "She is old and seeks peace rather than battle."

"*Really.*" The mocking note in Metkyi-as-Staul's voice deepened. "In my conversations with your Hidden One I have perceived nothing to make me think her powers have diminished with age. If anything, her cunning has grown." His tone changed again, now menacing. "So have you given your sword to Nitel?"

"No." The smaller of the other two Shadowwalkers spoke, her voice strong and clear. "But the Hidden One's interests lie far to the south, rightfully so given the conflicts there, and—compromises must be made for those of us who hold territory in the North."

"Ah, my sweetest and most devout." Metkyi-as-Staul turned a death's head grin on this Shadowwalker. "So what pledges have you and your kin sworn to this Zauril?"

"My Lord." This Shadowwalker dismounted, dropping her horse's reins to the ground. She marched up to Metkyi-as-Staul and knelt before him, keeping her eyes lowered and submissive as she struck her chest, every move equally as respectful as Gegarth's had been defiant. "I will show you the vows that were made to Zauril if you choose to read me."

"You betray us!" Gegarth bellowed. "You will show everything not just to the God but the one he rides!"

"The one I ride is also vowed to Me," Metkyi-as-Staul said. "You do not trust that vow?"

"You I trust, my Lord. But the one you ride is linked to *her* and these others." The Shadowwalker gestured toward Alicira. "That linkage I do not trust."

"Then I will cut that linkage."

"No." Alicira released Inharise and Heinmyets's hands, stepping forward. "I made the linkage. I do not consent to its breaking."

I need its protection.

Would Metkyi betray her?

"Ah. The lady in question speaks." Metkyi-as-Staul turned his focus on Alicira, Staul's looming *presence* dominating Metkyi and overwhelming her. "And what does this fugitive oathbreaker have to say for herself? Why should I not break your spell? What need would you have for it now?"

Dovré protect me! Alicira prayed as she faced the full strength of the God in front of her.

Staul carried by a shapeshifter was more magical power than she had ever faced before, even when Zauril had carried Nitel. Zauril's linkage with Nitel was imperfect and nowhere near as schooled as Metkyi's connection with Staul. It was one reason why Zauril's attempts to use Nitel to control Alicira had not gone well. Hopefully *her* Goddess would rouse from whatever restriction had been placed upon her to help, with Staul here in this much strength.

Warmth flooded through her.

I am here.

Dovré possessed Alicira more strongly than ever, even as the child stirred restlessly within her.

Be still.

The Goddess commanded the child. The child calmed, but the Goddess moved Alicira's body without her control, was an *other* looking through her eyes, pushing Alicira aside and isolating her as an observer of events.

So this is what it is like to have the Goddess ride me.

"I am here to protect my servant," Dovré spoke through Alicira. The sensation of her mouth speaking words she had not determined felt even more disorienting than her body being moved by another's volition. "Among other reasons, my beloved and brother, she is dear to me."

"We all have servants dear to us." Metkyi-as-Staul tapped his chest. "This one is particularly dear."

"Not all servants are as significant as this one and the one you ride," Dovré responded. "Breaking the spell my devoted one wove changes many things. It would injure the one you ride and impact the role he is to play."

"True." Metkyi-as-Staul scowled. "There is the question of that damnable Zauril and the questionable oaths he has elicited from my own servants. Much as I doubt their value, nonetheless I must consider their arguments."

"Allowing these partial servants of yours to carry out Zauril's wishes would advance the End of Days."

"No more than what may come from the child your vessel carries."

Alicira flinched deep inside at that statement by Staul.

The Goddess reassured her.

> Do not fear. Many choices lie between her and that possibility.

"But forcing her to go back to Zauril with them will advance that particular prospect and make that future more likely," Dovré countered. "Would you further Nitel's ambitions?"

Metkyi-as-Staul snorted. "And what of Karnoi and Cirdel's servant in Waykemin? What changes will she bring should she fulfill her goal in weakening or eliminating Nitel from Waykemin?"

"That is between the Twins and Nitel. Nonetheless, beloved, *do not break those links.*" Urgency tinged Dovré's statement. "Not if you value all we have sought."

"Then let your vessel speak for herself." Metkyi-as-Staul's lips tightened. "Let her defend why she should not be returned to Zauril, and I will not challenge my own or betray their vows, partial to one side of me though they may be."

"As long as you do not touch her magic!"

"I will honor that request. But she must speak on her own, without your presence in her."

"Hardly fair."

"We are speaking of vows My servants have made. I must be fair to them as well. You may choose to ride another to be physically present if you feel the need."

"I do feel the need, but there are none vowed to me here who carry my magic," Dovré said.

"Good Gods, beloved! You doubt my intent? Ride your non-magical follower and stand watch. You can jump to your favorite should you see the need."

"Without magic my follower will be overwhelmed."

"I am her uncle," Alame said. "Vowed though I am to Artel, I will carry you, noble lady."

Dovré turned Alicira to face Alame. "Your intent is good,

cherished of Artel, but your own linkages are questionable, especially the one to Waykemin."

"I will do it," Heinmyets said steadily. "I offer no bonds other than to my lady Inharise and the ties I seek with the lady Alicira. While I am also vowed to Artel, I also speak for those who lead Keldara. My ties are to this land. My ambitions are to this land alone. I want what is best for it, but I do not seek to rule an Empire. Will that be acceptable?"

Wonder swept through the Goddess and flowed into Alicira as their combined selves stared at Heinmyets. He met their gaze without flinching, Alicira gliding along with Dovré as she looked deep into his soul. Love of Keldara, desire to lead his people to be safe and secure should the Council of Keldara choose him as worthy (not that he questioned the likelihood of that happening), and commitment to the sister of one who had been like a brother to him as well as Inharise and Cenarth resonated throughout his being.

An honest and dedicated man.

Dovré concluded.

He will do well by you. More important, he will not take harm from me, vowed though he is to Artel. You accept this?

Yes.

"I accept your offer, Heinmyets of Keldara," Dovré said out loud.

Heinmyets released Inharise's hand and stepped forward. Warmth and power flowed out of Alicira until she was only herself, with no Goddess in her. Heinmyets did not change form but a shadowy shape bearing the silver-tinged black curls of the

Goddess hung over him, and Dovré's presence emanated from him.

"So. My lady Alicira. Oathbreaker and fugitive, what have you to say to me?" Metkyi-as-Staul asked.

Alicira turned to face him. "I swore no oaths to Zauril, much as he would claim otherwise."

"But you were part of a bonding ceremony."

"I was forced to participate. I did not speak the binding words. I spat out the drink."

"Words were spoken," Metkyi-as-Staul said.

"Under compulsion. I was bound and drugged." She met the God's eyes. "Do you doubt my resistance? *I* will not struggle should you choose to look at that memory."

"That would not be wise for him to do so," Dovré said through Heinmyets. "Not with the child you carry."

"The child. That is another concern entirely separate from your fate. I wonder what Zauril truly desires, you, your child, or both of you," the God mused.

"You know what he wants. He made no secret of his ambitions when bragging to me," Alicira snapped. "I am sure you, even your partial self, are well aware of what he aspires to."

"Aspiration and oaths are not necessarily the same thing." Metkyi-as-Staul looked down at the Shadowwalker kneeling before him. "Oh dearest of mine, one who worships but a shade of me. I will not look but I will ask. What does Zauril wish? The lady or the child?"

"Do not answer—" Gegarth began to order her.

Metkyi-as-Staul impatiently waved him to silence. "I am your God and you try my patience. Should I strike you down for your impertinence? It is very tempting right now, despite the blood and souls you have fed to me."

"My lord!" Gegarth tightened his hand on the red stallion's reins.

"I have to question your allegiance if you value your vows to Zauril over your vows to me."

"My lord, I am sorry." Gegarth looked down at his kneeling compatriot. "But we risk incursions by Zauril into our territory if we do not bring the lady back. I must think of my own. Perhaps my oaths to him were unwise—but they were made with the intent of protecting my people."

"Yes, oaths were made," Metkyi-as-Staul said irritably. "Oaths being thrown around with little to no consideration for their impact—or with trust in my favor."

"My lord. We are your hounds, and but mildly favored in your sight. We accept this, but all the same—I must protect my own. Zauril holds power. He threatens my clan, and the Hidden One's favors and interest are, as my sister says, elsewhere for good reason at this time."

"I understand. But I still would hear the answer to my question about Zauril's intent as disclosed to you." Metkyi-as-Staul glared at the Shadowwalker. "I will speak with my sister Nitel, and impress upon her to restrain her servant's impulses with regard to those I hold as mine. Is that enough for you to let her speak?"

"Thank you, my lord. I will object no more. Sesenth, you may answer."

The kneeling Shadowwalker—*Sesenth,* Alicira thought, studying this Shadowwalker closely so that she might recognize her in the future—swallowed hard.

"Thank you. My lord, while he of whom we speak would desire to have the lady, the child is the one he most wants."

"He cannot have her!" Alicira snapped. "She is mine!"

"Would you yield your freedom to him to keep her as yours?" Metkyi-as-Staul looked away from Sesenth.

"No."

Metkyi-as-Staul raised his brows. "You cannot have both your freedom and your child, my lady. Not without a price."

"And that would be?" She raised her chin defiantly despite the dread gripping at her.

"He is the child's father. He does possess rights with regard to her future."

"He raped me," Alicira said flatly. "He forced me. He bound my magic with Nitel's aid and kept me helpless until he was certain I was pregnant. I call for judgment upon him for those actions, and renunciation of his rights to control and influence his child's future because of the means by which he conceived her."

"You would feel this way even if the child turned out to bear his magic instead of yours?"

Alicira tightened her hands into fists and forced herself to release them, counting to calm herself so she would not explode recklessly at this God. Not here. Not now. Not when answering a God.

"You understand he intends to rule the world at the very least, if not fight and claw his way into Godhood using this child as his tool. I will resist that outcome until my last breath, even if my unborn daughter bears Zauril's magic instead of mine."

The God did not answer immediately but studied her thoughtfully, scratching Metkyi's chin while staring deep into her eyes. Alicira did not look away, even though she felt him pushing against her, testing her strength and resolution.

"How do you feel about games of chance?" he said finally.

"My Lord?" Confusion flooded through her. What did he mean?

"The people you would adopt as your own often use various games of chance for purposes other than entertainment and gambling. Is that not right, Heinmyets, Leader-to-Be?" He raised a hand. "I know the answer from my vessel here, but I would hear it from Heinmyets himself, Lady Dovré."

"Yes," Heinmyets choked out, his voice strained and tight

instead of its usual deep rumble. "But it is intended as guidance and not final determination. We understand that often the Gods gamble on our fate. My Lord Staul! You would not—"

Metkyi-as-Staul waved a few fingers and Heinmyets fell silent, though his brown eyes burned with his anger, not the Goddess's.

"My lady Alicira," Metkyi-as-Staul said slowly, carefully. "I propose that you and I throw chips to determine your future and that of your child. Do you accept?"

"My Lord Staul." Inharise spoke before Alicira could, determination set hard in her tightly held face. "It is not as simple as that, nor does the fall of the chips become the absolute determination of the questioner's fate. What the chips say is nuanced and advisory, and there is a ritual and process to make the message of the chips valid."

"Valid point, but I would hear my lady Alicira's answer first."

"Do I have a choice?"

Metkyi-as-Staul shook his head. "You want to challenge his rights to your child."

"I want to challenge his rights and I want him punished for what he has done to me and my family!"

"Alas, I cannot grant you the favor of vengeance. But I *can* offer you a means by which to challenge his claims to your daughter. Do you accept?"

The world swung around her. She dared not look away from Metkyi-as-Staul, dared not look at her uncle or Inharise or Heinmyets. Something in the expression of the God riding Metkyi suggested that this more than anything else might grant her the refuge she sought here.

"Will he leave me unharassed if I do this?"

Metkyi-as-Staul inclined his head. "If that is one of the questions you win."

She gestured toward the Shadowwalkers. "Will *they* be bound by this?"

"I will make them swear to this or they will experience my displeasure."

"Then my answer is yes. I will throw the chips to determine the future of my daughter and myself."

She could swear that the relief at her statement that swept across Metkyi's face was all of the God and not Metkyi himself.

Inharise cleared her throat. "The lady Alicira will need an advocate to observe and interpret each throw. Since she is of Dovré, we need one dedicated to her Goddess to be here as her advocate, especially given the stakes."

"My lady of Terat, and Leader-to-Be of Clenda." Metkyi-as-Staul inclined his head in respect. "I believe there lies a difficulty. If her Goddess had one with magic dedicated to her service present, she would be riding that person now."

"If you have the access to Metkyi's knowledge that you claim, you would be aware that one such is on her way." Inharise's voice remained level but Alicira could hear the anger within it. "I seek bonding with Alicira along with Heinmyets, and speak for him as well as myself in her behalf. If this is to be done, she should have full knowledge of what it is we will do, with an advocate present to oversee her interests."

"You would not be that advocate?"

"I am doing so now but she needs her own Goddess's Voice present. That is how it is done here, among my people as well as Heinmyets's."

Metkyi-as-Staul cocked a brow and looked at Gegarth. "I have spoken for you and now need to hear your consent. You would accept such results in Zauril's name?"

"Alas, that is one problem," Inharise inserted. "In some form or another Zauril would need to be present as well."

"Oh, that can be arranged," Metkyi-as-Staul said airily. "Those who have sworn oaths to Zauril would not face difficulty carrying him. Right?" He eyed Gegarth, a half-smile twitching the right corner of his lips as horror flitted across the Shadowwalker's face, to be quickly banished.

"If it must be done," Gegarth said slowly, his face ashen gray. "But I will need to prepare."

"There we are," Metkyi-as-Staul said. "You will ready yourself to carry him who appears to be your true master instead of myself—"

"My Lord!" Gegarth protested. Metkyi-as-Staul glared at him and Gegarth paled further.

"Do not interrupt. We will have that discussion later, when I am not riding this servant. You will agree with my verdict or accept my wrath?"

"I will," Gegarth said, forcing the two words out.

"Meanwhile, we will wait for the arrival of this coming Voice of Dovré, and this vessel I ride will rest and recover while *you* —" he fixed Inharise with a stern glare. "—will inform the oath-breaker and fugitive Alicira of what it is we intend to do. We will also need a Voice of Artel to judge."

"As you well know, we have a speaker for Artel riding with the Voice of Dovré," Inharise said. "Or Heinmyets himself could speak."

"It is good that another is coming. Heinmyets seeks a bond with Alicira, so he cannot be Artel's Judge. The other option would be Alame the Exile, and his ties to Terani of Waykemin as well as his blood connection to Alicira compromise him." He raised a hand as Alame opened his mouth. "No need to argue about it, Exile. It is my judgment."

"As you say, my lord," Alame growled. "But those ties to Terani are not what you would think."

"Nor are they what you think, either. That is immaterial. Are we all in agreement that once these speakers for Dovré and Artel have arrived, we will cast the chips to determine what is to be done with the lady Alicira and her unborn child?"

Alicira bit her lip to keep from further protests. *It can't be just that random!* she wanted to cry out.

Inharise glanced at her.

Trust us, Alicira. We will take care of you.

"Terms will be negotiated once all have arrived," Inharise said firmly. "The lady Alicira has her own rights as well. Meantime, she is under *my* protection, specifically, with all of the privileges I possess within Keldara and Clenda. My lord Heinmyets would say the same were he not carrying the Goddess."

"I would ask that all present swear not to take action during this waiting period," Alame said. "I say this as the lady Alicira's last surviving relative."

"Good." Metkyi-as-Staul nodded. "So. Sesenth and Gegarth, you are the named Shadowwalkers here. Do you vow not to act against Alicira and those with her while we wait, speaking for your riders and for the one with you who is not named?"

The Shadowwalker Sesenth rose. "I so vow for myself and my houndriders." She glanced at Gegarth. "*I* am true to the Hidden One, as is my companion." She gestured to the other Shadowwalker who sat quietly on its horse, the hood of its cloak still up and covering its features. "I will not speak for Gegarth. Not when he walks so closely with Zauril and away from the Hidden One's paths."

Metkyi-as-Staul turned to Gegarth. "Do you swear?"

"I so vow!" he spat out, jerking his stallion around. "But only for the time of this meeting and whatever comes of it!" He kicked the red stallion into a trot. The human riders and two houndriders followed.

Sesenth bowed to Metkyi-as-Staul. "We will watch to ensure he does not overstep his vows." Then she turned and strode to her horse, mounting and turning it with much more grace and ease than Gegarth had done. The other Shadowwalker and the remaining houndriders followed her.

Metkyi-as-Staul bowed to Alicira. "Then farewell until our meeting, our lady of Miteal. Prepare yourself well." He glanced at Inharise. "Listen to your advisors, including the lady Inharise. Keep in mind that I have a role I am bound to execute despite what my deepest wishes may be. May fortune ride with you." He nodded to Heinmyets. "Good sir, I thank you for your service, even though you are not bound to my lady Dovré. Sister, shall we confer?"

"We shall." Her presence faded and Heinmyets staggered sideways even as Metkyi collapsed to the ground on hands and knees, shaking his head. Inharise hurried to Heinmyets and Alicira followed her as others went to Metkyi.

"I am well," Heinmyets assured them as Alicira and Inharise reached him, though he leaned on Inharise as she moved in close. "Metkyi?"

He stood, supported between Ciren and Orlanden with his arms around their shoulders.

"I will be well with some rest." He coughed, spat, and swallowed. "My lady Alicira. My lord Staul means well by you, but there are many complications. The more specific you can be with the items to be cast, with as many details as you dare create, the better it will be for you. Consider this to be as complex as a trade agreement and it will go well for you."

"I hear and thank you, my lord Metkyi."

He shook his head. "No lordship. I am but the Voice of Staul."

"You have done well."

"Many thanks. But if I am to bear my lord Staul soon, I must rest and eat. I recommend you do the same, while planning. Remember, as many details as you dare create!" He coughed again, leaning hard on Ciren and Orlanden as they guided him back within the cordon.

Heinmyets sighed and swayed hard against Inharise. Alicira slid in closer to help support him, marveling to herself that he had born the Goddess with such ease.

"Let us plan while we rest," he said, his voice hoarse. "Inharise, dearest, we will need all of your negotiating skills." He rested his arms on their shoulders, squeezing them tight. "The Goddess gave me some insight. If we do well here, what we create—" His voice trailed away.

Alicira exchanged glances with Inharise, now sensing how tightly he held himself. They followed Metkyi, Ciren, and Orlanden back inside the cordon, her insides roiling with worry.

My future lies in the throw of chips. Goddess, how did it come to this?

Now that the determination of her future was upon her, she almost wished she were still a fugitive.

CHAPTER 10

It was full nightfall and the moon had yet to rise by the time the second party from Wickmasa arrived. While waiting for them, Metkyi slept as deep as if he were dead and Heinmyets napped inside the tent. Alicira, Inharise, Ciren, Alame, and Orlanden sat around the fire and planned.

Twana holds the chips we will use, Inharise had explained.

She showed Alicira her pouch that carried chips like the eight that Alicira and Staul would alternately throw to determine each question they devised. One side of the chip was blank while the other bore a single deep score. The sum of the scored chips referred to differing verdicts, ranging from eight blanks to eight lines and any combination in between.

Twana as the Judge would determine the meaning of the chip's verdicts, referring not just to Artel (Alicira was uncertain whether Twana would be carrying Artel or consulting with him) but also to a book she carried which contained summaries of each verdict.

Then they had broken down the questions to be wagered,

arguing over the priorities until Alicira firmly insisted that custody of her daughter was crucial.

"Everything else will flow from that decision," she said.

"It needs to be nuanced," Inharise said. "If Zauril is to have a voice in her upbringing, then you need to specify at what age and to what degree."

"There's also the question of her inheritance of the magic of Medvara," Alicira sighed. "I cursed Zauril and kept the magic for myself until I released the last shard at Delian's death. But I still have the right to call upon it. That will not fade. He may wish to argue my right to keep that to myself, especially if he has any degree of control over the child and her magic."

"So," Orlanden said. "Your freedom is one question. The control of Medvara's magic is another. Your daughter's inheritance of it is a third, and her custody is a fourth."

"I don't know," Alicira groaned. "Everything on four questions."

"There may be further tosses for each question," Inharise added. "The chips do not always speak specifically and clearly. There may be a time factor."

"The child needs to be first," Alicira insisted. "Will he be able to add more questions?"

Inharise shook her head. "You issued the challenge to Zauril, so it is between you and Staul to toss. Zauril cannot challenge the result since it is you tossing with the God."

"I don't know. I've never heard of the Gods determining someone's fate in this way before now!" Alicira wanted to scream with frustration.

"It has happened before," Alame said. "But it is not common among our people, and no one has faced what you do for a very long time. My father could have challenged Etikar like this, but feared the consequences if the dice went against him."

So I dare to do what my grandfather wouldn't.

"Am I being a fool, uncle?"

"Say rather that Alexran was the fool, to flee when he should have challenged," Alame said heavily. "That said, from what I know of the chip toss, it is more complex than the dicing our people used in the Empire-over-Sea. The outcomes will be more nuanced and not as black and white."

"All right." She swallowed hard. "The first question will be, *to whom does my unborn daughter belong, myself or Zauril?*" She looked over at Orlanden. "Write that down."

Orlanden nodded. A lump tightened in her throat at the finality of the scratching of his pen on the paper. She had wanted the judgment of the Gods on Zauril. While this confrontation was not going to be everything she had wanted, perhaps if she phrased her questions properly, she could gain her vengeance.

"If the question does not give a direct determination, ask to throw for when she would go to him," Inharise said softly.

"Write that," Alicira commanded. She waited for Orlanden to finish. "Next. Medvara's magic. Who now controls the right to use it?" She paused, until Orlanden looked up. "Then the third question. If I control the right to use Medvara's magic, then when does my daughter inherit it? Does she gain it at my death or sooner?"

"And if sooner, at what age?" Alame suggested.

"Yes. Write that." It seemed forever before Orlanden stopped writing. Heinmyets came out of the tent and joined them, dropping to the ground between Alicira and Inharise.

"Now. My continued freedom. Or will the previous answers be sufficient?"

"You are spoken for, if not formally bonded yet," Heinmyets said, taking her hand. "That should be the first question. Should you be held to the terms of a forced and incomplete bond, or is that bond to be erased with no terms to follow?"

Inharise smacked his forearm. "Beloved, she is most worried about the child."

"As she should be. But let's get the question of her forced and incomplete bond to Zauril out of the way first. It is my suspicion that the Gods will have their own opinion on the validity of Zauril's attempt to force that bond and that judgment will affect all other questions. Can you read them to me?" He raised his brows at Orlanden.

Orlanden read them aloud.

Heinmyets nodded. "If you would take my suggestion, Alicira, toss first for the bond's validity."

"It does simplify the remaining questions if the issue of my freedom is put forth in terms of the bond. Thank you."

"Riders coming!" one of Heinmyets's men on watch called to them.

"Are we prepared?" Heinmyets asked.

"We are, as best as we can be," Alicira said, the pulse pounding hard in her ears.

"I will wake Metkyi," Inharise said, rising.

"Come with me," Heinmyets said. "I will introduce you to Siljaren and Twana, and we will talk further."

Alicira took the parchment with the questions from Orlanden and walked with Heinmyets. Fear clawed hard at her gut.

It is time.

No more running.

THE MUNDANE NATURE of the meeting preparations squelched the jangling of Alicira's nerves by the time things were finally ready. Siljaren and Twana needed further explanation of what was happening; then Twana gathered five riders to prepare the site. Metkyi stood by the fire, blinking sleepily as he sipped a stimulant tea produced by Siljaren, who turned out to be Wickmasa's Healer. While they waited for the preparations to be done, Siljaren took Alicira off to a tent to examine her in private.

"How long has it been since you've seen a Healer?" was her first question once they were in the tent.

"Not since Midsummer."

Siljaren frowned. "And you're pregnant? Take off your tunic and let me look."

Her scowl deepened as Alicira reluctantly removed her tunic, revealing the slowly healing scars she had not shown anyone else since her escape.

"Gods above, what did Zauril *do* to you?" Siljaren exclaimed, fingers tracing the wounds.

"Torture. Rape. All after I refused the bond. Daily, until I was weakened to the degree he could overwhelm my protections and impregnate me." Alicira fixed her eyes on a discoloration in the heavy woven fabric of the tent. It was easier to talk if she couldn't see Siljaren's reaction.

"Goddess's golden tits," Siljaren growled. "So when did he succeed in breaking down your defenses?" Her voice was blunt and harsh, tight with controlled anger.

"The beginning of fall." Alicira blinked back tears that threatened to break loose as Siljaren continued to gently finger the scars on her back. "But I did not conceive until the beginning of winter."

"And since then?"

"Once he was satisfied that I was with child he put restraints on my wrists and ankles and left me alone." She gulped. "Delian —and Orlanden—brought charms that helped the injuries heal as much as they are now. But it took one of my jailers who objected to what Zauril did to get me free of those shackles."

"Those charms weren't strong enough." Siljaren dug into her bag and brought out a jar of salve. "As part of your chip tossing, you need to ask that all of his magic be pulled from you. I can do some things with this salve but there is a pernicious spell which keeps these wounds from healing like they should. I dare not do more until after your child is born."

Alicira flinched as the salve stung. Siljaren whispered a charm and the burning eased. The baby roiled inside of her, kicking at the new magic, painful enough to make Alicira double over, clutching at her torso.

"The child?" Siljaren asked.

Alicira nodded, unable to speak until the spasm passed. "She is strong in magic already," she gasped once she could talk. "I fear she may carry her father's power."

Siljaren shook her head. "Too early to determine now. If the spell remains in those wounds it is more likely that his magic will influence her. Otherwise, she could carry yours. You've had problems?"

"Yes. I've had a hard time keeping down food and she's been restless since she quickened. But the Goddess has been so remote—"

"The spells in the wounds," Siljaren said softly. "Just strong enough to keep the Goddess at bay, but weak enough for you to use your magic in a limited manner. Those charms—where did Orlanden and Delian get them?"

"Inharise."

"Her charms would be strong enough to ease his grip on you, at least. Just not enough to completely eliminate their effect on your body."

"You can't banish the spells?"

"I—" Siljaren hesitated. "I am reluctant to do that while you carry the child. It will be very hard on you and your healing is already impaired. Zauril or Staul in his name must remove them. Your uncle has some talent with healing. Have you not checked with him?"

Alicira shook her head. "No time, and—" Her voice trailed away. She hadn't wanted to think of him, of any man, seeing what Zauril had done to her. She hadn't shown Delian anything more than the wounds on her wrists.

"Probably better he not mess with this," Siljaren muttered. "Best handled by women and not men, even well-intentioned men." Her lips tightened as she finished with the salve. "I will make sure the Goddess insists that these wounds be cleared before we even begin the chip tossing. At least that should give you more rest and strength."

Alicira nodded, blinking back tears. Siljaren knelt before her, gently placing her hands over Alicira's womb. Her touch seemed to soothe the restless child, easing tension that Alicira hadn't noticed was there. At last Siljaren rocked back on her heels, pushing back a strand of dark hair that had worked loose from her braid.

"The baby is well. She develops normally, and will be powerful. Remove the spells from your wounds and her magic will mature as it is intended to grow."

"Of me or of Zauril?" Alicira's voice trembled.

Siljaren shook her head. "It is too early to tell. It is a good sign, however, that you have been struggling with illness and that she is so sensitive to your magic. She fights the influence of those spells." Her lips thinned. "They will be removed for the child's sake as well as yours. He seeks to influence what should flourish on its own."

"He seeks divinity."

"It will be a foul day if he succeeds." Siljaren stood. "Put your tunic back on. I'll give you a minor potion to fortify you for what lies ahead."

Alicira wordlessly pulled the tunic back on and drank the offered potion. They silently left the tent. Heinmyets met them.

"It is ready," he said. "Are you?"

Alicira nodded. He took her hand, and they walked to join Inharise, who took Alicira's other hand. As they walked toward the opening of the cordon, Metkyi, Alame, Ciren, and the others fell in behind them.

A fire crackled two hundred paces away from the cordon. Twana stood by it, wearing dark robes and the golden hat that marked her status as a shaman of Artel, a thick, leather-bound book in her hands. She looked young to Alicira, younger even than Metkyi, whose face was still drawn and tired after Staul's earlier possession of him. To her right stood Gegarth, looking human instead of Shadowwalker, and Sesenth, who still retained her Shadowwalker shape.

Alicira stopped on the side of the fire opposite from Twana. Inharise and Heinmyets remained at her side. Twana walked away from Gegarth and Sesenth, moving so that she stood halfway between Alicira and Gegarth. Siljaren and Metkyi joined her, and they spoke quietly, so soft that Alicira could not hear the words spoken, though from the intensity of Siljaren's gestures she could tell the discussion was angry.

"I will convey your concerns and make it happen," Twana said finally. "You are right in this. Voice of Staul?" she queried Metkyi.

His face was stony and hard as he replied. "*Fully* agreed."

Twana turned toward Gegarth. "Bearer of Zauril. Our lady of Dovré has a requirement for you. Artel's judgment and the Voice of Staul agree. The lady Alicira bears wounds that carry a spell which violates the rules of magical influence on an unborn child. Remove it now or forfeit your right to appear here."

"And if I do not?" Gegarth's voice carried enough of Zauril's deep tones to make Alicira shudder.

"Then *I* will remove it, and you will be forfeit for any harm done to Alicira and her child, as well as losing any right to claim what you desire."

Gegarth growled. But he raised a hand, and through him Alicira felt the slightest touch of Zauril's magic. She would have flinched away but gritted her teeth and closed her eyes, her wounds seeming to burn worse than ever.

Then it was gone. She swayed slightly and Inharise steadied her. Alicira opened her eyes to stare across the fire at Zauril glaring at her through Gegarth's eyes, the red in Gegarth's eyes replaced by Zauril's dark gray. The easing of pain made her realize just how much it had been a part of her life the past few months. Anger burned deep within her.

No matter what happens here, he will pay. Even if it takes the rest of my life, he will pay.

"We thank you, Zauril," Twana said. She looked at Siljaren, then Metkyi. "Siljaren. Metkyi. Are you ready to bear your Gods?"

"I will speak for Dovré," Siljaren said. A shimmer, and then the Goddess's form descended upon Siljaren, a translucent other that transformed Siljaren's dark braid into black and silver curls even as the darker shape of the Goddess shimmered in outline around her.

"I speak for Staul, both Balancer and Destroyer," Metkyi said, changing as he had before, no transparency about Staul as he took over Metkyi.

"Artel, king of the Gods and our Judge, hear our plea. We throw now to determine these questions brought before us, to decide the status of the lady Alicira and the challenges she brings to the claims made by the lord Zauril. My lord Staul will throw for Zauril, in his role as advocate of the Balance, since Zauril is only here through one of his servants."

"Why not my lady Nitel?" Gegarth-as-Zauril thrust his chin out defiantly.

"Nitel does not participate in these judgments," Metkyi-as-Staul said. "She never has. It is not her role. As two of the Eldest among the Gods, Dovré and I are God and Goddess of the judgment, as it always has been."

"Are you satisfied?" Twana asked Gegarth-as-Zauril.

He grumbled but nodded.

"My lady Dovré," Twana continued. "Do you throw for your dedicated?"

"My dedicated brings the challenge for herself," Siljaren-as-Dovré said, her voice modulated by the Goddess's smooth tones. "I will advise."

"Come forward, then, Alicira ea Miteal. Do you understand what is to be done?"

"I do," Alicira said, fighting to keep her voice steady. Both Heinmyets and Inharise squeezed her hands before she released them. Gegarth-as-Zauril also came forward.

"You will stand here." Twana gestured toward Siljaren-as-Dovré. She turned to Gegarth-as-Zauril. "You will stand next to Staul." She pointed toward Metkyi-as-Staul. Then she untied a pouch from her belt and knelt. First, she spread a cloth on the ground, then poured out eight chips that clattered against each other. "These chips are made from daranval bone. Handle them with respect." She rose. "My lord Staul, as representative for the challenged, please examine the chips."

Metkyi-as-Staul knelt, turning each chip over carefully, looking at each one to ensure that one side was blank and the other was marked. "They meet my approval."

"My lady Alicira. Would you examine yourself, or would you have a representative do it?"

"I—" she faltered, then swallowed determinedly at the cruel pleasure that flowed across Gegarth-as-Zauril's face. "I would have the lady Inharise inspect for me."

Twana nodded. Inharise came forward, knelt, and checked each chip. "They are acceptable," she said, rising and backing away.

Twana knelt and picked up the chips. "Blanks will favor Alicira. Marks will favor Zauril. My lady Alicira. Present the first question."

Alicira cleared her throat. "Am I to be held to a forced and incomplete bond that was attempted by my lord Zauril, or is that bond to be erased with no further binding upon either of us?"

"I object—" Gegarth-as-Zauril began.

"You are not the challenger," Twana cut him off. "You do not have grounds to object to how she phrases her questions. The throw will judge the rightness." She handed four chips to Metkyi-as-Staul, then four to Alicira. "Staul leads, as representative for the challenged. Any chip that falls off of the cloth is null."

Metkyi-as-Staul tossed. Blank.

Alicira tossed. Blank.

They repeated, until eight blank chips lay on the cloth.

"My lady Alicira prevails with no interpretation," Twana pronounced. "The Gods speak. She is not bound to Zauril." She gathered the chips.

Alicira would have reeled in relief but there were three more questions.

Gegarth-as-Zauril glowered. "My rights are denied!"

Twana's visage darkened, the shadow of a male form overlaying her. "Would you rather *I* issued *my* judgment?" Artel rumbled through her. "I assure you that the chip throw will be more nuanced and in your favor if my Voice judges than if the lady Alicira appeals directly to me."

"You fear a challenge to your authority." Zauril's presence grew stronger. "You fear I grow strong enough to become your brother."

"If you are indeed worthy to depose one of us, you will be powerful enough to withstand setbacks," Artel-as-Twana said. "You think you are the first human to aspire to Godhood by playing our political games? Little man, you are but one of many. I suggest you demonstrate the virtue of patience."

"And you attack those you would join," Metkyi-as-Staul muttered. "I will remember this."

The sense of Zauril's presence weakened. "Proceed," Gegarth-as-Zauril said.

Artel's visage faded from Twana. She looked at Alicira. "Ask your next question of the chips."

Should she ask about the child or about the magic? *Magic*, came to her.

"To whom does Medvara's magic rightly belong? Myself, Zauril, or the unborn child?"

"As the loser of the first throw, Staul tosses first." Twana gave Metkyi-as-Staul four chips, and Alicira the remaining chips.

This time, there were four blank and four marked chips, the blanks from Alicira, the marked from Metkyi-as-Staul.

"Inconclusive and even," Twana pronounced. "The claims of Alicira and Zauril balance. Wait." She held up her hand before Alicira could object. "There is a third to be considered, who cannot throw for herself. The judgment goes to her, not to you or to Zauril. The unborn child rightfully will hold Medvara's magic." Twana gathered and distributed the chips. "Because of the nature of the toss, Staul leads again. My lady Alicira, your next question."

"When does the magic of Medvara come to my daughter and who holds it until then?"

This time, the throw was six blank and two lines, with Metkyi-as-Staul's first and last throws providing the extra blanks, the lines coming from his second and third throws.

Twana picked up her book and thumbed through it. When she finally found the page she sought she frowned as she read, chewing her lower lip. At last she closed the book.

"A mixed verdict, requiring nuance due to the nature of who threw the blanks and when in the toss," she said. "The unborn child will come into magic at the normal age of thirteen. But this will be her own magic, not the magic tied to the land of Medvara. The full judgment waits for my lady Alicira's final question. Had the lines occurred on Staul's first throw, the interpretation would have differed. There is one further question to be resolved before the magic can be determined."

Who she belongs to, Alicira realized. "I apologize, my lady Twana and my lord Artel, for misordering my questions."

Twana shook her head as she knelt to gather the chips. "No, that was an appropriate followup to the verdict of the second question." She handed chips to Metkyi-as-Staul and Alicira. "Ask your last question well, my lady Alicira, remembering this verdict as you ask."

"May I ask this question in two parts?"

"You may ask, but Artel will decide if it is valid."

"To whom does my child belong, and how does her custody affect the magic of Medvara?" Alicira waited, tense, until Twana nodded.

"My lord Staul." Twana gestured to Metkyi-as-Staul.

First chip. Blank.

Alicira threw. Second chip. Blank.

Metkyi-as-Staul threw. Blank.

Alicira threw. Line. Behind her, Alame groaned. A sneer twitched Gegarth-as-Zauril's lips.

Metkyi-as-Staul threw. Blank.

Alicira threw. Blank. She allowed herself to hope now. Only one line. But she had thrown it, not Staul. Did that matter?

Metkyi-as-Staul threw. Line.

Five blanks and two lines. Whatever does that mean? Not a victory for Zauril but not a victory for her, either. Alicira shook the final chip in her hand, controlling the tremors that threatened to overwhelm her.

She threw.

Line!

Her throat tightened and she wanted to scream. Zauril gloated behind Gegarth's face.

What did I do wrong?

"A *very* interesting verdict," Twana said, kneeling to sort the chips before she opened the book. This time she flipped to her place without hesitation, and left the book open for all to see as she interpreted, her index finger following the lines. She pursed her lips as she read, looking up when she was done. "The first three throws, two by Staul and one by Alicira, are blank. My lord Artel interprets this as meaning that the child initially belongs to Alicira." She pointed to the writing. "Those who may question can look for themselves, but this is Artel's verdict. Do you wish him to speak the verdict, or shall I?"

A scowl spread across Gegarth-as-Zauril's face as he peered at the writing. "We see no need to have Artel speak," he growled after reading. "Your interpretation is not to our liking, but it is true."

Alicira let the breath she had been holding exhale slowly. She suspected that Zauril had no desire to expose himself any further to Artel, especially since the rest of the throw could swing in his favor. Or perhaps he was, like her, unfamiliar with this form of judgment by the Gods. Nuances of the dice, they both knew. Chips? She doubted he knew any more about interpreting these chips than she did.

"However, the fourth throw, by Alicira, is a line. Zauril will be allowed to request tribute for each year Alicira holds the child. Again, this is my lord Artel's verdict." Gegarth-as-Zauril made a satisfied noise and Twana glared at him. "Tribute will be the market price of a young, unbonded daranval, to be paid in silver or the equivalent. Should Alicira forfeit, Zauril can claim the child."

A groan escaped Alicira's lips. Heinmyets and Inharise moved closer to her, their shoulders touching hers.

"The fifth and sixth throws, by Staul and Alicira, are both blank. Medvara's magic will come by choice to the child, and Alicira will hold it for her until the child is thirteen. The seventh throw, by Staul, is a line. The eighth throw, by Alicira, is a line. A choice comes to the child, who is not able to represent herself here, so Artel's verdict is that we may go no further than this decision at this time. If the child chooses to take on the magic of Medvara at age thirteen, Alicira must send her to Zauril then. Had Alicira's final throw been blank, the magic would have gone directly to the child with no conditions. Because she threw a line, the child must go to Medvara at her age of magical majority. She does so with the provision that, at age eighteen, the child will have the choice of challenging her sire both for the magic and for the rightful rule of Medvara."

"And if something happens to the child?" Heinmyets asked. Alicira gave him a grateful look and he smiled at her before returning his focus to Twana.

"At that time we will meet in judgment," Twana said. "It will be best for all concerned if the child survives to a healthy adulthood. The Gods will not—" and at this point she fixed Gegarth-as-Zauril with a stern glare, "look favorably upon those who bring harm to the child." She spread her hands wide. "The Gods have spoken through our Lord Artel. Let none challenge his verdict."

"I demand tribute now," Gegarth-as-Zauril said.

"Tribute does not begin until the child's first birthday," Twana said. "The lady Alicira will inform you of that date. Meanwhile, you will not interfere further with her pregnancy, or with her work and life. Only on the anniversary of the child's birth will you or your agents make direct contact with Alicira. You will not attack her or those she takes refuge with. You will not hamper her use of magic and her access to Medvara's magic, until the child makes her choice."

"And her?" he demanded. "What keeps Alicira from raising an army to depose me?"

"In return, the lady Alicira will not act against you as lord of Medvara. She will not give aid and comfort to those who may seek to overthrow you, just as you may not do the same to her and those of her household."

A smirk briefly touched his lips.

"Is this for life or until my child is eighteen?" Alicira glared at Zauril.

You will pay. You will pay, drummed through her.

"The two of you are bound not to act directly against each other for as long as you both live." Twana fixed Heinmyets with a direct stare. "That will include those to whom you choose a bond with. They will fall under the same protection and restraint that you do." She picked up the book and closed it with a loud THUMP that made both Alicira and Gegarth-as-Zauril jump. "Zauril, this restriction extends to your servant that you now ride. Furthermore, your oaths bind you to this decision, even though you were only present through the gift of another giving you the use of their body. Do you understand?"

"Yes."

"Good. Now it is time that you leave." As Gegarth-as-Zauril turned to go, Twana continued. "That is for you, Zauril. Gegarth, you remain. My lord Staul would have words with you."

"You will not harm him," Gegarth-as-Zauril growled.

"It is not a matter of your concern," Metkyi-as-Staul said. "Unless you would choose to challenge me now?"

Gegarth-as-Zauril hesitated. Then he shook his head. "No. Not apart from my body. Nonetheless, my lord, should any harm come to him—"

"I will keep that in mind," Metkyi-as-Staul said dryly.

Gegarth stood still as Zauril's presence faded. Then he knelt to Metkyi-as-Staul, striking his chest with his right fist, all defiance gone. "I plead exigent circumstances," he said quietly. "It is as Sesenth said."

"You do well to fear my wrath." Metkyi-as-Staul glared down at him. "I will be watching you. It is in your favor that this one I ride serves the Balancer and not the Destroyer, else things would be different for you."

Gegarth hit his chest again. "I accept your rule, Lord Staul."

"Then you and yours will not further act against the lady Alicira and those with her. Your actions brought about the death of her brother."

Gegarth looked up. "My paths will not cross hers until it comes time for her daughter's decision. This is not my territory and I will not speak for those who control here. Nonetheless, I will remain at Nixyin and not intrude here. As for the lady's brother, I plead the protection of Zauril for his death."

Metkyi-as-Staul exhaled, the breath hissing through his teeth. "Do not expect favor from me in the future, Gegarth. You have made your choice. Now. Go. Before the Destroyer becomes dominant."

Gegarth thumped his chest one last time, then nodded, stumbling backwards as he rose, until he joined Sesenth and the other Shadowwalker. Then they mounted, turning to ride away. Metkyi-as-Staul glowered after them, fists tight.

Twana knelt to gather the chips and the cloth. After putting them away, she stood and broke the silence that hung around the fire.

"Unless the Gods would speak further, I pronounce this gathering to be complete in Artel's name. My lady Dovré?" She looked at Siljaren.

"I am satisfied with the verdict. However, I would speak to my dedicated before I leave."

"Go ahead."

Siljaren-as-Dovré went to Alicira, gently stroking her cheek. "Beloved. You have endured much. I know the rage that floods through you at Medvara's loss and for what was done to you. Restrain it for the sake of your child and her future. Seek to build what is positive, and what you create will be brighter and more memorable than anything you would have done as the

Lady of Medvara. But go to the negative and the creeping shadows, and your name will be a curse and the deepest red blight. Be mindful of your choices."

"I will, my lady." Alicira's voice rasped in her throat. "But I burn with what was done to me."

"Channel that anger. Use it to create, not destroy. I promise that what will come of your creativity will outweigh whatever you would do in vengeance."

"I will try, my lady."

Siljaren-as- Dovré's hand slipped from Alicira's cheek to the back of her head, pulling her forward until their foreheads touched.

"As long as you walk in the positive paths I will be with you. Let my healing touch you now."

Warmth flowed through Alicira, bringing tears to her eyes as the final remnants of pain faded, leaving her with sorrow at Delian's death. The child stirred within, but not with the frantic struggling against magic that she had done previously.

"I cannot remove everything that was done to you," the Goddess said. "But your brother Delian has given you strong companions. Trust them, depend on them."

"I will," Alicira repeated.

"Then walk in joy and beauty, my lady Alicira. Keep hope in your heart even when things are darkest. I will be with you." The Goddess kissed Alicira's forehead. Then she released Alicira and stepped back. "I am done." Her presence faded from Siljaren, who now collapsed on her knees.

"My lord Staul," Twana said quietly.

"I would speak to Dovré's dedicated as well."

"You may."

Metkyi-as-Staul waited as Ciren and Alame helped Siljaren up and away. Then he walked to stand in front of Alicira.

"My lady Alicira. When the time comes, this vessel of mine will swear to shadow and protect your child. She will not be of me but I will extend my protection as the Balancer until she is of age and has come into her power." He took her hand. "I give you this vow as man and as God. She will need much guidance as she navigates the world of shadows, a world she will must know should she choose to challenge her father in the deepest of red rage. Metkyi-my-voice can give her the training and support she will need."

"Thank you, my lord Staul." Emotion flooded through Alicira, the combination of fatigue and awe that Staul would so vow overwhelming her and keeping her from saying more.

Metkyi-as-Staul kissed her hand, then stepped back. As Staul's visage faded he collapsed to the ground.

Twana sighed. "My brother gives much of himself to the God." She drew herself up. "And with this, I pronounce this gathering done in the names of Artel, Dovré, and Staul. May all vows given be held true and may all remember the assurances they have provided. Go now in peace."

Alicira sagged and would have fallen, fatigue dropping over her. Inharise and Heinmyets steadied her. She tried to walk but faltered in her first step. Heinmyets swept her into his arms.

"What now?" she asked them.

"Tonight, you rest," Inharise said. "Tomorrow, we go to Wickmasa. There we will swear what threefold marriage vows we choose to make before Imnari their headwoman."

"And the vows?"

Heinmyets chuckled. "We will have time to discuss them as the three of us ride together tomorrow. It is done. We have done what Delian desired."

She was too tired to ask further questions.

CHAPTER 11

For the first time in what seemed to be ages Alicira rose in the morning without feeling the need to rush around to travel. A fire crackled in the center of the tent, smoke drifting out the opening at the top, and she was alone, the other bedrolls neatly rolled and tied.

A delicious odor of cooking meat wafted in from outside. For the first time in ages the scent didn't provoke an urge to be sick. Careful working of her shoulders and bending from to side to side revealed that the nagging aches and pain that had haunted her throughout the flight from Medvara were gone. She still felt tired and sore, but the deep hurts from her confinement had vanished.

Alicira quickly pulled on her boots and jacket, rolled and tied her bedroll, and went outside, hesitating as she let the door fall closed behind her. Tiny snowflakes drifted down slowly, falling from a light gray sky that seemed benign. Several people stood around the campfire while others steadily loaded the wagon. The protective magic cordon still shimmered around the campsite, but many of the logs that had been part of the barricade had been moved to a tall stack. Heinmyets directed the riders as they continued to disassemble the barricade. He flashed Alicira a smile before continuing to work.

One of the tents was down. Inharise and Ciren worked with two others to fold it. Siljaren held a plate in her hand as she spoke to Alame while they stood by the fire. She motioned to Alicira to join them.

"How do you feel?" she asked, as Alame went to the wagon.

"Tired and sore, but much better than before."

"Good. Metkyi and Twana still sleep in the other tent, but they should be awake soon."

Alame returned with a plate and a cup. "Are you hungry?"

Her stomach rumbled in answer. They laughed.

"I could eat," Alicira admitted.

Alame handed her the cup. "Your daranval milk. The hunters brought in a deer, so we have fried venison and pancakes this morning."

"That sounds wonderful." Alicira made a face at the cup but drank.

When she had finished, she took plate and utensils and took a chunk of meat and three cakes from the three-legged spider frying pan that sat at the edge of the fire. As she straightened, Metkyi and Twana came out from their tent. After greeting Alicira, they went to the wagon, Metkyi moving slowly and carefully.

"What happens now?" Alame asked Alicira.

She finished chewing the last piece of meat and swallowed. "We go to Wickmasa. I discuss terms of bonding with Heinmyets and Inharise, and—" she shrugged. "I don't know what happens after that. Except that I will be safe, and at some point next summer will deliver a daughter."

"You do not want more?"

"Uncle, after the past six months, knowing that I will live in safety, knowing that there will be a place for me to raise my daughter to her age of magical majority, that is enough." She ate a chunk of pancake, sweet with a flavor of tangy berry syrup unfamiliar to her.

"You could have done much more." The tone of his voice startled her with the depth of regret laden in it. "More *was* prophesied at your birth. You could have been an Empress."

The pancake seemed to turn dry in her mouth. She worked at it until she made enough saliva to swallow it in a large lump.

"Zauril would have made me an Empress," she said softly once the pancake had settled, staring down at her plate. "A puppet Empress, but one nonetheless. I rejected that path. Perhaps Zauril's ambitions were what was foreseen."

"Possible, but I don't think so. You could have found a means to fulfill that prophecy had you gone to Waykemin."

Alicira shook her head. "I think it is best I did not consider that path."

Alame looked at her sadly. "But it would have been great."

She eyed him thoughtfully, assessing his phrasings and the tone in his voice. "Who prophesied that future for me? Not my mother, or my father. Neither had one whit of magic in their blood. It would have been either you or Grandfather."

Alame sighed. "I was the one, yes. It was one reason why I was exiled. Alexran would not entertain the idea of that possibility for you. I do not remember the details. Only that Empress was one pathway that lay ahead of you."

She wondered if that was why her grandfather had been so standoffish to her when he had been so pleasant to Melaraen. Then she pushed those memories aside.

"My future is set now," she said firmly.

"As part of a ruling triad, as one who shares a spouse in a threefold marriage."

"You heard the Goddess."

Alame shook his head. "None of us heard what either Dovré or Staul said to you at the end."

"This is the path I have chosen, and both Dovré and Staul

look favorably on it. Uncle, I have no further regrets. I have many new things to learn."

Heinmyets brought her a cup of water, and took her plate. "Now that Metkyi and Twana are awake, we will be leaving soon. Metkyi says this storm will be slow but steady and that we should not delay leaving for Wickmasa."

"Metkyi says?" she asked.

"Part of his duties as the Voice of Staul includes weather observations and predictions." He smiled at her. "I listen to him, and would prefer a relaxed ride where the three of us can talk without worry rather than a hard ride to escape a storm and no time to speak."

"Then I will make ready." She glanced at Alame. "Uncle, I hear your concerns, but we must be leaving. Does your path follow mine?"

He sighed, as Siljaren walked by and patted his shoulder. "I have much to discuss with Siljaren. You are not the only one who needs healing and solace."

"Wickmasa is a pleasant place to spend a winter storm," Inharise said, coming up on Alicira's other side. "And I am certain that Headwoman Imnari will be honored to have us stay until the weather clears."

"If only brother Makri were here and not in training at the Healing House in Dera," said Twana. "We will not see the like of these events any time soon."

Metkyi frowned, but it faded when Twana looked at him. Alicira wondered what that meant, especially when Siljaren's face also clouded.

"We will have much to discuss," Inharise said. "But for now, let's finish packing and be on the road."

"I will help," Alicira said. "Best to start my new life now—or is travel going to be that common for us?"

Heinmyets laughed. "My lady, even should the leadership of Keldara pass to me, there will be traveling. I do hope you like it."

She smiled back at him. "My lord, after all those months spent imprisoned, it will take me a long time to be comfortable staying in any one place. Besides, how could I stay off of my sweet Narasin?"

He laughed again and patted her back, his hand resting oh-so-lightly on her shoulder, not enough to pressure her but just enough to let her know he was there.

Inharise's smile spread wider. "Spoken like a true daughter of Clenda. Oh, I do hope the timing of your daughter's birth allows you to see the high pastures next summer! Summer is sweetest there."

"I look forward to it." Alicira went with Inharise and Heinmyets to the tent, where the others were already carrying out the bedrolls.

Welcome to my new life.

Somehow she thought she would prefer roving to being stuck in even Medvara's court.

Medvara.

Thinking of her former home did not ache so much. It still hurt to lose it, true, but knowing that Zauril could not access its magic and that the magic might still come to her daughter eased the burden of knowing it was gone.

When we reach Wickmasa we will mourn all our losses, even as we prepare for a new future.

Still, she wondered how long the peace would last.

In the lifetime of one who would be a God, thirteen years was a very short time. But Zauril was impatient by nature. Would he wait to act upon his ambitions? Only the Gods knew —and by his actions this day he had angered three of the Seven Crowned Gods. To move further without reason would indeed show himself to be one beyond any honor and unworthy of deity, no matter how strong his magic. That would constrain him from moving too quickly.

But I have no such restraint beyond my vows to Staul and Dovré. I have truly gone beyond any need for honor.

She did remember the Goddess's warning, though.

I will heed and remember. Still, Zauril, vengeance will be mine. Our daughter will know what you have done. Our daughter will be mine—and my means for revenge.

When she thought about vengeance, it was easier to acknowledge her daughter's sire. Acknowledge but not honor or respect.

If she had anything to say about his fate, she would ensure that he remained beyond honor forever. Even if it took the rest of her life and power to make it so.

THE END

EXILE'S HONOR

SAFE....OR NOT?

Whoosh! Blood-red flames suddenly flare from the wall sconces in her cell. The temperature drops. She shivers in her thin cotton shift, magicless, her power bound by the shackles on her wrists and ankles. He is coming. He is coming. He is....

ALICIRA STARTLED UP, LOOKING WILDLY AROUND HER. NOW WHAT had thrown her into *those* memories? Another *whoosh* made the small fire flare in the hearth and she sagged in relief, realizing it was just a gust of wind roaring down the chimney. Then she drew a deep breath and released it slowly, calming herself.

It wasn't just the wind. She hadn't slept well last night, so she had drowsed off in this comfortable chair near the fire. Most of all, it had been seven long months since she'd been alone like this. Except for those dark nights when the guards chained her to the bed, leaving her ready should Zauril choose that night to impose himself upon her.

Those times are gone, never to return.

Still, it felt strange to be sitting in this comfortable chair, all by herself. More than that, she had no immediate obligations, no need to be rushing around. How long had it been since she had this kind of peaceful, solitary moment unmarked by dread? Too long.

So, of course, she drowsed off and frightened herself again.

I need to get over this. I am home now.

That is, if this afternoon's meeting didn't go wrong. Did Nateri, the Leader's wife, still wear the magic-suppressing bracelets from eight years ago? She didn't *feel* Nateri's magic stirring in the flows around her—but that didn't mean much. Nateri could have learned subtlety over the years. Or the bracelets binding Nateri's magic might still be serving their purpose.

If only I had known then what I do now.

She swallowed hard at the memory of Nateri's anguished, twisted face as Alicira's magic locked the bracelets on her wrists. Followed hard by her memories of *those nights* lying bound, at Zauril's mercy.

Nateri wasn't tortured and raped. A small mercy. But having her magic locked down, controlled? Bad enough.

Depriving or controlling any Aireii sorcerer's magic would still leave a mark, no matter how well-intentioned. Alicira would have to deal with that issue soon, but for now—*focus on the moment.* She was safe in this small sitting room in the suite she shared with her spouses. Had it only been a month ago that she was in the dark, dank, stone spell-encrusted prison cell in Medvare-the-city?

Less than that.

Concentrate on the world around you to calm your mind. Concentrate.

One of her first lessons as a sorceress.

Concentrate.

Bright morning sunlight spilled through the east-facing windows of real glass, not the greased paper or thinly sliced horn common for window coverings outside of Medvare. A neatly woven pink and gold carpet, made of non-magical materials, covered the oiled wooden floor. The sunshine illuminated the polished round table in front of her. A white rose-painted plate with biscuits, a teapot, and a delicate porcelain cup that matched the plate sat on the table. The real window glass was familiar but it felt out of place with Heinmyets' and Inharise's riding gear hanging on the wall, exuding the faint scent of horse.

I need to have my own riding gear made.

She had borrowed her brother's gear during her escape—and her eyes began to blur with tears as sorrow flooded over her at the memory of Delian, who had died during their flight from Medvara.

Riding hard after Zauril's Shadowwalker allies attacked us, Delian in the saddle in front of me, feeling him fade away as we rode. His final breath just as the sun came up....

The faint golden image of her daranval mare Narasin, currently in the stable, stirred. Wordless support and a visualization of Narasin gently nuzzling her neck and shoulder offered reassurance. Alicira clung to that image, letting her daranval comfort her. At last she straightened up, sending Narasin a wordless surge of grateful emotions.

Narasin snorted, and returned to her hay manger. Her aura faded from the main thrust of Alicira's thoughts, though a tiny golden presence lurked at the edge of her awareness.

What would I do without my daranval?

Before her flight from Medvara, she hadn't known what it was like to be bonded to one of the magic-bred horses out of Keldara. Now Alicira didn't think she could survive without Narasin.

Certainly not during my flight from Medvara!

Calmer now, Alicira refocused on her surroundings. A fire snapped and crackled in the small fireplace set into the wall between the sitting room and bedroom. The scent was familiar but the dryness of the cold was nothing at all like the damp darkness of the cell, where she anticipated the unlit sconces to flare with blood-red magical light that announced Zauril's immanent arrival.

So why do I keep thinking about it?

As of four days ago, Zauril had no further claim on her. The Gods had said so. Her marriage to Heinmyets and Inharise completed the Gods' ruling. She was fully bonded to a Keldaran daranval who would protect her.

All true—except for the unborn child she carried, the daughter Zauril had conceived upon her in an attempt to bind Alicira's magic.

And he would never, ever be able to claim Alicira's daughter, at least as long as Alicira continued to find refuge with Heinmyets and Inharise. Despite her history with Nateri, she was safe here.

Why does he continue to haunt me, then? Why do I doubt and worry?

A loud baby cry came from the nursery on the other side of the wall, where Inharise was with little Cenarth and his nurse, Danetna, centering Alicira even more. Inharise was not far away. Their husband—quick thrill pulsing through her at the thought of *husband*—Heinmyets was conferring with his advisors to prepare for their audience this afternoon with his father Thenil and stepmother Nateri.

Nateri again. Her heart drummed faster when she considered Nateri. What grudges might the woman still bear against her? And how justified was she in feeling that way?

I did not understand the corruption in Alexran's heart then. If I had—

But would it have changed things? If she had understood then, could she have stopped Zauril?

You were young. You did not fathom the depths of Alexran's folly.

Nonetheless, she couldn't banish the feeling that she should have grasped this reality then, even as a young woman of fourteen.

Magic straining against the shackles as Zauril locks them on her wrists. Memory of Nateri screaming as Alicira locks the bracelets on her wrists. Now Alicira screams just like Nateri did; white-hot, burning pain as her magic ignores her command and pounds fruitlessly at the shackles. Zauril's chuckle as Alicira collapses, her screams continuing as he claps the fetters on her ankles. Then magic is gone. Try as she can to revive it, nothing stirs. No magical awareness. No magic. NO MAGIC. She doesn't even feel his hands dragging her up and on her cot as she sobs, trying and failing to revive her magic. She's barely aware of his body on hers as she tries to find her magic.

Her hands trembled as Alicira shook her head to banish that memory. Narasin's faint golden presence loomed larger, worry projecting from her.

I am all right.

She sent reassuring thoughts to Narasin, and the golden mare's aura retreated again, though larger than it had been. Alicira focused on the steam rising from her cup of tea, waiting until breathing and pulse calmed, then concentrating on closer, tangible things.

She still needed to braid her hair. At least she had washed her face and performed her morning absolutions, and put on a dress appropriate for the day's events. But her dress was borrowed from Inharise, a simple brown and gold wool with a fitted waist that showed the slight curvature of her pregnancy, and long, flowing skirts.

Need to have some dresses of my own made as well as riding gear.

Zauril had kept her in long cotton shifts with no magic in

them, and once her brother Delian had freed her, she had worn his spare riding trousers, shirt and sweater while fleeing. It hadn't been until this morning that she had put on a dress, in—how long? Months, at least.

But ordering the construction of new dresses would have to wait until after this afternoon's audience with Thenil and Nateri.

Alicira sighed. She leaned forward and broke a corner off of the biscuit.

Aloneness. A dress. Simple things that a year ago she would have never considered important, but now marked the difference in what her life had been over the past—seven months? Yes. Seven months since Midsummer. Seven months since Zauril's invasion of the nation of Medvara and the massacre of her family. She nibbled at the biscuit corner, then took the cup in both hands, inhaling the fragrant warmth. A berry tea, with spicy undernotes.

Just like she had been drinking the morning that—it—happened.

Her gorge rose and she carefully set the cup back on the table with shaking hands.

The alarm raised as she drinks tea that morning. Scrambling to grab her shortsword, even though she knows her grandfather Alexran would not like her to do that. The screams of her sister Melaraen as Zauril's men cut her down before Alicira can come to her aid.

No. No.

She couldn't do this to herself. Why, by the Goddess's golden tits, was she so haunted this morning? She was safe now.

Alicira banished that memory before Narasin responded. Swallowing hard to keep the bit of biscuit down, she got up and went to the window to get away from that scent, dampening her emotions as best as she could to keep from disturbing Narasin. She was still new to the bond between daranval and human, and feared upsetting the golden mare when there was no need.

Just me and my memories.

Alicira gulped, half-laughing at herself, half-crying. She was safe. Safe. Just—dreading the upcoming meeting with Nateri. She leaned against the window frame, studying what she could see of the small city as a distraction from those worried thoughts.

At least part of the time this house would be her home. Heinmyets and Inharise only lived here in winter. The rest of the year, they either rode with the Leader's herds or made the rounds to the villages of Keldara, representing Thenil to the village leaders. Inharise still had duties in neighboring Clenda, and that would also require travel in summer and fall.

But for now, it was winter, and she was in Dera. Would be in this house for the winters. The Keldaran Leader's House here was nothing like the huge building kept up by the Leaders of Medvara in Medvare-the-city. The Medvaran House had three wings, one for her grandfather Alexran, one for her parents Richenax and Melara, and one that had been her own and her sister's, that would have been for their families.

Zauril's house, now. And only the Gods knew what atrocities he had visited upon it.

As they drag her down the hallway toward the Great Chamber,
writing and kicking and spitting when she can, Alicira hears the
crash of porcelain, glass, and wood breaking. Loud yells as soldiers
rifle through the rooms on either side of the hallway. They shove her
by her father's bloody body, lying over her mother, blood pooling
around them. She screams louder and tries to call on her magic. Before
it can do more than stir, a guard hits her in the face. She blacks out for
a moment. When she rouses, she is trussed so tightly she can't move
her hands or arms from her side. She's on the floor staring at her dead

parents. Someone has kicked Richenax's body off of Melara and she sees that her mother has been partially decapitated.

Another shudder as Alicira dug her fingernails into the windowsill, then leaned her head against it, thumping her forehead slightly against the sill to see if *that* would banish these memories.

They faded, but still lurked as an undercurrent. Alicira swallowed hard and stared at the snow-covered crags to the east, the great open space of the meadowed valley beyond Dera, and the buildings and streets below. The Keldaran Leader's House could fit in one of those vast wings of the house she had grown up in. This house was two stories high with no wings, and just a single Great Chamber that doubled as a dining hall.

And yet the Leader's House dominated the other houses around it. From what she had been learning about her new home over the past few days, big houses were rare in the much colder climate of Keldara. The villages of Wickmasa and Kinherit that they had visited on their way to Dera consisted of mat lodges and longhouses that could be moved easily to winter and summer locations along the river valleys. Dera was the first Keldaran city Alicira had seen with significant permanent buildings.

Different from what she had grown up with. Different styles, a different life. Hadn't that been what she yearned for before Zauril struck?

I was a fool. Young. She blinked back tears. *Revolution is not pretty.*

Thick, deep snow covered what she could see of the city. They had arrived too late last night for her to see much of Dera. Alicira tried to estimate the size and population of the city from what she saw, just as she had learned to do in her studies.

Dera lacked Medvare's easy access to the Great River Chellana that made it a port city and the heart of the nation of

Medvara. But the warehouses that stored trade goods were visible from the Leader's House. Heinmyets had pointed them out last night as they rode into the city. Far off in the valley, she spotted the flocks of sheep and cattle that were part of Keldara's strength. Smoke belched from a foundry and the attached mill that processed iron ore. The Keldara River was strong enough here to power other mills for grinding flour and planing timber.

Alicira pursed her lips, trying to estimate the size of trade, her thoughts falling into a trained, predictable pattern. There had to be enough to support a small army strong enough to protect its own borders. Once Jeinyet had established her rule over Keldara, she had rejected any aid from Medvara and Alexran. Her son Thenil had continued that tradition. Keldara was prosperous in its own way, even if it wasn't as ostentatious as Medvara.

And that would have mattered to Alexran.

Her grandfather scoffed at the small size of Dera, rejecting it as an inadequate capitol city for one of his granddaughters, even the one he despised for her independence.

And yet there was a strength present in the cityscape she surveyed, a wild, magical strength that was greater than Medvara's had been in those last days.

Oh Grandfather. Why couldn't you let me come to Keldara before things fell apart? That might have saved all of us.

Someone knocked at the sitting room door. Alicira turned away from the window, fighting back the worry that suddenly flooded through her.

You have nothing to fear here.

Except Nateri, and she wouldn't come to Heinmyets's suite without being announced. Alicira gulped and took a deep breath, extending her magic to let her see who it was.

A servant. Yamera, the same one who had brought her tea and the biscuit.

"Come in," she said, fighting to keep her voice steady.

Yamera glided into the room. "Your breakfast is acceptable?" she asked, frowning at the barely touched biscuit and the full teacup.

"It's fine, except—is there another tea I could have?"

"That is a fine tea for pregnant women," Yamera said. "You don't like it?"

"I would prefer something else—if you have another one suitable for pregnancy. This one has—unpleasant associations."

Yamera frowned and studied Alicira more closely. "Perhaps a rose hip blend?"

"As long as it doesn't have the same spices as the berry blend," Alicira said.

"I think I can find something different that is also beneficial for pregnancy." Yamera picked up both cup and teapot. "Heinmyets also sends word that he will be back shortly. The audience with his father and Nateri has been set for two bells after midday. He asked me to let you know."

"Thank you for bringing that message, and for changing the tea," Alicira said, her throat tight.

"You're welcome."

Alicira stood by the window until Yamera left the room. Then she returned to her chair and buried her head in her hands, trembling even as Narasin sent reassurance.

You are being silly. You have faced down Gods and Shadowwalkers over the course of the past few days. You resisted Zauril to the best of your ability. You've seen your brother die. Why are you afraid now? You are safe!

Except that wasn't exactly true. Yes, she was now married to Heinmyets and Inharise; the three of them now bound together with vows to their patron God and Goddesses that only the Gods could break. But the marriage had been hasty, presided over by a village headwoman, and without the approval of the Keldaran Council and the Gathering of the nation of Clenda, Inharise's home.

Not that the Gathering of Clenda would be a problem. When Inharise had first bound herself to Heinmyets, their patrons the God Artel and the Goddess Terat had said there needed to be a third partner to make their marriage whole. Clenda would rejoice that the third was Alicira, exile though she was now, and that their Leader-designate Inharise was now firmly established in her position with Heinmyets and Alicira.

But the Keldaran Council would be a different story. *Nateri* would be a different obstacle to encounter, with the grudges she could still be carrying.

Alicira shuddered and raised her head. Why was she so worried about Nateri after all else she had faced over the past seven months? True, if Nateri could accept her presence here it would make her life easier, but Nateri was not powerful enough to cause this dread digging at her. Not powerful enough to dredge up the horrors of her captivity.

At least I didn't have that haunting me during my escape!

Perhaps it was being back in a real city and not the small villages of the nation of Keldara that made the difference in how she felt this morning. Perhaps it was as ordinary wearing a dress again.

She clenched her hands into fists, nails digging into her palms. The fear hadn't dug into her like this while she was fleeing Zauril.

Am I really so worried about Nateri? Or is it something else?

Perhaps it was because she was now in almost the same position that Nateri had been at the court of Medvara eight years ago. Exile. Disgraced. Dependent on the good graces of one who had good reason to dislike her.

I didn't cause my spouse's death, though. Nor did I cause the failure of the Cooscol berry trade.

True, the proof of Nateri's ties to these events was tenuous and contradictory, depending upon which account one listened to.

Flight from Medvara and marriage to Thenil in Keldara had solved most of Nateri's problems. But would the same strategy work for Alicira, even though she hadn't made Nateri's mistakes?

It will simply be unpleasant, nothing more. Having these memories revisit is not an omen of any sort.

And yet the dread persisted. Narasin sent her an image of a skittish and spooky filly, shying at shadows. Alicira chuckled despite herself, and thought about hugging the golden mare's neck.

Yamera returned with a fresh pot of tea, and a plate of cheese and apple slices.

"Inharise suggests you eat this with the biscuit," she said. "And this blend is rose hips and lemon balm. It should not give you trouble."

Alicira lifted the teapot's lid and sniffed the tea. It smelled flavorful and, best of all, it didn't trigger any memories.

"This is very good, thank you," she said.

Yamera set the pot and the plate down on the table, and went to the sideboard to get another cup. "Is there anything else you would need?" she asked.

Alicira shook her head. "I should be all right."

Yamera hesitated. "Inharise said you should eat."

Alicira gave her a quick smile. "Tell her that I have heard her worry and will do so."

She poured herself some tea and nibbled on a cheese slice. At least it didn't have the strong flavor of daranval milk. Milk from the magical breed of horses was supposed to be good for pregnant sorceresses, but by the Goddess's gold necklace, gulping a cup every morning was more than she could face sometimes! Yes, five days of drinking daranval milk every morning had eased the debilitating morning sickness that had plagued her flight from Zauril, but still—

Yamera waited until Alicira had taken a bite from the wrinkled but flavorful apple slices and another morsel of biscuit, then left the room.

Alicira ate slowly, alternating bites of biscuit with bites of cheese and apple, occasionally sipping her tea. Her shakiness settled as she ate.

Inharise entered the sitting room, her long dark braids rippling blue-black in the sunlight as she got a cup from the sideboard. She poured herself some tea, eying Alicira's plate.

"Good. You've eaten."

Alicira put her cup down and leaned back in her chair, closing her eyes as the baby stirred. She placed a hand over her abdomen. "Easy, little one." A bitter taste came into her mouth and she choked it back.

"You're feeling all right?"

"Feeling disconnected and strange," Alicira admitted. "Memories haunting me like in my dreams last night. And worried about this afternoon." She opened her eyes as Inharise knelt beside her, taking both her hands.

"Sister-wife, I promise you. No matter what happens, you have us beside you now. The Gods have spoken. Nateri is not more powerful than Heinmyets, and she bears nothing more than marriage right to Keldara. She cannot exile you. We stand with you."

Alicira tightened her grip on Inharise's hands, noticing how pale hers looked next to Inharise's red-brown—*a legacy of Zauril's bindings?*—and leaned forward to rest her forehead against Inharise's, seeking a brief moment of comfort from her worries.

"Thank you," she whispered. "But I worry, even though Narasin supports me. Nateri is from the Ralsem family, and they betrayed my family years ago, before we crossed the ocean from Daran. Plus—I was not kind to her before my exile. I was a young and arrogant sorceress."

Inharise slipped one hand free and rose, pulling Alicira close in a hug. "Nateri may need to be reminded that you were young. And we stand with you, along with your daranval," she repeated. "But I don't understand. If her family betrayed yours, then how did she come here? I know she was exiled from Medvara, but why was she even allowed into Medvara with that family history?"

"Nateri's parents were betrayed by the Usurper and they fled to Medvara, like my family did, only later," Alicira said, straightening back up. "Her mother became Administrator in Cooscol after she convinced my grandfather that they, too, had been betrayed. When her mother died, Nateri and her husband were elected to replace her."

"I know what happened in Cooscol. That got her exiled, correct?"

"After the details of the destruction of the berry trade came out, yes."

"It will be well," Inharise repeated. She rose to stand behind Alicira, and began to run her fingers through Alicira's loose hair, a touch that soothed even as she straightened out the tangles. "She can't blame you for Alexran's choices, after all."

Alicira drew a deep breath. "As I said, I was fourteen, fully come into my magic and full of the strength and foolhardiness of a young magician." She swallowed hard. "It fell to me to execute my grandfather's orders as the youngest and strongest Miteal sorcerer, an object lesson in the hard choices I would have to make as Leader."

Inharise stroked Alicira's cheek. "That was his decision, not yours."

"Does Nateri still wear green and black bracelets that she never takes off?"

"She does."

"Those bracelets bind what magic she has. I put them on her. At my grandfather's behest, true, but—I was fourteen, and she had said hurtful things about my family." Alicira winced, her memories of Nateri's binding intertwined with what Zauril had done to her. "I did more than I should have. She will have good reason to be angry with me."

The steady stroke of Inharise's fingers through Alicira's hair did not falter. "She can only advise. Thenil and the Council will keep a rein on what she can do."

"Still, I worry."

"No blame for that." Inharise finished combing out Alicira's hair. "Come. It is a sunny day. Let me show you around the grounds and a little bit of the city. Better for you to be doing something rather than brooding. That will make Narasin happier, too. Best for you and I to be seen together, as well."

Alicira let Inharise urge her to her feet, then followed her into the dressing room. Of course, she had to borrow a nicer jacket than the one she had been wearing ever since she had escaped Zauril.

So many things I have to borrow.

So different a life from what she had anticipated just a short year ago.

A CHALLENGE ISSUED

ALICIRA, HEINMYETS, AND INHARISE SAT ON A BENCH OUTSIDE OF the Great Chamber where Thenil and Nateri were finishing their early afternoon meeting with petitioners.

Memory roiled over her once again, her breath quickening.

Sitting shackled on a narrow bench outside the Great Chamber in Medvara. Her grandfather Alexran's decomposing head on a pike, staring at her. Shivering as a guard yanks at her chains, dragging her to her feet. Jeers as she falls to her knees.

"Alicira!" Heinmyets' sharp call brought her back to the here and now.

Narasin's thoughts circled worriedly around hers until Alicira carefully shielded herself with a careful reassurance toward her mare. She hated to do it but Narasin didn't need to be fretting about stupid human emotions. When she had visited Narasin during her walk with Inharise, she had needed to curry off the dried sweat.

She was fretting and sweating this morning, the hostler had said. *Not colic, but something was worrying her.*

Alicira had known, then, that she couldn't keep asking her daranval to relive her own anxieties.

"Sorry. Memories," she gulped.

"It is all right, beloved," Heinmyets continued, projecting thoughts of *safe, comfort.* He pulled Alicira close. "Both of us are with you."

"I am here," Inharise breathed. She pressed tightly against Alicira's other side. Heinmyets reached over as far as his arm could stretch to bring her even closer, his hand resting on Inharise's neck. Inharise slipped her arm behind Alicira, wrapping her hand around Alicira's waist. "The three of us are together, dear. You have us and you have your daranval."

Alicira blinked back tears, remembering how both of them consoled her last night when she had roused, screaming from a nightmare of Zauril. The resonances from that nightmare had been doubled by Narasin's agitation at Alicira's upset. Inharise leaned closer. Her hand slipped up to Alicira's shoulder, squeezing gently.

"Thank you," Alicira murmured, hiding her face in Inharise's shoulder. Heinmyets's hand slipped from Inharise's neck and stroked her cheek. "I'm sorry I'm so weak."

"Weak? After what you have gone through? Dear one, I've known warriors who could not endure what you did," Heinmyets said."

"I'm no warrior," Alicira protested.

"We are all warriors," Inharise said, kissing the top of Alicira's head. Alicira let them hold her like that a few moments longer, drinking in the comfort as the dread slowly drained away. Then she straightened up and their grasp on her eased, though her spouses remained pressed close to her.

"Thank you," she breathed. "It's just—moments. I dread

facing Nateri. I dread her resentment. I dread what she may want to do to us. What if she wants to exile us? Break up our marriage? What if I'm not safe here after all?" Tension tightened her voice again. "And when I worry, I still don't know enough to keep Narasin settled, which means we both fret."

Heinmyets' arm tightened around her waist. *"You are safe,"* he said firmly, emphasizing each word with a gentle squeeze. "We will not let anything dire happen. And you will learn to calm and not worry Narasin. Your bonding to her is yet new."

"Your fears are to be expected after all you have been through," Inharise said. "You keep saying you are no warrior—wrong. You have been battling for a long time, Cira, and now you are safe enough to let yourself think about what you have suffered. I have seen this in our warriors, men and women alike."

"As have I," Heinmyets said. His voice dropped lower. "I understand your worries, dear one. But my father is not Alexran, nor is he like any of those you said Nateri bespelled. And the Council will not hold with exiling any of us. The Gods have witnessed our marriage. The Council has proclaimed me as my father's successor. Unless another candidate for the Leadership comes from outside Keldara, they have no other options."

"Keldara's trade with my homeland has expanded," Inharise added. "Clenda has more grazing than my people can use—and benefits too much from Keldaran herds grazing there in summer —to have any objections to our marriage. Worst case, we simply make our return to Clenda in winter instead of early spring, to let things blow over here. But I do not anticipate it will be that bad."

"Nateri will demand something," Alicira countered weakly.

Inharise stretched her hand between them. A faint blue flame flickered from her palm, then faded. "We should offer to tame Keldara's magic. No one has been able to do that for a long time. My water magic can temporarily tap it but—" she shrugged. "—about as long as that flame."

"The same for my earth magic," Heinmyets said. "My grandmother Jeinyet did it with my grandfather Thenor's help. My mother and father tried after Jeinyet died, but to no avail."

"Why do you think your grandparents succeeded in controlling Keldara's magic?" Talking about a magic strategy calmed Alicira. It was something tangible to think about, to grasp in place of her dire fears. Maybe the unsettled nature of the land's magic was what disturbed her now.

"Jeinyet was of two nations, of Keldara and Clenda. Old Keldara, not of the Aireii that Alexran sent to settle here after the plagues. She was one of the last Tauri survivors in Keldara, and had fled to her kin in Clenda when my grandfather came to the land."

Alicira snorted. "I heard my grandfather often enough on the subject of mixed peoples. He was wrong and imprudent to banish your grandfather and others like him." *And foolish enough to turn down suitors from other peoples for me. Even though Zauril never identified his family, he was Aireii-kin—and that kept Grandfather deluded until the end.* "But wouldn't your father's descent from Jeinyet be enough for you and Inharise to control the land's magic on your own, without me?"

Inharise shook her head. "Something is missing from the mix when we try to spin and weave the magic. I felt that your magic is a part of what we need when we wove magic to stop those Shadowwalkers chasing you. It's not everything required —but it's a large part."

Alicira closed her eyes, taking her spouses' hands as she opened herself to magic. It was a strain to visualize Keldara's magic, but she remembered that night when dire need drove them to weave protection.

There it was—she reached for the magic. Quicksilver-like, it trickled through her fingers, dancing free. She sighed and opened her eyes.

"That's longer than we have been able to grasp it without a great need," Heinmyets said in a low voice.

"Didn't Jeinyet weave a Great Tapestry?" Alicira asked. "Even though the magic within it would have faded upon her death, it would still provide a key to Keldara's magic."

"No," Heinmyets said. "I have never seen anything like that for Keldara. Not like the one your grandfather wove for Medvara."

Alicira swallowed hard, remembering the agony that had spilled over her when Zauril burned Alexran's Tapestry. He had not wanted to risk that she would find some way to access it and challenge his authority. Her hand clamped down tightly on Inharise's, fighting to keep another torrent of memories from pouring over her.

"Gentle, gentle," Inharise murmured, her free hand's fingers working under Alicira's.

"Sorry!" Alicira concentrated on making her hand relax. It seemed so difficult—and then her hand eased. "I just—that might be what is needed. A Great Tapestry to control Keldara's magic, that the three of us spin and weave."

"Would doing that be so bad?" Inharise asked.

"No. But there's more to what I have to face—the further issue of what lies between me and Nateri," Alicira said. "Those bracelets have constrained her magic for eight years. Weaving a Tapestry to make Keldara's magic accessible might not be enough recompense for her."

"She can only go so far," Heinmyets said.

But there are things Nateri can demand of us.

With those bracelets removed, Nateri could insist that Alicira accept the same restraints she had been forced to accept.

"There are many ways she could display her vengeance," Alicira said slowly. "She'd have enough magic with her bracelets removed to snap them on my wrists instead, to lock my magic down for two times eight years. Some would think she would be entitled."

"You can't let that happen to you," Inharise said firmly. "We won't let that happen. What if Zauril disregards his oath to the Gods? You need your magic free and unfettered for that circumstance."

"It wouldn't be the first time someone broke their oaths to the Gods," Alicira muttered.

"Sooner or later they pay for that oathbreaking," Inharise said.

Before Alicira could respond, the doors to the Great Chamber slammed open. They stood as ten people made their way slowly out the doors, chattering.

"*She* is certainly in a mood," one man said. His face lightened as he spotted Heinmyets. "Heinmyets! It is good to see you again." He cast a curious glance at Alicira. "And who is this? She's pale like the Aireii."

"She *is* Aireii, and our new spouse," Heinmyets answered. "May I present Alicira ea Miteal, late of Medvara, who is now wed to Inharise and myself as my First Wife."

That pronouncement made even the stragglers pause and stare. Alicira released Inharise and Heinmyets's hands and stepped forward. She bowed to the group that pressed close.

"I am honored to be in Keldara," she said softly. "Honored to be the spouse of Heinmyets and Inharise. I can only hope that I will do well by the peoples of Keldara and Clenda." She reached for the hand of the man who had spoken. "I am Alicira. And you are—?"

"Yetklet, a sheep farmer of the village of Sassin, in the south end of the Keldaran valley," he said, taking her hand gently and squeezing it. "I am honored to meet you, Lady Alicira." He gave her an appraising gaze. "Medvara, hmm?"

"I am no longer any Lady," Alicira corrected. "But yes, I am from Medvara, and I will want to see your sheep at some time to check your fleeces for magical uses."

"Yetklet produces some of our finest wool," Heinmyets added. "He has some of the sheep that Delian brought from the Medvaran herds last spring."

Delian. Alicira swallowed hard to avoid tears at the mention of her brother. "I see. Then, Yetklet, I will certainly be looking at your herds."

She moved through the crowd, shaking hands and getting names and villages as Heinmyets briefed her. Most of the ten were sheep farmers, like Yetklet from the southern valley. She knew how to talk to shepherds, had grown up talking to shepherds as part of her duties. A couple pressed around Heinmyets and she heard brief mention of border concerns and Saubral incursions. *Saubral.* She shivered at that. It had been a Saubral Shadowwalker, Gegarth, who had killed Delian. Goddess, was that only a few days ago? It seemed like it had been an eternity.

"So this is Alicira ea Miteal." A husky voice as deep as Heinmyets made her turn away from the last shepherd. She immediately saw the resemblance between Heinmyets and this man— who must be his father Thenil.

She knelt in her deepest formal curtsey, nearly sinking to the ground. One knee wobbled and she would have fallen, save for Yetklet quickly steadying her elbow. Inharise and Heinmyets moved to her side, Heinmyets softly breathing thanks to Yetklet as he took Yetklet's place.

Alicira rose. "I am Alicira ea Miteal." She met Thenil's gaze directly, not flinching. Easy to do after those months dealing with Zauril.

Was that a quick smile that twitched his lips? "Come, now. We have things to discuss."

Heinmyets and Inharise slid their arms into hers, part support, part a show of unity. The shepherds moved aside to let the three of them march together toward Thenil. He raised a brow, but stepped aside to hold the doors open, then close them.

The Great Chamber was less imposing than Alicira had expected. It was a quarter of the size of its Medvaran equivalent, which still meant it would take about twenty of her strides to reach the edges, big enough for a dance. Polished benches lined the high walls that were at least two stories tall. Light spilled from around the edges of narrow, shuttered openings near the top of the outside wall. A narrow walkway provided access to those openings. Great ceramic oil lamps with glass chimneys illuminated the room.

No magical tapestries lined the walls to support Thenil and Nateri's magics, not like there had been in Medvara's Great Chamber. Alicira didn't sense any magic in the rugs covering the wood floors.

How do they manage and control the magic to rule in a space like this?

The rugs and tapestries in the Great Chamber of Medvara had been created over the years by her grandfather to support, enhance, and control magic.

It hadn't been enough to stop Zauril. And he had burned every single one of them to cripple Alicira's tie to the land.

Still, the lack of magical rugs and tapestries gave her hope.

This is a task we can offer after all, and it will fulfill a need here that will require my magic to be unrestrained.

Thenil limped past them and only then did Alicira let herself look at the chairs in the front of the room. A row of empty chairs faced the two chairs on the platform against the wall. One of those chairs was empty, and the other—

Nateri smiled a slow sneer that was more sinister than happy. "So. Lady of Miteal. We meet again."

"Lady of Ralsem," Alicira replied, giving Nateri a short bow, less deep than the formal curtsey she had given Thenil.

Nateri looked much older than she should, her black hair

streaked with silver and her face more wrinkled than Alicira would expect from—how old would Nateri be now?

She was thirty-four eight years ago, that would make her—forty-two years old now?

Not much younger than Alicira's deceased parents would have been had they survived Zauril's attack. Both Richenax and Melara had not shown this much silver in their hair or looked this haggard before their deaths. Nateri looked like she was the same age as Alexran had been at his death.

Has the restraint on her magic aged her that much?

Alicira vowed then and there that she would free Nateri.

No sorceress should be forced to endure that.

Her eyes met Nateri's firmly with that resolution. Nateri raised her brows, then nodded.

Alicira didn't know if she was relieved by that response.

I will have to find some way to restrain any retribution she may exact from me when I free her.

She hoped that being cooperative would reduce that likelihood.

Thenil dropped into the chair next to Nateri and gestured toward the chairs in front of him and Nateri. "Sit, sit."

They sat. Alicira reached for Inharise and Heinmyets' hands.

Thenil sighed. "So. Imnari of Wickmasa sent a messenger to tell us that she wed the three of you five days ago. You could not wait to come here for the Council's approval?"

"Very hasty," Nateri added. "Did you not think of the potential consequences?"

"After the Gods spoke to us, we thought it best not to delay," Heinmyets said.

"The Gods!" Nateri scoffed. "A pretty enough excuse—"

"Hush, love! If the Gods speak—" Thenil leaned forward. "Which Gods?"

"I diced with Staul for myself and for my unborn child to be free from Zauril," Alicira said. "Artel was present, as was Dovré.

The verdict went in my favor, and they blessed our union. We decided it was best to follow their wishes as quickly as possible, with the support of those of Wickmasa dedicated to Dovré, Artel, and Staul."

Nateri scowled as Thenil leaned back in his chair, rubbing his chin.

"Shadowwalkers had pursued Alicira and her party within the bounds of Keldara," Heinmyets added. "We consulted with Imnari and felt it best to act quickly for Alicira's protection."

"The three of you wed but not Ciren and Delian?" Thenil asked. "Heinmyets, I would think that your sister would have taken her love as spouse at the same time. Surely the Gods would not have objected?"

"Delian died on the border of Keldara," Alicira said, swallowing hard, remembering once again how her brother had died in her arms, at sunrise, shortly before meeting Heinmyets and Inharise. At least describing it out loud kept her from being immersed in the details as she had been all day. "We were attacked by those Shadowwalkers in alliance with the Goddess Nitel—who bore Zauril."

"We would not leave Alicira unprotected," Inharise said. "Not against *that* Goddess."

Thenil shuddered and Nateri made a warding sign at the mention of the reddest of red Goddesses. "Given those circumstances, I can understand the urgency," he said. "Still. You could not have sent a bird with the message?"

"I did not think delay of any sort was advised," Heinmyets said. "And Alicira spun magic with me and Inharise to protect us from the Shadowwalkers."

Nateri sat straight up, staring at Alicira. "You dared work Medvara's magic *here*? When Alexran exiled me for invoking what bit of Daran remained to me in Cooscol to try to save the bushes?"

"I severed my last tie to Medvara's magic the night Delian

was attacked," Alicira said flatly. She stood up, releasing Inharise and Heinmyets's hands, spreading her own wide. "Not only did I sever my magic from Medvara's, but I banished it so that Zauril can not access it. Only my unborn child can take up the magic of Medvara."

Nateri blanched. "You lie! As tied to Medvara's magic as you must be, you couldn't have done that and remained sane!"

"It was difficult," Alicira conceded. "But my daranval eased the pain of severance, and my bonds with Heinmyets and Inharise replaced my ties to Medvara."

"That can't be," Nateri whispered. "Without bonds to the land a sorcerer or sorceress goes insane." She stared wide-eyed at Alicira. "Especially one with the power you displayed at your age of magical majority." She thrust her wrists toward Alicira, shaking the black and green bracelets on them. "If you had truly banished all ties to Medvara these bracelets would no longer restrain my magic!"

"My personal magic is greater than my ties to Medvara," Alicira retorted. "And even without restraints your power would not be strong enough to tame Keldara! What I have tasted of Keldara's strength is that of a strong and unruly sorcery that needs nuances that you didn't have eight years ago! Your disruptive magic runs counter to what it needs. The Twin Gods are not what this land needs, any more than Medvara will thrive under the rule of one dedicated to Nitel. Dovré linked with Artel and Terat will benefit Keldara and Clenda!"

"Liar! How would you know anything of my magic! Alexran blunted it before you did his bidding!"

"Remember who it was that bound you and how!"

"Enough!" Thenil raised his hand, then rested it on Nateri's. "I understand your upset, dear one, but this is eight years past."

"My lord, she owes me compensation," Nateri insisted, her voice softening. "If she had not restrained my magic the two of us might have been able to spin Keldara's magic—still might be able to do so. We might have stopped the Saubral incursions on the southern herders."

"The three of us may be able to spin and weave Keldara's full magic to achieve the same goal," Heinmyets said, rising to stand with Alicira. "We spun our magics together to stop the Shadowwalkers pursuing Alicira. The Gods have spoken in favor of our union. Father, Alicira's strength compliments both Inharise and me. The three of us together can spin and weave the Two Nations into a unity that I have not felt from any other, including Nateri. Besides, remember Grandmother Jeinyet's prophecy."

"Yes," Thenil said slowly. "My mother did say that a trifold leadership would bring the Two Nations into ascendance to rival Medvara."

"But she is from that cursed line of Miteal," Nateri insisted. "She will bring doom and disaster upon us, her and her ill-gotten child. How do we know she is free of Zauril's influence? What curses does she bring down on us because of Zauril's ill will?"

"*I diced with Staul to win my right to my daughter,*" Alicira hissed. "And Ralsem is a fine one to speak of curses! What family was it that brought about Elithra's downfall and deposed my grandfather from his rightful place as Daran's Emperor? Your family, the Ralsem!"

"The Miteal family had withered and grown corrupt," Nateri retorted.

"As if Ralsem was any better!" Alicira shivered. Parts of the Ralsem family had served Nitel, the Goddess that Zauril was pledged to. "After all, whose magic was it that brought on the Great Plague?"

"Miteal had its part," Nateri said. "And more recently, why is it that so many fled Medvara under Alexran's rule?"

"It was policy. Policy and treaties with Larij and the survivors of Keldara."

Nateri shook her head. "It is a bad thing that the last survivor of Miteal has come here. What curses do you drag behind you, Alicira? What doom do you bring to Keldara?"

"I severed all that!" Alicira snapped. A hope stirred in her. Nateri was not aware that her uncle Alame yet lived in exile. "And another Miteal survivor has made his home as a wanderer in Clenda and Keldara. My uncle Alame still lives."

"Alame!" Nateri spat. "No more than an exile!"

"As am I. And so are you. We are all exiles, and of those of us here, only Inharise can claim non-exile status."

"Playing with words again, Miteal!" Nateri stood, fists clenched, glaring down at Alicira from the platform. "As has always been your wont. What makes you any different from me? Why should Keldara grant you the mercy that Medvara failed to give me?"

"I didn't destroy the Cooscol berry trade and bring about my husband's death through my own magical mistakes!"

"No. But you bear Zauril's child." Nateri closed her eyes for a moment. "It doesn't require much magic for me to see the hooks he still has in you because of her."

"My daughter will be born free of Zauril's taint! The Gods have spoken."

"Enough, ladies," Thenil interjected. "The marriage is done. Whether it was done recklessly or wisely will remain to be seen. I am concerned about our vulnerability to Zauril's powers, as well as the deal Imnari spoke of between Alicira and Zauril with regard to her child. Keldara and Clenda both will need stronger protections."

"We assume responsibility for the tribute to be paid to Zauril until Alicira's child reaches the age of magical majority," Heinmyets said. "That will come from our personal herds, not those of the Two Nations."

"The Red Goddess will be looking for further means to achieve vengeance for her beloved, however," Thenil said. He took Nateri's hand in his. "And then there is the need to make things right with the lady Nateri. I for one am not convinced that what was done there was correct." He fixed Alicira with a sharp gaze. "And it is my understanding that you were the tool of her judgment."

"I acted on the command of my grandfather Alexran," Alicira said. "And I now believe that it is wise to free Nateri. However, I will not do so without protection for myself above and beyond my one living relative, along with a vow from Nateri to release any vengeance."

"Easy enough to regret now that you are the petitioner for mercy," Nateri growled.

"What I did to you then was more than what was required. I plead youth and ignorance."

"An excuse."

"But it is the truth."

"Enough," Thenil repeated. "We gain nothing from this. Alicira. Restoring Nateri to full strength will only benefit us. When will you do it?"

"She deserves a taste of what I have suffered," Nateri muttered.

"As if she hasn't!" Inharise snapped, standing next to Alicira.

"Thank you, Inharise, but let me defend myself." Alicira stepped forward. "Releasing Nateri must be done. I must keep myself safe as well, however. Let me think."

She studied Nateri, drawing on her magic. Eight years ago, Nateri had claimed a commitment to the God Karnoi and his twin sister, Cirdel. But when Alicira had cuffed Nateri, she had seen a shadowy purple-red glow, suggesting that the Goddess Nitel reigned dominant within Nateri, and not Karnoi and Cirdel. In reaction Alicira had called upon her patron Goddess, Dovré, to intensify the power of those bracelets.

The purple of Nitel still simmered under the magenta and bright red shades of Karnoi and Cirdel.

"I would be reluctant to release Nateri without protections for myself," she said slowly. "I still see elements that suggest Zauril could use Nateri willingly or unwillingly to attack me, without penalty from his oath to Staul." She sighed. "I cannot do it, not with what I see."

Thenil rose. Three strides brought him close to Alicira. "Show me."

Alicira hesitated. "I—"

"I will protect you," Heinmyets said, taking her hand.

"As will I." Inharise stood and took Alicira's other hand.

"Then show me," Thenil insisted.

Alicira hesitated.

Inharise mindspoke to her.

We will protect you.

Heinmyets put his hand over both of theirs.

We stand with you.

She looked at Thenil and nodded. He took their joined hands into his, his presence a sudden, jolting fourth to their triad. Alicira looked deep into Nateri's other self, guiding Thenil to where he, too, could see that faint trace of purple in her magical presence.

Then he lifted his hand and stepped back, shaking his head. "There are traces of Medvara in that purple."

"The rot in Medvara began long ago," Alicira said, her voice going harsh. "It is not necessarily Nateri's fault. Things—have been going off for some time."

Nateri grimaced and nodded in an agreement that surprised Alicira. "Disagree though we may in other ways, I concur with the lady Alicira in this. I saw much more of the problems in Cooscol than Alicira would have seen in Medvare."

Their eyes met and for a quick moment Alicira felt kinship with the older woman. As administrator of Cooscol and daughter of the previous administrator, Nateri most likely had gone through much of the same sort of challenges from the older magicians and Court politicians as Alicira had. Alexran had little tolerance for outspoken women, as Alicira had discovered upon returning to Medvare from fostering in Larij.

Perhaps that was Zauril's influence early on.

After all, the Usurper had wormed his way into overthrowing her grandfather from inside, becoming a close advisor and influencing his policies bit by bit over the course of ten years.

"Then what do you suggest?" Thenil scowled. "In spite of the agreements you may have made with the Gods, Keldara still needs to have a defense against Zauril."

Alicira glanced around the room again. "One thing lacking in this chamber is the presence of a Great Tapestry to focus and center the land's magic. You don't even have lesser tapestries or rugs."

"A Great Tapestry," Nateri mused. A mischievous light came into her eyes. "You say that you think the three of you can spin and weave the magic of Keldara?"

"Yes," Alicira said.

"So if there were a Great Tapestry in this chamber, then you would feel safe in releasing my magic?"

"I—suppose." Alicira feigned a hesitation she didn't feel.

A Great Tapestry in return for her freedom and my safety. Good enough, especially since we can weave protections to restrain Nateri into it.

"There we have it." Nateri plopped back down into her chair. "In order to win our approval, Thenil, we should have them spin and weave a Great Tapestry for this chamber incorporating Keldara's magic." A wicked grin twisted her lips. "But it needs to be done quickly. Overnight."

"That's impossible!" Inharise exclaimed.

"Either that or I claim the right to restrain Alicira's magic."

"No one can spin and weave a Great Tapestry that quickly!" Heinmyets objected. "Over several days, yes. But overnight?"

"Nobody?" Nateri's voice turned coy. "Tell me, Lady Alicira. How long did it take Alexran to spin and weave Medvara's Great Tapestry?"

Alicira swallowed hard. "Three days, Lady Nateri. Three days without sleep. You know the tales as well as I do."

I should have thought of this possibly before bringing up the Great Tapestry!

It was true that the lesser weavings could be done easily. She had thought that even if they had been called upon to create a Great Tapestry, however, that they would have more time than this.

A week would be better.

Alexran had been pressed to provide a defense quickly, to protect against an attack he feared would happen the very next day.

"There's three of you instead of just Alexran." Nateri's smile expanded, but didn't spread to the rest of her face. "Might that mean that the three of you working together could create a Great Tapestry for Keldara in one day, instead of the three days it took Alexran?" Her expression reminded Alicira of a snake's just before striking at its prey.

"I—um—I don't know." *Oh Gods, I don't want to commit us to this.* "An ordinary magical tapestry, possibly. A Great Tapestry? I don't know if it is possible."

"Three magicians, bound together to spin and weave. Is there any reason why the three of you shouldn't be able to do this task overnight, if you have adequate control of Keldara's magic?" Thenil asked. "My mother wove only small pieces to control Keldara. A Keldaran Great Tapestry may not need to be large—and doable overnight."

"That's the question. It's not always possible to gain control of a land's magic that quickly," Alicira said. "The Great Tapestries require magic to be produced."

"Alexran did it in three days straight, without sleep," Nateri said. "Or so my mother told me. Don't the Great Tapestries start weaving themselves once the foundations are set?"

"You're bold to be telling me about my own family's magic!"

"Perhaps this is a sign of the degradation of the Miteal."

"Have the Ralsem families ever been able to weave a Great Tapestry?" Alicira snapped, goaded by the coy note in Nateri's voice.

"You know I can't attempt a Great Tapestry with your magical restraints upon me!" Nateri snarled.

"Ladies. *Enough.* We know the stories of Alexran's weaving. I was still a young boy in Medvara before my family came here on Alexran's orders, to assist in rebuilding Keldara after the Great Plague. I *saw* the Great Tapestry after Alexran had created it. I know some of what goes into the making of one." Thenil eyed Heinmyets. "My son. Do you feel you have an understanding of Keldara's magic?"

"Some. It is an elusive and fey thing, not as straightforward as Clenda's magic."

"Lady Inharise. What say you?" Thenil continued.

"I would agree with my spouse. We have tried to work Keldara's magic together before. It needs skills we don't have. After what magic we worked with Alicira before our bonding— I have hopes that she will provide our third to master Keldara's magic. But overnight? I do not know if we can do that."

"Lady Alicira. What impression do you have of Keldara's magic?"

Alicira drew a deep breath and closed her eyes for a moment, allowing her senses to be open to Keldara like she had been with Medvara before severing that link.

Quicksilver. Fast, darting, and flowing. Neither water nor earth, but not quite air either.

Something about the magic reminded Alicira of a wild unbonded daranval, less docile than her own daranval mare Narasin. She visualized a herd of mixed regular horses and daranvelii running free on the great mountain summit prairies.

That would make sense. Daranvelii come from Keldara, so they may be an expression of the land's magic. Remember that.

She opened her eyes. "I would need to handle fleeces and an artifact made using Keldara's magic to be certain."

Thenil nodded. He reached in his pocket for a small woven square. "This was made by my mother Jeinyet. She used it as part of her foreseeing once she became Leader of Keldara in her own right, while the land was still raging from the agony of the Great Plague. It is no longer magically active. The magic faded upon her death."

Alicira took the square from him. The brown and gray wool was soft and well-worn, and carried a feel of Thenil about it as an overlay for the magical foundation that had once supported the magic it had bound. That sorcery was exhausted, completely used up. She pushed deeper, visualizing the foundations for the weaving. What she could trace of the base spell was complex and nuanced, incorporating all four elements of earth, air, fire, and water.

Despite the fact that the weaving was no bigger than her palm, it was clear that much effort had gone into creating the underpinnings of the spellwork that had contained Keldara's complex magic. Once again the image of a mixed herd of horses and daranvelii running free came to her. Alicira thought she spotted a black daranval stallion like Heinmyets' Elantai following the herd, led by two mares, one golden like her Narasin, one brown like Inharise's Rianja.

Is that the key? Visualizing through our daranvelii?

If so, that was different from what her grandfather had done with the Medvaran Tapestry.

Every nation is different. Every land is different. Medvara has its own personality, as does Keldara.

She looked at Thenil. "It will be complex," she said. "It took much work for one person to master this weaving, small as it is." For some reason she didn't feel comfortable sharing her vision of the daranvelii.

"But there are three of you. One of Keldara, one of Clenda, and one of Medvara."

"I am no longer of Medvara," Alicira said. "As yet, I have no land bond."

"You are married to Heinmyets and Inharise," Thenil said. "It is time you formed your new bond to this land—and this may be just the task to do it. Do you accept this challenge? It is either that or surrender your magic, Alicira. We dare not have one of your power—and bearing a child of Zauril's—roving unbonded in this land." Authority resonated through his voice with just enough magic to emphasize that Thenil spoke as the Leader of Keldara.

Alicira let her breath out slowly, bowing her head. Put that way, she had no other options. Thenil was correct. She and her unborn daughter were a risk to the land and to those who ruled it, even though she was bonded to Heinmyets and Inharise. Nothing for it but to agree. She looked at her spouses. Could they do it?

Inharise's mindvoice whispered to Alicira.

I support you and will do my best.

We will not fail,

Heinmyets thought confidently.

Alicira squeezed their hands. "My spouses and I agree. We will have a Great Tapestry ready to present by sundown tomorrow."

Thenil nodded, the sternness fading out of his features. "There is one thing I would ask, if possible. Would you be willing to incorporate some patches like this of my mother's work into your Great Tapestry?" He paused, chewing at his lower lip and glancing down at the small square Alicira still held. His voice was even quieter when he spoke again. "I would honor her memory and summon her protection. Jeinyet was a great Leader and I hope that in some small way we can still invoke her blessings upon Keldara. Our nation would not be what it is without her foundation."

"If—if I could include some tokens for my brother, who had the vision that I belong here," Alicira said.

"His memory honors Keldara," Thenil said. He started to speak but Alicira held up her hand.

"I would also include any others who might want to be a part of this weaving." She looked at Nateri. "That includes you, Lady of Ralsem. It would be easier to incorporate protections for both of us if you and I contributed some small pieces to be pieced or woven into this tapestry. I have a scarf I can contribute, that I wove myself in Medvara. You?"

"A magical weaving?"

Alicira nodded.

Nateri scowled. "You ask much."

"No more than what I myself am willing to give. That scarf is all I have left of Medvara." *And useless other than a source of warmth to me, any more.* "It lacks magic, but it still carries my essence." She touched the scarf at her neck. "Would you care to check it?"

Nateri heaved a heavy sigh and shook her head. "Once magical but no longer active?"

"Yes."

She reluctantly drew a folded kerchief square out of a skirt pocket and extended it to Alicira. "Will this work?"

Alicira handed Jeinyet's square to Heinmyets. Then she took a moment to whisper a protective spell—not to shield herself on initial touch, but to react should the kerchief be tainted. Then she took the small square of white linen with purple and green embroidery on it. A trace of residual magic flared as she touched it, but quickly faded.

Made in Cooscol.

Once it had contained magic, but now it was no more active than Jeinyet's square. She unfolded the square delicately. The embroidery was of Coos berry bushes, and the kerchief was worn, the fabric almost transparent in places. A token, not something for everyday use. She probed deeper. Elements of Daran as well as Medvara lingered in the cloth.

Is that a wise choice?

Given that Daran still remained a threat—perhaps so. She sensed an image of three generations of women—grandmother, Nateri, and a shadowy infant.

A child Nateri lost.

She had not known about that. Alicira glanced at Nateri.

"Are you certain you want us to use this?" she asked. "Those memories are deep and special."

"It has no other use now," Nateri said bitterly. "It was my first working as administrator of Cooscol. That magic faded long ago. And as for the other—it is long gone and best forgotten. My daughter died before I left Cooscol, and I would much rather not remember losing both her and Feyanit."

Alicira nodded. She delicately refolded the square. "I am honored, Lady Nateri. It is a great gift."

Nateri lifted her chin and tightened her lips. "It is lesser than your gift, but it is the best I can do."

"Lesser in size only. It will be a pledge for Ralsem and Miteal to work together peacefully once again," Alicira said.

"If you can weave the tapestry," Nateri said pointedly.

"We can do it," Alicira said.

We have to be able to do it. Dear Goddess, I hope we can tame this magic!

A CHALLENGE ACCEPTED

They returned to their suite in silence. Once safely inside Alicira sank into an overstuffed chair and buried her head in her hands.

"What have I gotten us into?" she moaned.

"It did go better than I expected," Heinmyets said.

Alicira raised her head. "Better than you expected?" Her voice rose in pitch as she continued. "We have to weave and piece a Great Tapestry in a day's time! However are we going to do it? We need a big loom. Fleeces to spin together. Gods help us, we have to master a magic that is quixotic and takes in all four elements—and we are only masters of three of them."

Heinmyets rested a hand on her shoulder. "With the Gods' help we can do this. Listen. You will need to be the binding and uniting force as we meld our magic."

"But without a tie to the land—" Alicira's voice trailed away. She had hoped to gain a connection with Keldara's magic once she had wed Heinmyets and Inharise. She had reached out to the land on her wedding night, expecting it to yield to her touch like Medvara's magic had. Instead, it still resisted her.

"We have time," Heinmyets said. "We need to gather the wool for spinning before we start trying to work any magic. Perhaps we can talk our way through strategies."

Think like a leader of Keldara, not a rejected and usurped leader of Medvara.

"There may be something different that we should do," she said. "When I reached for Keldara's magic at your father's behest, and then again when I examined that working of your grandmother's, I caught images of a mixed herd of horses and daranvelii running free. I hadn't gotten that picture before."

"That's interesting," Inharise said, twining her fingers together and pressing her index fingers against her lips thoughtfully. "I have not seen anything like that when trying to reach for Keldara's magic."

"Nor have I," Heinmyets said. "Do you think we should call upon our daranvelii to aid us in spinning and weaving, Alicira?"

Alicira began to pace the room. Movement helped her think. Daranvelii. A magic-gifted horse breed, with their own internal rankings based on magic strength within herds. Her first experience with daranvelii had come when Delian had brought Narasin as a gift to her from Heinmyets and Inharise to help her escape Zauril. It had not been until they reached Keldara and upon Delian's death—and her severing of her last ties to Medvara's magic—that she and Narasin had fully bonded. Even now she depended on Heinmyets and Inharise to teach her more about how the daranval-human bond worked.

What would happen if they called upon their daranvelii to support their attempt to control and bond with the land's magic? Would they need to draw on the greater links between daranvelii, perhaps call on those linkages to all daranvelii within Keldara?

She stopped and turned to face them. "Daranvelii rank themselves within herds. Do they rank themselves within the land? Heinmyets, I tried to use Narasin to communicate with

Elantai when Delian was injured but couldn't—and I couldn't borrow his daranval, though I was told Delian's daranval could speak to other daranvelii freely across the land. But it would make sense that someone bonded to the land's magic might have that skill—if daranvelii outside of their herd regularly communicate with each other even when not bonded with humans."

"They do rank themselves across Keldara as well as within herds, but—I hadn't thought of that. Not every daranval has that ability, and not every daranval is capable of speaking across the land," Heinmyets said. "Elantai can in theory speak to every other daranval in Keldara at once but I've never tried it with him. I have sensed him speaking to whole herds, though. What are you thinking, Alicira?"

She resumed pacing. "If we could meld our daranvelii's minds like the three of us did with our thoughts when I diced with Staul, and reached out to the daranvelii of the land for their support, that might be sufficient to bind Keldara's magic. Daranvelii are of this land. It is only reasonable that their agreement and support may be needed to control its magic."

Inharise frowned thoughtfully. "That makes sense. I hadn't thought of that before, had you, Myets?"

"I hadn't either. Jeinyet did not share what she did to tame Keldara's magic, and even so, it was a wild thing when I remember her wielding it. She may not have called upon daranvelii."

A knock on the door brought Alicira up short from her pacing. "Who's that?"

"The shepherds have probably gathered what unspun magic wool we have available right now," Heinmyets said. He opened the door.

Zeinyn, one of the shepherds they had met before their meeting with Thenil and Nateri, stood there. "The wool is gathered for your selection. I apologize but it is a small amount. We have had much demand for unspun wool this year."

"If there is enough magic, a small amount will suffice," Alicira said, projecting a confidence she didn't entirely feel. "Perhaps we can add to the Great Tapestry over the years."

"We will inspect the wool shortly, thank you, Zeinyn," Heinmyets said. "We still need a few moments."

Zeinyn nodded and bowed. "We will be waiting for you."

"Thank you," Heinmyets said. Zeinyn left. "So. How do we best proceed? Do we need to set up a special lodge so that we are close to our daranvelii?"

"Closer to the daranvelii may be better," Alicira said. "Anything that will help."

"All right," Inharise said. "I will start the lodge preparation. My people may even have a lodge already erected that we can use. I will have spinning wheels and a loom brought to the lodge when it is ready. Then we can select the wool. Cira, Myets. You plan how we are going to proceed once the wool is chosen. Alicira should rest. It will be a long night."

"We do have books that speak of both Jeinyet's and Alexran's spinning," Heinmyets said thoughtfully. "My grandmother's journals are in the library, and I believe we have a copy of *The Chronicles of Alexran* that Delian brought here years ago. Alicira and I can review them."

"That would be perfect," Alicira said. "My grandfather wrote about preparing to create the Tapestry in the *Chronicles.* I remember reading it early in my magical training."

"Good. I will tell Zeinyn how we are proceeding." Inharise left.

Heinmyets took Alicira into his arms, holding her close. He kissed her forehead. "Ris is right, Cira. You rest while I bring the books. We need you at full strength. Take what respite you can."

"I will," she said back to him.

He squeezed her. "I will bring the books to our bedroom."

Alicira frowned. "I can help carry the books."

He brushed a strand of hair out of her face. "There is no need. You will be bearing the heaviest burden of melding and guiding us. You are the one who will need the most rest."

Reluctantly, she nodded. He kissed her again, then left. Slowly, Alicira headed for the bedroom and plopped down onto the bed that wasn't quite big enough for the three of them.

Deal with the Tapestry first, and then we'll figure out beds!

She lay back and closed her eyes. Sleep came quickly, a slumber filled with images of many horses and daranvelii running together.

Those dreams remained in Alicira's thoughts when Heinmyets woke her. As she sat up, he dropped a small stack of soft leather-bound journals into her lap. She opened the first one to see notations in a careful hand.

"I thought it might be best for you to review my grandmother's journals while I look at *The Chronicles of Alexran,*" Heinmyets said. "Unless you think otherwise?"

Alicira shook her head, scooting herself upright to lean against the headboard. Heinmyets joined her, wrapping his right arm around her shoulder to bring her close as he opened his book. She glanced at his book, recognizing it as one she had studied in her early years of learning magic. She turned back to the first of Jeinyet's journals, settling in against Heinmyets as she began to read.

MEETING THE CHALLENGE

The winter sunset's reflection glowed bright red and gold on the snowy mountains to the east of Dera as Alicira led Narasin down the main street of the city, Heinmyets and Elantai on their left, Inharise and Rianja on their right. Inharise had not said much about the lodge she had prepared for the magical weaving, other than it belonged to a cousin and that it was well away from the Leader's House.

The packed snow under her feet was slick and Alicira had to wrap her fingers tightly in the golden mare's silver mane to help keep her balance. She tried to emulate the flat-footed stride of Heinmyets and Inharise, but occasionally forgot and walked normally for a couple of steps, only to slip again. After the third slip she remembered and did not slip any more, walking slowly in flat-footed, mincing steps.

I wish we could ride.

But they were petitioners to the Gods and Keldara's magic. Conquerors rode. Supplicants were humble, and walked.

As the red and gold brilliance of the sunset faded, cold crept even further around them. Despite the chill, people lined the rough-planked covered boardwalks in front of the main street shops to watch them go by.

"Dovré's blessing upon you!" one woman called out. Other voices picked up her cry and added calls to the other Gods.

"Dovré be with you!"

"Lord Artel walk with you, Heinmyets!"

"Weave well and show the power of the Three! Lady Terat, Lady Dovré, and Lord Artel bless you!"

"For the Three! The Three! The Three!"

The Three kept echoing down the street, people chanting loudly.

"They accept us," Alicira said wonderingly. "But how do they know what we are doing?"

"I'm sure the shepherds have been talking," Heinmyets said calmly.

"My preparations were no secret," Inharise added.

"But acknowledging us as the Three?" Alicira asked.

"It is auspicious," Inharise said. "And well-known that Myets and I could not fully wed until we found our third spouse. Plus —" she smiled at Alicira. "You have made a good impression on the shepherds. I heard talk and received many blessings while my cousin Sosuwis and I were preparing the lodge. Word has gone out—not that there are any secrets in Dera, right, Myets?"

"Not when it comes to something like this," Heinmyets said. "Besides, for many this is their first chance to see the three of us together."

Before Alicira could say more they turned down a narrower street where there were fewer shops and no covered board-walks. The packed snow here was less slick than the main street, with a layer of rough-tracked snow up to her ankles that provided a better footing. The people here stood at the edges of snow-covered yards, fewer in numbers but their chants of *The Three! The Three!* were no less enthusiastic.

Some Clendan lodges, both with board walls and reed mat

walls, were staked amongst the houses, including longhouses like Alicira had seen in Wickmasa and Kinherit. As they passed the corrals mixed in with the houses and lodges, the horses, mules, and daranvelii confined in those enclosures added their nickers and brays to the human chants. Elantai pranced and snorted back at them but the two mares ignored the other equines.

Inharise stopped them at a longhouse with rough-planed plank walls. Smoke poured out of two chimneys in the ridgeline between the support poles. A young woman waited by the longhouse door. She pulled it open as they approached. Bright light poured out from the inside of the longhouse, exuding warmth and welcome. Inharise led Rianja in. Heinmyets stepped back with Elantai to be last, and Alicira tentatively followed Inharise and Rianja inside.

To Alicira's relief Narasin strode into the longhouse without hesitation, her hooves clomping on the rough wooden floor. Three small log pens big enough for the daranvelii to lie down in lined one wall, bedded with straw and wooden water buckets. Alicira put Narasin into the pen Inharise pointed to, and Heinmyets put Elantai in the pen between the two mares. The mares sniffed around their enclosures as Elantai stood alert, watching them. Then Rianja touched noses with Elantai and buried her nose in a pile of hay, followed by Narasin touching noses with Elantai and turning to her own hay. The black stallion heaved a sigh, nosed around his pen, then began to eat his hay.

That settled, Alicira turned to look around the longhouse. Glow lights of a type she recognized from Medvara, magically powered discs contained within a glass bottle, hung from long cables connected to the rafters. Two great iron stoves connected to stone chimneys that rose in the center of the longhouse radiated heat.

A permanent installation, then.

Bags of wool sat between the two stoves, Zeinyn and Yetklet

standing nervously next to them. Three spinning wheels sat amongst the bags and a great loom waited on the far side of the longhouse from the daranval pens. To one side was a small pile of the patches of Jeinyet's weaving to be pieced into the tapestry, also including some pieces from Heinmyets' late mother, Jarleni.

"Is this a good place to work?" Inharise asked Alicira and Heinmyets. She gestured to the young woman who waited calmly by Zeinyn. "My cousin Sosuwis owns this longhouse, but has not been using it this winter. We were going to offer it to Ciren and Delian…." Her voice trailed off.

Alicira bowed politely to Sosuwis. "Thank you so much for the use of your longhouse. It is my regret that it could not be used for its original purpose." She blinked back the tears that suddenly filled her eyes at the thought of Delian.

"I am grateful to be able to offer it," Sosuwis said.

"It is more than acceptable," Heinmyets said. "Sosuwis, you are indeed generous. My thanks as well."

Sosuwis inclined her head. "When I heard what was required, I knew this would be the right place. I am honored that a Keldaran Great Tapestry will be created here." She pointed to the lights. "We traded for these glow lights several seasons ago. They should last until sunset tomorrow without needing a new charge." She frowned. "Will you need me here to keep the fires going and to bring you food and drink?"

Alicira shook her head. "Once we begin working with the magic, it will not be safe inside for anyone but the three of us. It would be best to ensure that we have everything we need available here."

Sosuwis nodded. "Kegs of water are along this wall—" she pointed toward two great kegs opposite the door. "—and the wood is by the door. That should be enough to last until sunset tomorrow. I can bring in bread, jerky, and other food you might need while you are setting up to spin."

"Thank you so much for this work, cousin!" Inharise said. "We are indebted to you."

"I am honored that the Great Tapestry of Keldara will be made in my lodge," Sosuwis said. She hugged Inharise, and then left.

Alicira walked over to the bags of wool. Even before she opened the first one she could feel the magic emanating from it. She reached in to grab a fistful of carded fluff, noticing that it was the long, stiff fibers preferred for tapestry weaving. The wool itself was a mix of gray, brown, and white.

"Stardance breed?" she asked Yetklet and Zeinyn, relieved.

These were some of the best of the Medvaran long fiber sheep breeds, a spotted sheep. Just feeling the fiber brought back pleasant memories of summers spent surveying the Medvaran sheep herds, consulting with the shepherds there about bloodlines and which sheep to keep, which ones to cull. Those memories she welcomed.

"Yes. We had some that came with Jeinyet from Medvara years ago, and then the others arrived last spring," Yetklet said.

"Some of Delian's gift," Heinmyets said.

Alicira nodded, a lump in her throat making it difficult to speak. She went on to the other bags, quick bittersweet reminiscences of past wool checks with Delian and their sister Melaraen welling up as she worked. Unlike earlier in the day, though, the vivid flashbacks seemed to have calmed, so she wasn't vividly reliving those moments like she had been. At last she finished examining the last bag.

"All these are acceptable. Thank you," she said.

Yetklet and Zeinyn visibly relaxed.

"Good weaving, then. We are honored to be a part of this Great Tapestry," Zeinyn said.

"It is *we* who should be honored by your fine wool," Alicira said. "We owe you a blessing. Please give me your hands."

Yetklet and Zeinyn glanced at each other, then stepped

forward to offer their hands, each wrapping both of their hands around Alicira's.

"Blessings be from the Goddess Dovré upon your flocks for this great gift you have provided," she said, closing her eyes to help her recall Alexran's standard blessing upon the herders. "May they increase threefold, and may you prevail against any predators that dare threaten your herds. I say it will be so." As she finished, she felt the warmth of active magic pass from her hands to theirs. Both Zeinyn and Yetklet smiled.

"We are honored with your blessing," Zeinyn said, eyes widening. "I have not felt such a strong one in years. Our blessings to the three of you and your endeavor in return. We are privileged to be a part of this making." He and Yetklet unclasped their hands and bowed to Alicira. Then they left.

Sosuwis bustled in, followed by two men lugging another water keg, and two men carrying loads of wood. She supervised the placement of the wood and the water keg. When the men left, she turned to Alicira, Heinmyets, and Inharise.

"I believe all is ready," she said.

"Cousin, once again I thank and bless you," Inharise said. "May your trades be good!"

"May your weaving be productive," Sosuwis answered. She left, closing the door to leave the three of them with their daranvelii.

Inharise arched a brow at Alicira. "Now what?"

Alicira drew a deep breath. "From what I remember of *The Chronicles of Alexran* and what I've seen in Jeinyet's journals, we need to start by summoning the magic."

Heinmyets nodded. "Alexran spoke of directly contacting the land, addressing it as if it were a person. I've never encountered such a figure when working with Clendan magic."

"Nor have I with the Medvaran magic," Alicira said.

"Myets, that's because you came to the magic of Clenda through me. Cira, you were born to the Medvaran magic and your grandfather wielded it. You may not know Keldara's magic in the same way that Alexran and others coming into the land would have needed to be aware in order to wield it," Inharise said. "When my mother brought me into the Clendan magic, I met Clenda and petitioned for her support. I tried to find such a figure for the Keldaran magic, but—nothing. Keldara eludes me."

"Perhaps that's the meaning of my vision of daranvelii," Alicira said. "Let's start by linking through them. Then Myets, let's use your earth-seeking ability to reach into the land and perhaps find a channel to its spirit." She walked over to Narasin, calling the mare to her with a soft whistle, taking Narasin's head in her hands and leaning her forehead against Narasin's.

NarasinandAlicira,

she thought at the golden mare.

AliciraandNarasin,

Narasin thought back.

Wordlessly, Alicira shared their need. Of her image of daranvelii running freely, then gradually coming under restraint, channeled by human riders but not dominated or controlled. Then she visualized the land of Keldara and the quicksilver, darting magic.

A wordless affirmation came back from Narasin.

Alicira spread her awareness to Heinmyets and Elantai, Inharise and Rianja, then of Keldara's magic. The world around them expanded to include the brightness of *HeinmyetsandElantai* and *InhariseandRianja* as together their consciousness moved into the magical plane, the six now three. Alicira found she was mounted on Narasin in that world of sorcery. She reached her hands out. *HeinmyetsandElantai* and *InhariseandRianja* sidled up next to *AliciraandNarasin.* Alicira seized their magic and braided it together, like she had done a few days earlier. They became a six-fold but single being in this magical plane, under Alicira's guidance.

She had Heinmyets lead them toward Keldara's elusive magic as he delved deep into the earth, searching for a channel like he had done only days ago. The magic danced to the surface, then shimmered into a form. A silver daranval snorted at them, then whirled away. They followed the silver daranval through open fields toward the center of the Keldara Valley, the land shifting from winter to spring to summer to fall to winter again as they gave chase.

Finally, the silver daranval stopped beside a grove of aspen trees, bare and leafless in the winter. Gray and black eldritch sigils marked the white bark of the aspens. Next to the grove was a lake that steamed slightly, iceless even in the sharp winter cold. The daranval turned to face them.

Alicira slid off of Narasin. The sigils carved into the trees glowed bright blue and silver as she passed them. She approached the daranval and bowed to it, aware of Heinmyets and Inharise behind her dropping to their knees. She remained on her feet, however, somehow aware that this was the right thing to do.

She spread her hands wide as she mindspoke.

came back to her, sharp and pointed like the sharpest of crystal shards.

Alicira dropped to her knees in supplication now, stretching her hands out to the silver daranval.

I am no longer of Medvara, or of any land. I seek only the safety and benefit of Keldara, along with my spouses.

You bear a child that is of Medvara. You still carry ties to Medvara.

Yes. But I have renounced my link to Medvara, in her favor. Spirit of Keldara, I seek your blessing and your strength to protect this land. We seek your blessing and your strength to protect us from the shadows over Medvara that threaten to spread even here.

What can you give me?

The silver daranval tossed its head and stomped with its right forefoot.

Alicira bowed lower, remembering Jeinyet's account. Keldara had demanded Jeinyet let Keldara's spirit ride her from that time forward.

I give you myself. Everything but my child. She is not mine to give.

The silver daranval transformed into a dark-haired, brown-skinned woman in silver robes that shimmered as the daranval had. She came to Alicira and raised her to her feet, placing both hands on Alicira's temples in an imitation of what Alicira had done with Narasin.

Cold fire burned within Alicira as Keldara probed her, a jumble of memories good and bad pulsing through her thoughts. The collage of images and past events slowed as

Keldara reviewed the events of the past few days, the pace easing even more as Alicira recalled her wedding. Their first night together. Her joy at realizing the strength and depths of her beloveds on the magical plane, something she had not expected to encounter outside of Medvara or Daran-over-Sea. Her utter commitment to Inharise and Heinmyets after that first night, waking to find their arms twined around her as she lay sandwiched between them.

Keldara stepped back.

I name you Alicira the Outcast. You are now known to me.

And my spouses? Will we be able to wield your magic?

Hmm.

Keldara looked at Heinmyets and Inharise.

You have pursued me before, but without your daranvelii. Why did you not petition me through them? Heinmyets, I would have thought you knew better!

Heinmyets answered her.

We did not know, honorable Keldara.

You demanded my magic of me, Heinmyets, not asked.

My mistake. I beg pardon for the presumption, and join my wish with Alicira for your blessing and the use of your power.

Heinmyets genuflected and placed his palms on the ground.

A hasty mistake, but one that will remedy itself with the aid of your wives.

> I will hope that they will keep me on the correct path,

Heinmyets said.

> Glorious Keldara, I am dedicated to you. I want nothing more than the safety and security of this land.

He raised his head to steadily meet Keldara's gaze.

> This is as it has ever been. My union with Inharise of Clenda and Alicira the Outcast, as you name her, seeks only to keep this land safe for our people. Besides the threat that my Alicira speaks of, I sense a greater need, a menace that may not come in my lifetime but will require us to prepare to stop for the good of our land. I have no desire for greater power than this.

For long moments Heinmyets and Keldara stared at each other. Then she nodded, and stepped forward to take his head in her hands. Brightness glowed around them.

> My lord Heinmyets, when you told Delian of Medvara that his sister could find safety with you and your Inharise, I began to show you my favor in small ways. You have already given all you can give to me, and you are worthy of my blessing. Heinmyets of Keldara, you are now fully known to me.

> Thank you, my lady Keldara. I will do my best not to fail you.

Keldara stepped over to Inharise.

> Inharise of Clenda. You are blessed of my sister Clenda, and she has spoken well of you. But will you give me primacy over her?

> As much as I can, yes,

Inharise answered.

> I must owe allegiance and responsibility to my people in Clenda, however. For me, I would ask that you stand with Clenda in me, to the benefit of both lands. I would see the Two Nations stand strong together, each a support to the other. I will give what I can to you, honorable Keldara, but Clenda is my affinity and my home. Will that be enough? My son will bear the same responsibility as I do to both lands.

Once again, Keldara placed her hands on Inharise's temples. A softer brightness flared around them, and Alicira thought she saw a second figure join Keldara. It faded as Keldara stepped back from Inharise.

> Inharise of Clenda, I see you and know what I can of you. My sister is generous in her gift. I will respect her needs. Alicira the Outcast. Heinmyets of Keldara. Inharise of Clenda. I see much honor in you, even in she who is exiled. Hear my words. I will gift to you my power. May you do well with it. Spin and weave me well!

Then Keldara was gone. They abruptly dropped out of the magical world, leaving the three of them standing by their daranvelii. Alicira stepped back from Narasin, flexing her hands. Days before, when she had cut her last ties to Medvara, there had been a vast emptiness within her that Narasin's presence had only partially banished. Now Keldara's quicksilver presence filled the void where the personification of Medvara had lived.

"I feel it," Inharise said.

"I do as well," Heinmyets said.

Bright joy throbbed through Alicira, filling her with an energy she had not been aware of for over a year. "The land has accepted us! Now let us get to work. We have a tapestry to create!"

Heinmyets chuckled. He reached out his arms to them and brought both Alicira and Inharise close in a great hug. "We will do great things! But for now—let us spin and weave a tapestry!"

"Yes!"

For the first time in ages, contemplating the working of magic felt like pleasure instead of a dreaded dire necessity. The power pulsing through Alicira was enough to make her dance over to the bags of wool. As she picked up the first bag, the intoxicating throb of magic poured over her as she hauled it to a spinning wheel.

Even better, Keldara within her further drove out the haunting memories that had been plaguing her all day.

EXILE'S HONOR

Later that night Keldara's presence was more demanding and less intoxicating. Alicira stood up from the spinning wheel when she finished spinning her final sack, pressing her hands against her lower back as she stretched, to work out the kinks. Sorcery streamed around her while Heinmyets and Inharise continued to spin, the threads coming together faster than they would normally. It was easy to get sucked into the flow, absorbed by the seductive attraction of melding the magic to the thread, until she was finished with a bag of wool. Only then was she aware of her aching back and sore fingers.

But then she would pick up the next sack, and be entranced all over again. Now, though, there was no more wool to spin. Time to begin the weaving while Inharise pieced together the small tokens to be included in the tapestry. Alicira fingered the thread. Magic simmered there—but she felt as if something was still lacking.

Heinmyets had already set up the loom. Alicira eyed it, then tottered over to the water keg. She drank deeply, then turned back to the loom. The threads had broken on the loom again. She sighed, and began to unstring it. They could keep the magic strands together while spinning, but they went dead once placed on the loom.

An unbinding spell?

But all three of them had probed the loom after the first stringing had popped too many threads. There was no reason for it to resist their magic.

Three times we've strung it and all three of us have tried and failed. Now what?

Narasin stomped and Alicira looked over at her. The golden mare tossed her head impatiently and nickered low. Elantai added a sharp short bellow, pawing at the floor. Alicira looked back at the loom and the now-tangled and broken threads.

Quick flash of the image of daranvelii and Keldara dancing together in the moonlight.

Alicira piled the broken threads from the loom by her wheel. She went over to the daranvelii and slipped into Narasin's pen. The golden mare shoved Alicira with her head, swishing her long silvery tail—*her tail.* Alicira grasped the end of the tail when Narasin lashed her with it. Magic stirred within those hairs.

"May I?" she asked Narasin. The mare swung her haunches closer to Alicira and stood still. Alicira gently combed through the tail with her fingers, easing long strands loose and pulling a few hairs free at a time. When she had several handfuls from both mane and tail, Narasin snorted and pushed Alicira toward Elantai.

Alicira bowed to the big stallion. He nuzzled her, then gracefully presented her with his rump. She collected another fistful from his tail and a third from his long, curly mane, longer than either Narasin's or Rianja's. After she collected more hair from Rianja, she went over to the water, cleaned her gatherings, then returned to her wheel. She picked up the broken strings and placed them in her lap, then whispered an unbinding spell as she ran her fingers through the threads. Then she began to spin thread again, this time feeding strands of daranval mane and tail hair along with the wool.

At first it was clumpy and awkward. Alicira stopped several times to redo her spinning. She closed her eyes and thought of Narasin. The mare's awareness joined hers, an air of impatience from Narasin as she projected herding the strands as if they were fractious cattle. The spinning smoothed out.

When she was done, she brought this thread to the loom and began to restring it.

This time the strings held.

Heinmyets joined her. He sat at the loom while she worked the shuttle. Once again, magic enthralled Alicira, and she was conscious of nothing more than the weaving, occasionally changing places with Heinmyets. Inharise pieced together the patches to be worked into the tapestry.

Once the tapestry was woven, Inharise brought over her piecework. The three of them worked together to stitch it to the main part of the weaving. Finally, they were ready to whisper the spells that would make images appear on the tapestry in lieu of dyed wool. Alicira traced in protections for herself against both Zauril and Nateri.

And then it was done. Inharise and Heinmyets carefully carried the tapestry over to show the daranvelii. In turn each daranval sniffed of it, then stepped back, Rianja and Narasin nickering soft approval while Elantai trumpeted his agreement.

Only then did Alicira let herself touch the work and marvel at the images their magic had created. The silver daranval they had seen in their vision pranced in an open meadow in front of a gathering of horses and daranvelii, humans standing behind the herd. If she looked closely at it, it almost seemed as if the silver daranval danced upon the weaving. It was not as big as the Great Tapestry of Medvara had been, but she felt as if as much power, if not more, radiated from it. As she watched, the seasons seemed to shift until they settled upon winter.

"We should consecrate it," she said. "Not just in the name of our dedicated Gods, but the Seven Crowned Gods."

"I agree. According to the *Chronicles,* Alexran only blessed the Medvaran tapestry in the name of Artel and Dovré," Heinmyets said. "If we dedicate it in the name of all Seven, even though we represent three, then that might appease Nitel at the least."

"And ask the daranvelii to join with us as well," Inharise suggested.

"Good." Alicira watched as Inharise and Heinmyets hung the tapestry on the wall. Then she went over to Narasin. The golden mare nuzzled Alicira and she rested her hand on Narasin's neck.

"Let's let them out," Inharise suggested. "That way we can all remain in contact. It has been a long night and day's worth of work, and it will make our linking easier."

"That sounds good."

It took a moment to line up daranvelii and humans in front of the tapestry, shoulder to shoulder with the daranvelii's heads resting on their bonded humans. Alicira took a deep breath, and then began a chant to summon Dovré. The daranvelii responded to her call with soft whickers, as befitted those beloved of the Goddess. Heinmyets chimed in with the counterpoint for Artel. Lastly, Inharise's contralto called upon Terat and balanced Alicira and Heinmyets's voices.

When their joining in sorcery was steady once again and the daranvelii blended into the magical meld, Alicira then began the general invocation, through Dovré summoning first Staul the Balancer, then the trickster Twin Gods Karnoi and Cirdel. Lastly, and not without reluctance, she called upon Nitel. That Goddess grumbled, and Alicira shivered as Nitel's reddish-purple malevolence joined the devious green and brown synthesis of Karnoi and Cirdel, holding back slightly but still part of the mix.

Heinmyets led the next phase. "In the name of the Leaders of Keldara, I dedicate this Great Tapestry as a safeguard and a blessing upon the land of Keldara. I petition you, oh Gods and Goddesses, to look upon this creation with favor."

Alicira swallowed. As Heinmyets's First Wife, it fell to her to call upon the Gods next. But how to identify herself to them when she was no longer of Medvara?

Something that felt like the magic of Keldara stirred within her.

I know you and have named you, Alicira the Outcast, Alicira the Exile.

Then she knew what to do.

"By my honor as Alicira the Exile, Alicira the Outcast, I dedicate this Great Tapestry as a safeguard and a blessing upon the land of Keldara. I petition you, oh Gods and Goddesses, to look upon this creation with favor."

Keldara touched her yet again, approvingly.

"In the name of the Leaders of Clenda, I dedicate this Great Tapestry as a safeguard and a blessing upon the land of Keldara," Inharise repeated. "I petition you, oh Gods and Goddesses, to look upon this creation with favor."

As Inharise finished speaking, thunder pulsed through Alicira's body, vibrating deep inside of her. She trembled as the power reached beyond her to descend upon Inharise and Heinmyets. A form of Artel, the leader of the Seven Crowned Gods, shimmered before them.

"We have heard your petition, Heinmyets, Alicira, and Inharise. We grant our blessing upon this creation. You have done well."

And then the gods were gone. The Tapestry glowed with a brighter light. Alicira leaned against Narasin, only now beginning to feel her aches and pains and a dragging heaviness in her arms in legs. But they were not done yet, not until the tapestry was presented to Thenil and Nateri.

And I need to remove her bracelets.

She groaned at the thought of the work still ahead of her.

Inharise shot her a sharp glance. "We will take the tapestry down and carry it. Alicira, you ride Narasin and lead us to the Hall."

"All right."

"I'll give you a leg up," Heinmyets said. He popped her up onto Narasin's back, then he and Inharise took down the tapestry and rolled it up. Inharise threw the door open. To Alicira's surprise it was light, almost dusk.

We wove the whole day?

The sounds of Dera suddenly crashed in on her. Somewhere the bells tolled three in the afternoon. The sun hung low over the western mountains, but not quite descended. She urged Narasin out the door, followed first by Heinmyets and Inharise carrying the rolled tapestry between them, then Elantai and Rianja. Sosuwis rose from a bench sitting next to a bonfire that burned in a stone pit next to the longhouse.

"Have you succeeded?" she asked Alicira.

Alicira nodded.

Sosuwis began a loud, piercing, ululating cry. She ran down the street, calling, "The Three have succeeded! The Three have succeeded! Keldara now possesses a Great Tapestry!"

As Alicira rode along, she heard others take up Sosuwis's chant. Before long a crowd had gathered around them, until they reached the Leader's House.

Thenil and Nateri stood on the steps to receive them.

"Your task is fulfilled?" he asked when they had stopped.

Alicira gestured to Heinmyets and Inharise. They handed her the top of the Tapestry as she sat on Narasin. She held the Tapestry while they unrolled it, first to show to Thenil and

Nateri. Then she used her legs to move Narasin into a slow and careful turn toward those who had gathered to watch, to show them as well.

Soft cries of approval echoed from around them as she turned Narasin and the Tapestry back toward Thenil and Nateri.

"You have done well," Thenil said.

Nateri reached out to touch the Tapestry's silver daranval. "Ouch! It rejects me!"

"No, no," Alicira hastened to reassure her. "Only because of the bracelets. Once I remove the bracelets, you can touch it freely."

"Of course," Nateri grumbled. "And why a silver daranval? Why do I see the three of you and Thenil but not me?"

"You are right there," Alicira said, pointing out the section where Nateri stood amongst a throng of others.

"Not my best image," Nateri snorted.

Alicira fought back the temptation to roll her eyes. "Things will look better once your bracelets are off. That keeps you separated from the magic."

"Trust her, dear," Thenil said. "I assure you, *I* see you standing next to me, along with Jarleni. All is well."

"If you say so," Nateri sighed. Still she reached out delicately one more time, brushing the back of a finger across the patch of Coos berry bushes off to the side. Her touch lingered on the bushes. "Could this mean that we might be able to cultivate the Coos berry here?"

"I don't know," Alicira said. "We could try."

Nateri chewed her lip. "We may want to let the magic mature. But if we could find a means to grow Coos berries here through your role in spinning this tapestry, then—that alone atones for what you did." She stepped back. "I suppose I approve of it, especially since you do, Thenil."

"Good." Slowly, Heinmyets and Inharise rerolled the tapestry. "Shall we mount it now?" he asked.

Thenil and Nateri exchanged glances. "We should wait until tomorrow," Thenil said. "You have worked hard, and this feat is worthy of a feast. Keep it with you, and we will put it up with all proper ceremony tomorrow."

Alicira slipped off of Narasin. "I believe there is a further task I am bound to do by my honor," she said. "I promised to remove the restraints on Nateri's magic. I will do so now."

But as she took her first step, she faltered. Her knees gave out as fatigue crashed over her. Alicira shook her head, and tried to push herself up.

So tired. So heavy.

Narasin squealed and pressed close, nuzzling Alicira's back.

Before Heinmyets or Inharise could reach her, Nateri took Alicira's arms and guided her up. To Alicira's surprise, Narasin did not challenge her but stepped back.

"I have lived with this for eight years, I can wait another day," she said dryly. "I am not so impatient or so vicious as to ask you to do this when you have given so much of yourself to such a great work."

"Thank you," Alicira breathed. Their eyes met.

"Perhaps Ralsem and Miteal can find the peace here in exile that we could never find in Medvara or Daran," Nateri said.

"It is a new land and a new start."

"Exile's honor for both of us."

As Heinmyets took their daranvelii to the stables and Inharise guided Alicira toward their suite, Alicira mused upon Nateri's words.

Exile's honor, indeed.

And that part of herself that had still clung to the tiniest part of dread released itself. Perhaps two exiles could work together to make this land a home for both, after all.

We both want to defeat what Medvara has become. We both want to keep the Two Nations free from that taint.

Nateri's question about the Coos berry bushes already had her considering that prospect.

If we manage to grow Coos berry once again—what else could we do here?

She shivered at the thought of that potential.

Take that, Zauril! The exile and outcast you abused and scorned will someday bring about your demise.

She placed her hand on the gentle swell of her belly. She could not bring about her revenge through her own actions— her vows to the Gods constrained her from directly taking vengeance, in exchange for him to leave her alone.

But their child had taken no such vow, nor had she taken such an oath in her unborn daughter's name. Exile's honor did not go that far.

Keldara the Land of Exiles will yet be your undoing, Zauril. And I can only hope that I will survive to see it happen.

THE END

BIRTH OF SORROW

BIRTH OF SORROW

It could be forgivable for an observer to assume that the shimmering of the air over the high mountain ridge's grassy, flat top was nothing more than early summer's heat.

It could be—except for the edgy silence that accompanied the flickering air as the midafternoon sun beat down on the broad, flat expanse. No crickets droned, no hawks screamed. Even the camp of Keldaran and Clendan kinfolk summering on the high ridge lay mute; no children running, the camp herds clustered together, adults doing only what was urgent. Otherwise, they, too, watched as magic spread out from the large mat lodge belonging to their leaders, Heinmyets of Keldara, Inharise of Clenda, and Alicira the Outcast.

The long shriek of a woman in childbirth echoed through the camp. The air on the open flat quavered stronger than ever and the strong, thrumming vibration that announced a God's impending arrival rolled over the ridge in response to the cry. Another scream burst from the lodge, followed by sobbing gasps for air. Magic thickened around the camp, its heavy hand spreading fear even among the adults so that they signed protections for themselves and their children.

Orlanden en Selail's fingers itched to pull his short horn bow out of its case as he stood head of the guard around the Leaders' lodge. He was no stranger to powerful magic, but this high sorcery of the Seven Crowned Gods made his skin prickle, as if Saubral desert scorpions were crawling all over him. His normal response to this sensation would be to prepare for a battle.

But not this time. Not when a sorceress of the Miteal gave birth to another sorceress of equal or greater potential power. Alicira the Outcast, exiled though she might be, still carried significant magical power that she had needed to put away during the last part of her pregnancy. Now, with the impending birth of this child, Alicira's magic rebounded with renewed strength to protect her against the uncontrolled fledging power her daughter would wield in her first breaths.

What was the old saying?

When sorceress gives birth to sorceress, the Gods themselves may tremble.

Given that the sire of this girl was none other than Zauril the Usurper, cause of Alicira's exile and a strong and powerful magician with aspirations to join the Seven's pantheon by over-throwing one of them, there was no doubt in Orlanden's mind that the Gods were trembling. No doubt that at least one of the Gods, if not all of them, would come to witness this child's birth.

He wished he wasn't here. That he was back home in Larij's capital Leithra with his lover Haran, youngest son of the Mershaunten, Larij's ruler. But the Mershaunten had exiled Orlanden precisely because of that relationship with Haran. And Haran had sent Orlanden to help protect Alicira in her flight from Zauril, thanks to the fostering ties Alicira and Haran had from their youth. Orlanden had sworn an oath to protect Alicira—and gods or no gods, magic or no magic, he would not go back on it.

Alicira screamed again. The magic pounding down on the camp weighed even more oppressively.

Orlanden swallowed hard. He had witnessed the chip throw that won Alicira free from Zauril. Then, three Gods plus Zauril riding the bodies of their servants had been present.

What he felt now was stronger than the *presence* of those three had been then— Artel, Dovré and Staul. How many more Gods coming that meant he did not know. The thought of being near Nitel, Karnoi, Cirdel, or even gentle Terat made Orlanden tremble.

Then again, before, the Gods had attended through their mouthpieces.

This time, with this ominous birth, the three Gods who had participated in Alicira's deal with Zauril might well choose to attend in their own selves rather than through intermediaries.

Gods above, he hoped that was all this heavy feeling meant.

Meanwhile, Orlanden swallowed again to lubricate his dry throat.

Gods above, he wanted to be with his beloved Haran and not here.

ALICIRA GROANED as another wave of contractions tightened her body. She clutched to the birthing pole with both hands and leaned her head against it, screaming as it seemed that every muscle in her body tightened beyond tight.

We are here.

Her sister-wife Inharise supported her left side, murmuring reassurance and sending soothing thoughts as she rubbed Alicira's back, pushing down her spine with a muscular fist.

We are here.

Their husband Heinmyets supported Alicira's right side, mirroring Inharise's actions.

The contraction released her. Alicira sprawled against the birthing stick, Heinmyets, and Inharise all at once, gasping for breath. She stared out the open lodge door. At least one God if not two or more waited for this child to be born from the way magic roiled outside the lodge. She just wished she could see some sort of sigil, some indication as to which God this child would favor. But the magic vibrating in the grassland kept its own secrets, the Gods clearly waiting until the child's arrival before revealing themselves.

By Dovré's golden necklace, I hope Nitel isn't one of them!

Zauril claimed that Goddess as his patron, using her to fuel the reddest of his red magics.

"Getting there," Siljaren the Healer said. "Just a few more pushes. Next one should be the head. She's not eager to join the world just yet. Stubborn little thing."

Alicira tried to laugh but choked. Heinmyets wiped her forehead and Inharise gave Alicira a damp cloth dipped in honey water to suck on.

Then another contraction tightened Alicira's body. This one seemed to go on forever, dropping Alicira to one knee as Siljaren followed her down. But things were moving, things were moving—she could feel her daughter pushing out as Siljaren reached to ease the little one's way into the world.

The child screamed, her first vocalization ripe with a power that stirred the unknown Gods lingering just beyond the boundaries between worlds. Alicira pushed with another contraction. Power flooded through her, the like of which she hadn't felt for months. She matched her daughter's cries, binding and shielding that untrained power from those who would prey on it.

Another push, and the baby's cries grew even more stronger, this time free of magic.

"She's here," Siljaren breathed.

Alicira collapsed against Heinmyets's thigh as he stroked her cheek. She grunted as another contraction squeezed through her. The afterbirth. Both Inharise and Siljaren had told her about this. Supposedly the afterbirth would tell them what god this child favored.

Supposedly.

Heinmyets sat on the ground after this contraction, propping Alicira's head up on his legs as Siljaren placed the baby on her stomach. Alicira caressed her daughter's small head, afraid to look at her until she'd had a chance to study the afterbirth. What if Zauril stared back at her from this baby's eyes? What God dominated this child's magic? She had worried about this moment for months now.

One more contraction.

"That's it," Siljaren said, relief filling her voice. "The afterbirth."

Alicira struggled to sit up. Inharise took the baby and handed her to Siljaren as Heinmyets helped Alicira sit.

"Are you ready?" he asked.

She nodded. Together, he and Inharise cut the cord, and Alicira whispered a spell to contain the magic glimmering in the afterbirth. Then she picked it up. The trapped power within the spell containing the afterbirth shimmered smoky red and gray with shots of blue swirling in it.

Red. Nitel's color. But blue for Dovré as well, and the gray— Staul?

Inharise held out the juniper bentwood box the three of them had crafted for the afterbirth. Alicira eased it in and Heinmyets secured the lid.

As he put the box down, Siljaren handed her daughter back

to Alicira. Then, and only then, did Alicira look at her daughter, dread tightening her heart.

Three gods showed influence in that afterbirth. What did this mean for her child? Which God would she claim for her power? She stared down at the tiny face to try to make sense of this outcome, the baby's blue eyes staring back at her with a sharper focus than one would expect from a newborn. Her daughter had the black hair of her grandfather and great-grand-father, not Zauril's brown or Alicira's silver-streaked gold. A silvery splash that looked as if someone had carelessly run a paintbrush through her hair ran thick from her forehead, thin-ning until it trailed out into black at the back of her head.

Alicira shivered. Legend told of this mark at birth, the sign of a powerful sorcerer or sorceress. She unsuccessfully tried to push away the uneasiness rising higher in her, focusing instead on learning her daughter's face. Those brows did not look like any Alicira recognized from her family, nor did that snub nose. But the lips, the eyes, the high forehead and high cheekbones—those features marked this child as unmistakably of the house of Miteal.

My daughter. My heir. The future of Miteal.

"Welcome to the world, my daughter," she whispered. "I name you as my daughter, potential heiress of Medvara and rightful heiress to that land's magic."

"Yes. Welcome." Heinmyets placed his hand over the girl's tiny head. "I name you as daughter of my heart, if not by my blood, and extend the protection of Keldara over you, little one. I claim the title of Heartfather."

Alicira smiled quickly at him.

Inharise rested her hand on the girl's chest. "I name you as daughter of my heart, and welcome and claim you as your Secondmother. I extend the protection of Clenda over you."

"Thank you." Alicira kissed her daughter's forehead. "Wel-come, little one," she repeated.

"Have you decided on a name?" Inharise asked.

Alicira shook her head as she held her daughter to her breast. "I couldn't think of a good name from my lineage. And with the Gods here…" she hesitated as the baby's lips fumbled around her left nipple. Then she latched on and began to suck.

"She's strong and nursing early. Good. As for the name, it's wise to wait until the Gods have had their say," Siljaren said. "You wouldn't want a mismatch between her name and any fate they might want to gift her with."

"Three Gods, at least. What does that mean for this little one? What kind of fate awaits her?" Alicira bit her lip. "And the power's thick out there." She heaved a sigh. "I had hoped they'd let us be to rest and eat but from the way things feel, the sooner we hear them, the better. I'd like to feed her first."

"Feed her, clean both of you up," Inharise said. "Then we'll meet the Gods." She fixed Heinmyets with a stern glare. "One of us has to make the announcement and let the Gods know they need to wait. Best it be you."

Heinmyets pursed his lips thoughtfully. "As Heartfather, I suppose that task falls to me. You don't worry that they'll strike me down in their wrath at the delay?" A small smile quirked the right corner of his mouth.

"They can wait," Alicira said. "By Dovré's tits—ouch!" She winced as the child fumbled the nipple, then bit down.

"Aggressive little girl." Siljaren set a wide wooden bowl half-filled with water down next to Alicira. "Let's get you cleaned up."

"Go," Inharise shooed Heinmyets. "Artel loves you and even Staul the Destroyer won't dare do you harm because his brother loves you so. Besides, you are but Heartfather relaying the mother's wishes."

"True enough," Heinmyets conceded. "Though if Nitel is one of the gods out there, that could mean trouble."

"If you're worried, take my uncle with you," Alicira said. "He has studied with Terani the God Killer. Nitel will respect that."

"Besides, he'll be the first to want details." Heinmyets's smile widened. He kissed Alicira's forehead and then the child's head. "I'll go tell the Gods they need to wait." He chuckled. "Only you would have the courage to tell the gods to wait upon you, First Wife."

Alicira snorted. The child fumbled more at Alicira's left nipple and she switched her daughter to her right side.

"They certainly made me wait long enough before they came to my aid in Zauril's prison," she retorted. "So they can wait to see my daughter until I'm ready to meet with them."

Heinmyets laughed outright. He kissed the top of Alicira's head and left the lodge.

Alicira looked down at her daughter. Despite her brave words, fear pulsed through her.

The Gods had a purpose for this child, and she dreaded what it might be.

IT HURT Orlanden's eyes to look toward the flat. The air rippled with as much energy as the rough rapids of the Kitskan River deep in its impassible gorge, and the pressure from the Gods waiting pounded through him harder than ever. No more cries came from the lodge; only the soft sounds of people talking.

The child must be born.

Heinmyets emerged from the lodge. Alicira's uncle Alame, returned just this morning from a supply run to Wickmasa village, stepped forward from his post near the doorway, a strained look on his face.

"Is all well?"

Heinmyets clapped Alame on the back. "The babe has arrived. She and Alicira are well. Now I need your help. I am to tell the Gods that they need to wait to view the child and make their pronouncements until the baby is fed and she and Alicira are cleaned up." He made a face. "I need you to come with me for moral support, lest they take out their impatience on me."

"They won't take it well."

"Which is why I need your support." Heinmyets turned serious. "Formal presentation might be best when Alicira and the babe come forth to meet with the Gods. After we speak with them, I need to prepare my people so that we can show our support of Alicira." He glanced over to Orlanden. "If you could have them gather at the Council Fire?"

Orlanden nodded, and moved away from the Leaders' lodge, glad to have something active to do.

THE MAGIC still weighed heavily on the camp by the time Heinmyets and Alame joined the gathering at the stone ring where the Council Fire burned on cool nights. Uncharacteristically, even the pack of young children that normally raced throughout camp sat quietly with their families, waiting. Orlanden noticed that the pale shadows lightened Heinmyets's dark skin while Alame's face appeared more lined than ever.

Heinmyets joined Orlanden at the large rock that served as the Leaders' speaking stone. He bowed to the gathering, then placed his hand on the waist-high rock. His lips moved soundlessly as he bowed to the rock, whispering acknowledgement to the power it conveyed to him. The small twinges that spoke of great magic vibrated through Orlanden. Then Heinmyets straightened and turned back to his people.

"My people. The Lady Alicira has given birth to a healthy daughter."

The crowd's cheers were muted, some members casting worried glances toward the meadow where the Gods awaited.

Orlanden schooled himself to remain quiet, impassive, not reacting even though he had been present at enough portentous births during his time at both the Larijian and the Medvaran courts to know that this much divine presence did not bode well.

What fate does this girl bear?

Once this meeting was done, he would beg the use of a messenger bird from Otoken, the manager of the messenger flocks. Sending a message to Haran was risky given his own exile from Larij, but he hoped the Mershaunten would understand and not begrudge him this small communication. Haran was closer now than he had been since Orlanden and Alicira had come to Keldara. His father the Mershaunten had sent Haran to manage the Larijian resort of Wixtnal, just over the Keldaran border. Haran had not sent a message to Orlanden directly, but one of Alame's excursions a month ago brought back the news of the change in Wixtnal's management.

The news about Alicira's daughter is gossip that Haran can pass on and perhaps help enhance his stature in the Court.

Everyone knew that Haran and Alicira had been fosterlings. It would only be expected for Orlanden to pass on the news of this birth himself to Haran.

I ask you to be my eyes and ears around Alicira, Haran had said during their last sad hours together. *My father is a fool not to seize this opportunity to gain Alicira's power and favor as well as whatever sorcery her child will carry. But Larij's loss is Keldara and Clenda's gain.*

He made himself pay attention again.

Heinmyets continued. "She will present her daughter to the Gods soon. We expect this presentation to be—difficult. There were at least four Gods waiting when Alame and I spoke to them, and there may be more coming."

Four out of the Seven.

Heinmyets scanned the group, nodding to himself. "I would ask a favor of you in her name."

"Ask!" most of the group answered.

"Find your best celebration attire available in this camp. Dance her to the meeting with the Gods. Let us show the Gods that we support the lady Alicira and honor her child. Let them know she is not alone. Will you do this?"

Calls of "yes," "of course," "But I don't have my best outfit here in summer camp!" answered him.

"How many Gods await her?" one woman asked. Orlanden recognized the woman as Kenarjé, head of one of the Keldaran families.

Heinmyets swallowed hard. "At least four," he said quietly. "Dovré, of course."

Some of the crowd nodded. The Goddess Dovré was Alicira's patron.

"Staul," Heinmyets continued. "Artel, and—Nitel."

The crowd murmured at the mention of that last goddess.

"What does the Red Goddess want with our lady Alicira?" one young Clendan girl, Tekasné, wondered.

"Didn't Terani the God Killer banish Nitel?" asked one of the men.

"The child's sire is dedicated to Nitel, and Terani's actions only banished Nitel from Waykemin, not the rest of the world. She still is here, though weaker," Heinmyets said flatly. "She would have an interest and a presence because of her connection to that sire, even if she were banished here."

"Well, we'll see that the Red Goddess doesn't touch our lady or her daughter!" Tekasné's grandmother Weticasu, head of the camp's Woman's Council, retorted. She rose. "The lady Nitel does not belong in either Clenda or Keldara. Come." She gestured to those around her. "We will show that reddest of red goddesses that she is not welcome. Let's get our finery together;

such as it is here in summer camp. We will support our lady and her daughter! My lord Heinmyets, the Woman's Council will be at your lodge as soon as possible." She turned and marched away from the fire circle.

Her movement galvanized the others into action, the people hurrying off to their various lodges.

Heinmyets heaved a relieved sigh. "Perhaps it will be enough," he said out loud to no one in particular. "Nitel is quite insistent."

Alame rested his left hand on Heinmyets's shoulder. "I would not bet against either of your wives in this matter. Or you either." He glanced at Orlanden. "Watch well and report to Haran after. I've had no time to share this news with you yet, but the latest word from Larij is that the Mershaunten is in poor health."

"I will report to Haran," Orlanden said. He schooled himself not to hope too much. Who knew how Haran's eldest brother would react once he ascended to the title of Mershaunten?

"I wish we had more of us with magic to speak for the gods, however," Heinmyets fretted. "The summer camp is light on sorcerers this year." He tapped his fingers on the great stone.

"We have you and me for Artel, Alicira and Siljaren for Dovré, and Inharise for Terat," Alame reminded Heinmyets. "And then there's the Woman's Council."

"True, true," Heinmyets acknowledged. "The ladies of the Council will support Alicira and Inharise as far as possible. Weticasu lacks magic herself, but together with the Council she is still a force that even the Gods must reckon with." He straightened. "Let us prepare for this meeting with the Gods. I can feel Alicira's nervousness even here. Time for me to be with her." He strode toward the lodge.

Orlanden followed, Alame at his shoulder. He burned to ask questions about the rumors of the Mershaunten's declining health, but bit them back. Now was not the time.

No more delays.

Alicira used the birthing stick to rise to her feet, shaking her head at Heinmyets when he would have helped her. She needed to be able to stand without his help, now that she was on her way to meet with the Gods. She could not afford any sign of weakness.

Her daughter slept, newly fed and changed. Inharise and Siljaren had helped Alicira wash and dress. She desperately desired food and sleep, but the pressure of the Gods' presence demanded that she deal with them before she allowed herself any more comforts.

At least once on her feet she could stand without needing support from Inharise and Heinmyets, much less the stick.

"My scarf," she said to Inharise. "One from Medvara. I must appear strong in my own right."

Inharise nodded and went to the large bentwood box that held Alicira's summer clothing. One of the Medvaran scarves that carried the power from Alicira's early spinning and weaving lay folded neatly on the top. Inharise brought it to Alicira. She draped it loosely around her neck.

"I hope you don't mind that we wear our marriage scarves," Heinmyets said, looking up from carefully lacing the high tops of his ceremonial boots. "Perhaps you should wrap the child in your marriage scarf, to show the Gods that we protect her as well as you."

"I would feel better if you had something from us on you even though I know you want to appear strong for the Gods," Inharise added. "For her sake as well as yours."

It was a good suggestion. "I agree. If you could find it for me, Inharise?"

"I will." Inharise turned back to Alicira's box.

Heinmyets rose, shaking the sleeves of his formal summer

fringed tunic so that the fringes fell into place. Both he and Inharise wore summer formal tunics, boots, and leggings, their attire a mix of Keldaran and Clendan designs. Instead of her Keldaran summer formals, Alicira wore a long summerweight wool and linen skirt and blouse from Medvara that her uncle had somehow managed to find on his last trade run to Nere. The Medvaran designs lacked the specifically devised magic woven into the clothing Alicira had left behind, but they still carried an element of plain Medvaran magic.

Not that any of the Medvaran magic was now available to Alicira. She only chose the Medvaran wear because she wanted to remind the Gods of her own losses. The rough boundaries of her child's fate had been determined several months ago when Alicira had gambled with the God Staul to determine her own freedom from Zauril. But the child had not been born yet. No God or Goddess had conveyed their blessings and protections— or curses—upon her.

It was not a good thing that so many Gods were here. Especially Nitel, Zauril's patroness.

Dovré, guard and protect us!

Warmth pulsed from the pendant she wore under her clothing. It was an Eye of Dovré, sent to her from the Healing House of Keldara as a wedding gift. The Goddess was with her, at least. But could Dovré hold against her sister Nitel?

Ah well, it was time they found out.

"I am ready," she said, her voice rasping in a throat still sore from her cries during the birth.

Siljaren picked up the child and nested it carefully in Alicira's arms. Alicira faced the closed door. Heinmyets stood on her left, Inharise on her right. Alicira nodded to Siljaren and she opened the door. She processed outside, Heinmyets and Inharise with her while Siljaren followed, and stopped dead two strides out as the entire camp cheered, clustered around their lodge.

All of them. Most attired in summer formals, only the children casually dressed. The men whooped and four pounded hand drums as Weticasu and Kenarjé emerged from the ranks of the Woman's Council, carrying a formal blanket robe the likes of which Alicira had not seen before.

Weticasu and Kenarjé bowed before Alicira. "The Woman's Council presents the lady Alicira with this token of our support. We would be honored if you wore it to your meeting with the Gods," Weticasu said.

What could she say? Alicira blinked back quick tears. "I—I am honored. But to wear your token may endanger all of you who worked on it, should the Gods choose to burden my daughter with the reddest of curses."

"We accept that burden," Kenarjé said. "The Woman's Council would have the Gods know that you and the babe are cherished and loved."

"Then I accept your gift." Alicira stood still as the two women draped the blanket robe over her shoulders.

Teomoje, one of the Man's Council, came forward with an intricately worked silver and shell pin to secure the blanket. "We also show our support for you, beloved of Heinmyets and Inharise. The Man's Council also seeks to show our support for you."

"Thank you. Thank you," Alicira repeated. She continued walking toward the flat. The camp fell in behind and beside her, dancing and drumming and chanting. As they left the trees for the open flat, the shimmering air spread around them, enveloping the entire group in the power of the Gods. The world distorted around them, then steadied. Five Gods appeared ahead of her. Alicira swallowed hard and kept walking. Dovré. Staul next to her, his aspect as the Balancer more dominant than his Destroyer side today, for which she was grateful. Artel the Judge next to him. The welcome surprise of Terat of the Waters, Inharise's patroness, next to Artel. Last of all, Nitel of the Battles glowered at Alicira, standing an arm's length apart from the other gods.

Only the Twins are missing.

And who knew what chaos Karnoi and Cirdel would create if they were here? Alicira bit her lip, focusing on the precious weight in her arms and on the Eye on her chest.

Terat is here, to balance Nitel. Thank you, Goddess, for that.

She stopped ten paces from the Gods. Slowly, carefully, she went to one knee, bowing low and not looking at the Gods as she balanced her daughter in her arms. "Goddesses. Gods. I give honor and thanks to you for coming to greet my daughter."

"We have unfinished business," Staul said.

Alicira dared to look up at him. "My lord Staul, I thought all had been settled when we tossed chips for my daughter's future when I arrived in Keldara."

"All but what God she would be dedicated to," Staul said.

"My lord, she is but a newborn!"

"Old enough to determine who owns her loyalty," Nitel snarled. The hissing tones in that Goddess's voice made Alicira want to tremble, and it was only through the force of her will that she remained steady. "This way we can determine her affinity without undue sway from all of you." Nitel gestured at the people surrounding them.

"You already have had your influence!" Alicira snapped back at Nitel. "Zauril couldn't restrain my magic without your help!" The memory of the swirling red lights in the afterbirth flashed into her thoughts, and she tried to banish that image lest Nitel pick it out of her mind.

But the cruel smile on the goddess's face let Alicira know that Nitel had also seen that thought.

"Ah, but three of us can potentially be the god who is your daughter's patron, given what was revealed in the afterbirth." Was that triumph in the look that Nitel shot at Dovré?

"Stop it, Nitel," Staul rumbled. "It could just as easily be me who is her patron. There was more gray there than red or blue."

"She is born of *my* servant," Dovré insisted. "She has the potential to serve me well, *if* she is not unduly affected by those seeking to regain power!"

"Just you wait until one of mine targets *you*, sister!" Nitel scowled even more at Dovré. "You and your sanctimonious healers are not the only ones without blame when it comes to seeking power in twisted ways!"

"And how often have regimes been overthrown in my name?" Dovré glowered at Nitel. "How much torture has been done in your name; how much destruction of human lives and spaces in your name?"

"You are far from innocent, sister, especially in your patronage of Medvara and the Miteal. And shall we speak of the atrocities enacted by your former servants in Daran?" Nitel's voice dropped in volume but was no less poisonously malignant. "I know you've schemed against me. All three of you scheme against me now!" Her voice rose, trembling with rage. "How many of you cheered when Terani banished me from Waykemin in the name of our brother and sister? How many of you whispered guidance to Karnoi and Cirdel on how to do it, or appeared in visions to Terani?" Dark red pulsed under brown in her face. "But I got my vengeance on her. Karnoi and Cirdel consumed her even though she was their servant. Terani fell into the dreamless sleep and will never waken, nor will she dance with her loved ones in the Afterworld. *I got my vengeance!*"

Alicira saw the dread she felt reflected on the faces of the other gods, even Staul, as Nitel continued to rant. She clutched her daughter close. The child nuzzled into her chest, whimpering as the pressure from Nitel's anger rolled over them. Alicira tried to soothe her but she continued to fuss, her cries growing louder to match Nitel's shrieks.

"Stop it!" she screamed finally. "Stop scaring my baby!" She fought back the angry shivers that threatened to overwhelm her as she clutched the baby close. "You! You destroyed my family using Zauril as your tool. Now you're trying to take my child away from me by claiming her as your follower! I won't have it! I won't!"

Silence fell around them. The Goddess stopped, staring at Alicira.

"You dare to challenge me," she said finally, her voice low and poisonous. "Even after what Zauril did with my help, you dare to challenge me again."

Alicira met the Goddess's glare without flinching. "I challenged you every moment that Zauril held me prisoner. You may have vanquished my body, but you did not vanquish my mind. *And you will not have my child.* Even if it means my death, *you will not be my daughter's patron.*"

"Ha! You and who else will stop me?"

"I will," Heinmyets said.

"I will," Inharise said.

Scornful laughter from behind them. "We of the Woman's Council will challenge the goddess who screams like a spoiled brat!" Weticasu said as she and Kenarjé strode forward to stand next to Alicira, Heinmyets, and Inharise. "We're familiar enough with spoiled children."

"You dare." Nitel raised herself tall, becoming bigger than the others. "You mere humans *dare* to mock me? Then be willing to pay the price."

"No." Dovré spoke, her voice clear and firm. "Sister. You shame all of us if you take your humiliation out on these good people. All they are doing is supporting one of their own. Perhaps your reaction to their defiance is forgivable given your frustrations in Waykemin, but you shame us if you continue."

Terat stepped forward, taking Nitel's hands. "Sister. Our sibling speaks truth. Such wrath unbecomes you. You are a God, not a human!"

Nitel yanked her hands away, sending Terat staggering. "Do not mock me with your sly smile and slippery words, oh water-dreaming sister of mine. You couldn't wait to claim those dedicated to me in Waykemin that Karnoi and Cirdel didn't want, could you? You want to do the same thing to my followers here as well. I won't let you have any of my own!"

"Sister." Artel spoke low and firm, his voice cutting through Nitel's shriek. "You have had a grievous harm done to you by our siblings. But here and now is not the place for us to speak of it, with these humans. We are here to determine which one of you three will be this child's patron. Nothing more than that."

"She should be *mine.* Her father is mine."

"And I say not," Alicira insisted. "Artel's judgment on the chip throw gave her to me. That means she should follow Dovré. Don't most children follow the patron their mother belongs to?"

"But the power manifesting at her birth could well be from any of the three of us," Dovré said gently, a sad smile on her face. "Lady Alicira, I understand your passion. You have felt Nitel's wrath as channeled through your oppressor, and do not want to see her manifested in your daughter. Nonetheless, we must put your daughter to the determination."

"Does it have to be now?" Alicira choked back a sob. "Why can't it be when she is older, when she chooses her magic?"

"She will need one of us to guide her," Dovré continued in that same sad, soft voice. "She will be a powerful sorceress. Such strength cannot mature without guidance, lest it turn into the reddest of red paths. Even if she is of Nitel, would be best if she has a guide." She stroked Alicira's cheek, then leaned forward, lowering her voice. "And if she is of Nitel, still there are ways to avoid the twisted paths you fear for her. But we have to determine who her patron is, the sooner the better. Let us see the child."

Reluctantly, Alicira lowered her daughter from her chest,

exposing the little girl's features to the Gods. She bared her teeth at Nitel as the red goddess leaned close.

"No further," she said. When the Goddess would have reached for the child, Alicira flicked a tiny spark of magic to sting her.

Nitel snorted and pulled back. Alicira tensed, expecting the Goddess to lash out.

"You mean to guard your daughter well," Nitel said. "Pity you're of Dovré. Such devotion is well worth a reward."

"I want nothing from you," Alicira said through gritted teeth. "Even if you turn out to be her patron."

Nitel cackled. "Oh, you'll receive something from me. No doubt about it."

Artel moved forward. "Step aside, Nitel." He stood at the baby's head while Terat went to her feet. "The judgment begins now. Dovré. Staul. Nitel." He placed each God around the baby, facing Alicira. Then he extended his hands. Without speaking, the other Gods joined him. Artel put his left hand on Alicira's right shoulder and Terat put her right hand on Alicira's left shoulder. She felt a jolt, and then a vibration as if her magic had suddenly quintupled.

The gods through me.

Artel began a high descant. Alicira was familiar with the words, having heard them before in various chants and ceremonies throughout her life. But as the other Gods joined in, she realized she had never heard the Gods themselves chant before. Images flowed before her as they sang. The figure of a little dark-haired girl dancing around a fire appeared, someone who resembled what Alicira's daughter might well become. The three Gods shimmered into the vision. One by one they danced with the child.

Staul was the first to bow out, ruffling the child's dark hair affectionately before he stepped back, bowing low.

The dance between Dovré and Nitel intensified, the little girl whipping back and forth between them. She nimbly dove and weaved in and around the two Goddesses, enticing them into a faster and faster dance until it became a chase. Then she grabbed at Nitel and pulled a gold ring with a red gem from the goddess's fingers, crowing with triumph. Nitel began to cheer, except then that the little girl turned and grasped Dovré's gold necklace, yanking it free. Holding the gem and necklace high, she capered around the two Goddesses as Nitel stared numbly and a smile started to spread across Dovré's lips.

The little girl stopped dancing. She brought ring and necklace together, stringing the ring on the necklace. She hummed until the ring shrank so it was just another pendant on Dovré's gold necklace. The little girl smirked at that. Then she fastened the necklace around her neck. As she dropped her hands and the necklace began to glow, the little girl began to grow, her smirk transforming into a knowing smile. Her eyes met Alicira's, and she bowed low to her mother.

Then the images were gone. Terat and Artel dropped their hands from Alicira's shoulders and stepped back. Staul looked triumphant, Dovré flushed, and Nitel angry.

"The child is of Dovré," Artel pronounced. "She will have influences from Staul and from Nitel, but she is most of all of Dovré. Her spirit is strong and indomitable. Many paths are possible for this child. We will need to watch closely that she does not follow the wrong ways." He sighed, and if a God could look old, he did at that moment. "I will do what I can through her Heartfather and her uncle to guide her, but my influence will not be great. I will gift her the wisdom and courage that come from both those men in her life. Lady Terat?"

Terat stepped forward. "My only impact on this child will be through her Secondmother. But I gift her a strong and devoted Secondmother, one who will bring much perception and control to a headstrong and powerful child who will need it." She bent and kissed the baby's forehead, then stepped back.

Next was Staul. "I have already promised the support of my devoted to help this one in her power and magic. I repeat that support as my gift, and extend my own blessings to her." He kissed the baby's forehead and joined Terat.

An awkward pause followed. Then Nitel flounced forward. "To her who stole my gem, I do not give a blessing," she growled. "I curse her. I gift her with the curiosity to seek the paths and the red ways, the courage to look for the unconventional and the alternate way. It may seem to be a blessing at times, but make no mistake. I curse her. She may find a means to turn this curse into a blessing, but she will need to work for it." Then the Goddess turned and marched away, fading into the shimmering air around them.

Another awkward silence. Then Dovré came forward. "The child is of me," she began. "I cannot change what my sister Nitel has done. But I can build on it. Nitel's curse is open to becoming a blessing. I gift my beloved with the strength and the power to turn that curse into a blessing. To seek the paths that will change the world, and make things right." She looked at Alicira. "Have you a name for this child as yet?"

Alicira shook her head. "No. I have not found a name that would match her from my lineage."

"Then I will name her. Rekaré. I name her Rekaré. She was conceived in sorrow, so Rekaré—Sorrow— her name will be. But the sorrow she will bring will change the world."

Alicira couldn't speak. *Sorrow. Rekaré.* It was not a name she would have chosen.

"Such a name to encumber a child with," Inharise said. "My lady, are you certain?"

"I did not say to whom she would bring sorrow," Dovré said. "She will be Sorrow to her foes, quite possibly to a god or two as well." She smiled down at Rekaré and stroked her cheek. "Oh little one, what a power you shall be." Then she, too, kissed Rekaré's forehead. She straightened. "And to Alicira, my beloved. Be strong, be brave, and do not fear for the fate of this little one." She gave Heinmyets and Inharise a steady, measuring gaze. "All of you. Guide and shape this little one well. Much potential is here for either good or bad. It will be your work to make of her what she will be." Then the Goddess kissed first Alicira's brow, then Inharise, and last Heinmyets. "I gift all of you with the strength you will need to raise this child." Then she joined Artel, Staul and Terat. The four Gods bowed.

Then they were gone, taking with them the shimmering weight that had hung over the flat. Now the camp stood alone, no Gods nearby.

Alicira sighed, and stroked Rekaré's cheek. Then she peered more closely. Did she see a faint shadow of the Goddess's gold necklace with an extra red gem around the baby's neck? She blinked, trying to focus harder. It faded away.

"Let's get you back to the lodge," Siljaren fussed, guiding Alicira back. The dancers and drummers took up their chants again, singing them back into the lodge.

Once Alicira and Rekaré had been tucked into the waiting bed, Alicira curled around her daughter.

Tired as she was, it took her a long time to fall into sleep, thinking over the words of the Gods.

Late the next day, Orlanden was busy repairing hunting arrows, seated at the edge of the trees and looking out toward the grassland that had been so menacing the day before. Now it was just a high ridge grassland flat, with no power shimmering over it.

Otoken cleared his throat behind Orlanden. "A message from Haran."

Orlanden took the sealed message, heart pounding in his ears. He cracked the seal.

Portentous news of the birth of Rekaré. And I have more news for you. My father has passed. My brother the Mershaunten, while not yet ready to bring me back to court, has need of both of us to be his eyes and ears given these events in distant Clenda. It is reported that Zauril's reaction to the news was a blinding rage that took out ten of his guards.

Give Alicira and her spouses my blessings, and advise them that I will be meeting all of you in Dera this fall as the Mershaunten's representative, when they return to show Rekaré to her people.

We will speak of our future then, beloved. Things are in motion.

Haran.

Orlanden refolded the message, smiling to himself.

Rekaré might have been born of sorrow, but he suspected that her birth had changed the world.

He hoped he would live to see what those changes brought.

NEWSLETTER

Like this story and want to know what's coming out next, or what deals Joyce is offering on her book?

Check out Joyce's monthly newsletter at

https://joycespublishingnewsfromwideopenspaces.kit.com/ a65eaa89cd

And get a free download snippet from the Martiniere Multiverse!

BOOKS AND PUBLICATIONS

Goddess's Honor

Beyond Honor and Other Stories: Goddess's Honor Book One
Pledges of Honor: Goddess's Honor Book Two
Challenges of Honor: Goddess's Honor Book Three
Choices of Honor: Goddess's Honor Book Four
Judgment of Honor: Goddess's Honor Book Five

The Cost of Power

Return
Snippet: Outtakes from Philip Martiniere
Crucible
Snippet: The Criminal Injustice Interview
Snippet: Sibling Warfare
Redemption
Omnibus Ebook Edition

The Martiniere Legacy

First Meetings: A Martiniere Legacy Short Story
Inheritance: The Martiniere Legacy Book One
Ascendant: The Martiniere Legacy Book Two

Realization: The Martiniere Legacy Book Three

A Belated Christmas Honeymoon: A Martiniere Legacy Short Story

The Enduring Legacy: The Martiniere Legacy Book Four

People of the Martiniere Legacy

The Heritage of Michael Martiniere: A Martiniere Legacy Novel

Broken Angel: The Lost Years of Gabriel Martiniere: A Martiniere Legacy Novel

Justine Fixes Everything: Reflections on Mortality

The Martiniere Multiverse

A Different Life: What If?

A Different Life: Now. Always. Forever.

A Very Multiversal Christmas Miracle

Netwalk Sequence Author Preferred 2022 Editions

Life in the Shadows: Book One

Netwalk: Book Two

Netwalker Uprising: Book Three

Netwalk's Children: Book Four

Learning in Space: Book Five

Netwalking Space: Book Six

Bright Star Fair Witches

Becoming Solo: A Bright Star Fair Witches Novella

Non-Series Titles currently available:

Alien Savvy: A Western SF Novella

Klone's Stronghold: Reeni

Beating the Apocalypse

Bearing Witness

Fabulist and Fantastical Worlds: A Short Story Collection

Federation Cowboy

Vision of Alliance

Vella Titles:
Falcon of the Martinieres (part of *Justine Fixes Everything*)
Bearing Witness
Beating the Apocalypse
A Different Life—What If? An Alternative Martiniere Legacy Novel
Becoming Solo
A Different Life—Linda's Story: An Alternative Martiniere Legacy Novel
Federation Cowboy

Audiobooks Available:
Alien Savvy: A Western SF Novella

Released from other publishers:
"Queen of the Snows," in *Once Upon A Winter: A Folk and Fairy Tale Anthology*, edited by H. L. Macfarlane
"My Man Left Me, My Dog Hates Me, and There Goes My Truck," in *Black-Eyed Peas on New Year's Day: An Anthology of Hope*, edited by Shannon Page
"Lost Loves," in *All Worlds Wayfarer*
"The Wisdom of Robins," in *Whimsical Beasts: A Campcon Anthology*, edited by Joyce Reynolds-Ward
"The Cow at the End of the World," in *Well...It's Your Cow*, edited by Frog Jones
"To Plant or Pull Up Stakes," in *Pulling Up Stakes: A Campcon Anthology*, edited by Joyce Reynolds-Ward
"The Notice," in *Children of a Different Sky*, edited by Alma Alexander

ABOUT THE AUTHOR

The work of Joyce Reynolds-Ward includes themes of high-stakes family and political conflict, digital sentience, personal agency and control, realistic strong women, and (whenever possible) horses. She is the author of *The Netwalk Sequence* series, the *Goddess's Honor* series, *The Martiniere Legacy* series, *The People of the Martiniere Legacy* series, and the recently published *The Cost of Power* trilogy as well as standalones *Klone's Stronghold, Alien Savvy, Beating the Apocalypse,* and *Federation Cowboy.* Joyce is a Self-Published Fantasy BlogOff Semifinalist, a Writers of the Future SemiFinalist, and an Anthology Builder Finalist. She is a member of the Science Fiction and Fantasy Writers Association and a member of Soroptimists International.